Jeremiah 31:3

A Lily at Dawn

A Novel by

REBECCA FELLRATH

WESTBOW®
PRESS
A DIVISION OF THOMAS NELSON
& ZONDERVAN

WestBow Press books may be ordered through booksellers or by contacting:

WestBow Press
A Division of Thomas Nelson & Zondervan
1663 Liberty Drive
Bloomington, IN 47403
www.westbowpress.com
1 (866) 928-1240

Because of the dynamic nature of the Internet, any web addresses or
links contained in this book may have changed since publication and
may no longer be valid. The views expressed in this work are solely those
of the author and do not necessarily reflect the views of the publisher,
and the publisher hereby disclaims any responsibility for them.

Any people depicted in stock imagery provided by Thinkstock are models,
and such images are being used for illustrative purposes only.
Certain stock imagery © Thinkstock.

ISBN: 978-1-4908-1468-1 (sc)
ISBN: 978-1-4908-1467-4 (hc)
ISBN: 978-1-4908-1469-8 (e)

Library of Congress Control Number: 2013920232

Printed in the United States of America.

WestBow Press rev. date: 03/12/2013

To my beloved husband, Joshua Fellrath.

 *Chapter 1*

Matt's strong hand caressed Zuriel Rawson's as they walked through the woods. It was beautiful, romantic, and horrifying. Could this be the night? Each step seemed to be one step closer to her lifelong dream.

She heard their footsteps on the paved walkway, and it felt as though she were walking into the center of her heart. Did she really want to spend the rest of her life with this man? Could she put her faith in love, an emotion that had always betrayed her? It felt so right, but that's the excuse everyone used. Zuriel always wanted to fall in love but wasn't sure she believed in it. She had been through countless relationships, and not a single one of them could compare to this. She had never dated anyone this long before, and she had never let herself become so vulnerable.

The evening breeze tossed Zuriel's dark-blonde hair into her face, making her aware of her lack of preparation. The parks in Detroit were so pretty in May; she wished she could match it. She regretted not putting more endeavor into her appearance. She knew Matt didn't care about how she dressed, but her skinny jeans and black cardigan didn't feel *good enough*. Matt, on the other hand, was well prepared. His dark Silvers jeans and Polo sweater displayed his innate sense of fashion. His wavy black hair stayed in place, never wavering from its dresser's placement. He seemed so certain of what he was about to do. His love was without reserve.

Zuriel's parents had found love a long time ago. She could hardly imagine how her rough, emotionless father had fallen for an ex-hippie who named herself "Amour." The two had met in high school, and Amour's sense of adventure somehow won over the affections of her father. After school, he had dreams of getting married and starting a life with her, and for a while it almost seemed possible. They fell in love and had a little green-eyed girl, whom Amour named *Zuriel*. Only a few months later, Amour left, never to be seen again, leaving Zuriel in the care of her lonely and bitter father.

Zuriel slowly exhaled the evening air, vowing again to never forgive her mother for leaving. She wanted a normal life, but the events that formed her were far from ordinary.

Her father had somehow managed to keep her. He moved back in with his folks so she could be properly taken care of. She had been raised by her grandparents and dad, along with a burning desire to be loved. Despite her guardians' best attempts, Zuriel did not feel loved, or even liked. Her father hated the fact that Zuriel reminded him of his ex-lover, and her grandparents seemed to subconsciously blame her for their son's irresponsibility. It wasn't exactly what you would call an auspicious beginning.

Zuriel wanted love so desperately that she was willing to try almost anything to find it. She had even tried religion for a while, but that had been just another lesson on love's frailty. The small Catholic church she once attended hadn't treated her father very kindly. Her grandparents brought her to Mass every Sunday, leaving her now atheist father at home. Nothing seemed wrong with the church until Zuriel's first communion. Her father refused to come to the ceremony, although she had begged him to.

Devastated, she refused to take part in the ceremony without him. Many of the church members were judgmental when they found out she wasn't going to join in the sacraments. Her grandparents felt ostracized instead of loved and eventually stopped going.

Zuriel's desire for approval continued throughout high school. There were so many people to keep up with, compete against, and impress. She went from boy to boy for the first several years. By the time she entered her senior year, she was sick of all the drama surrounding the dating scene and didn't want to date anymore. Everyone pressured her though, so she made an agreement with her friend Nick. They would pretend to date for the whole year but secretly just be friends.

Their fake dating relationship worked fine for a while, but Nick became very attached to her. Zuriel hadn't realized how seriously Nick had been taking their relationship until it was too late. After graduation, Nick begged her to move in with him. She was astonished and tried to remind him that they were "just friends." Nick was furious. She could still remember his wounding words: "You're no better than your hippie, runaway mom! You just use people and then leave them like they're trash. I thought I meant something to you. Did you honestly think I put myself through all this just so you would be safe from high school gossip? I was wrong to ever love you, Zuriel!"

Nick's words had severely wounded her, but her pride kept her from giving in. She knew Nick had fallen in love, but she had refused to let herself love him in return. Or had she? The whole situation still made her cringe.

Her best friend, Suzy Baker, had come to her aid during that time, helping Zuriel through the breakup, or whatever it was. They rented an apartment together and got a job at the same department store. Things appeared to be going great, until Suzy's boyfriend turned out worse than Nick could have ever been.

Broken and depressed from the split, Suzy buried herself in drugs trying to mask the pain. She was a heavy user and rapidly declined into becoming an addict. It was apparent to Zuriel that Suzy cared more about the drugs than she did about their friendship. So once again, love failed her.

After Suzy left, Zuriel felt abandoned. The void in her soul had grown, and her hunger for love deepened. It was easy to fall in love with Matt. The affection he had for her was overflowing, and it filled her vast emptiness. Still, the fear of abandonment and disappointment made her hesitant to get too close. Zuriel wondered many times if she should get out before it was too late and she got hurt. Matt's consistent respect and care was the only thing keeping her from running.

Zuriel felt Matt's steps slow to a stop. She looked up at him and could hardly breathe. He was so handsome in the light of the park lamppost. His dark bangs brushed against his eyebrows as he intently studied her. She faintly saw her own reflection in his brown eyes and wasn't sure what to do. He was the only person who seemed to have truly loved her. Could she reject him? It seemed impossible that anyone else could show such genuine care. He was her last hope.

"You're so beautiful," Matt said. "You know how much I love you."

She leaned into his arms, his words spinning in her head. They had been together for six months of heaven. She almost broke up with him several times because she knew what he wanted. He desired a wife, but Zuriel wasn't sure if she could trust matrimony. She wasn't sure if she could trust him. Every date had been so perfect and beautiful that she wondered why she even had doubts. Hadn't he been faithful? He had loved her like no one else had ever loved her before.

He knew what it was like to be alone. Matt once told her how he grew up as the only child of a single mother. His mother had died of cancer a few years ago, so he understood what it was like to only have one parent, and he also knew what it felt like to lose everything. His story had comforted her, and she knew she wasn't going to get empathy like that from anyone else.

Zuriel knew she didn't deserve him. She was the one who had done so much wrong, the one who had sin to hide. She had to choose redemption! How could she not accept the one thing she wanted more than anything else?

Matt slipped a ring on her finger. Her heart pounded more rapidly, and she sighed. Was it a sigh of joy or of pain? She didn't know what she was feeling. The adrenaline rush she felt put every amusement-park ride to shame. She was so close to giving herself away.

Every clue had hinted that tonight would be the night of the proposal. It just wasn't normal for them to walk through the woods after midnight on a Monday. She had heard Matt talk before about marrying her like it was a solid plan. He'd insisted on getting her ring size. She wasn't blind to his intentions, although she wished she were.

The crickets chirped around them, and the wall of trees on each side of the path were enclosing. She wanted to prolong the stroll and avoid the prospective inquisition. Zuriel noticed a bench nearby and feared what awaited there. She felt his tug toward the bench, but she resisted. Pretending not to sense his directing, she kissed his hand and took a step backward. He followed her lead and wrapped his arms around her.

He held her, clearly waiting for some sort of response. She tried to say something. She was going to tilt her head and let him see her smile, knowing it would make him happy, but she couldn't move. In fact, she could hardly stand. She loved him so much. She wanted him so profusely. Why did she still fear getting closer?

"Zuriel," Matt whispered, breaking the silence. She felt his breath against her ear as she felt her heart melting. Mesmerized, her thoughts swirled into a mass of confusion. The only feeling that seemed to distinguish itself was pleasure.

"Marry me," Matt implored, "and make me the happiest man alive."

His words made her tremble. She felt like she had been standing on the edge of a cliff and Matt was urging her jump off. Her thoughts were interrupted as his lips pressed against hers, and she knew there was no going back. She felt secure for moment, resting in his arms of love. She had to choose to trust him and fight the urge to shy away. This was the man she would marry. She would be Mrs. Lowell, even if it cost her all the pieces of heart she had left.

"Yes," Zuriel managed to say, looking up at her husband-to-be. "I wouldn't have it any other way." Tilting her head, she received each of his kisses with growing reassurance. Perhaps this was meant to be after all.

Zuriel rolled out of bed to the sound of her alarm. Was it morning already? She had officially been engaged for one week and for the most part, it had actually been wonderful. She managed to survive without giving in to guilt and fear. That is, until last night. She had visited her family to tell them the news. As expected, they hadn't taken it well. Things were always the same with them, and Zuriel wondered if anything would ever change. She recalled the awkward exchange.

"Well, it's good to see you. Why don't you ever visit? You're too obsessed with that man of yours," Dad accused. "Aren't you ever going to be thankful for all we've done for you?" He paused when he noticed the frown starting to form on her face. Abruptly changing his tone, he continued. "Oh well; it's good to see you. I know your grandparents missed you."

Her grandparents rushed into the room.

"Zuriel, you're here!" Grandma exclaimed, running at her with open arms.

Grandpa as usual trailed behind and found a seat at the kitchen table. He nodded a greeting and picked up the paper.

"So, what brings you here today?" Grandma asked.

Zuriel knew she had put off this visit for way too long. The longer she stayed away, the longer she had to stay when she came.

"Well, I have some big news," she said as she looked around at her relatives. She wanted to laugh at their synchronized lean forward. Even Grandpa looked alert. "I'm engaged."

Silence. No one even breathed. After a few painful seconds, she felt tears gather behind her eyes. She looked down at her red ballet flats, which clashed profoundly with the golden-brown linoleum. She didn't want them to see her face and know just how much they hurt her. She hated giving them power, and every second of quiet screamed their disapproval. They were all skeptics of love, and of her. No one spoke until a tear trickled down her cheek.

"When did this happen?" Grandma asked, breaking the silence.

"This week." The emotion in her voice made it impossible to continue. Her eyes found their way back to her red shoes.

"Don't rush into this, Zuriel!" Her father's voice sounded strained. "You're not ready for this. In fact, knowing you, you'll probably call it off. It's not as if you could stick with one person. You can't even stick with us." His words drove ice picks into her heart.

"How do you know what I'm ready for? You don't know how I feel. You don't even …" Zuriel stopped mid sentence. She felt herself starting to lose control. There was so much hurt stored up inside her that she knew if she let it out, there would be no stopping it.

This conversation would just be fuel for the next fight, but she couldn't hold back her biting words. "I can make my own choices. Just because Mom hurt you, doesn't mean Matt would hurt me!" The arrow hit its mark. Her dad glared at her without replying. She always won their battles when she used that one against him. It wasn't fair, but neither was the fact that he was comparing his life to hers.

It took them all several awkward moments to recover, lock up their emotions, and speak again. They talked about the wedding plans without enthusiasm or feeling. The dryness of the conversation was the only thing that kept Zuriel from losing it. She was so thankful when she could leave and escape the nightmare that this visit had become. She had to remind herself that this was why she was marrying Matt. She was going to be an independent woman, and then her family would finally see her as a success. They would regret the things they had said, but it would be too late. At least she would have a life when all was said and done. What did they have?

And now here she sat. It was time to get on with her day. She loathed the fact that their opinions and feelings affected her this much. Why did she allow their words to creep into her mind and replay over and over again?

Her cell phone vibrated, and her thoughts were drawn back to the present. Matt was calling. Zuriel smiled, thankful to talk to the only person who would ever understand her.

"Good morning! How did last night go?" He sounded hopeful.

"Well, they didn't say much."

"Oh. Well, what did they say?"

"My dad said I wasn't ready and something about my not being able to stick with anyone." She felt awkward telling him about it and wondered how things would go when her family actually met him. She wished she were better at handling them so Matt wouldn't have to deal with their problems.

"Oh, I see. So your dad doesn't want to let you go? Ah, I should have talked to him before I asked you. Maybe that would have smoothed things over."

"Why would you do that? You've never cared about his opinion before," she asked, wondering why Matt's voice seemed different. It wasn't different in a bad way, it just sounded heartfelt. Usually they joked about her parents, but now he seemed almost remorseful.

"I'm not really sure. I guess I just feel like I haven't been doing things right lately, like maybe I should have respected him more."

"He's just my dad, Matt; it's fine. You've done everything perfectly."

She assumed he felt nervous about the upcoming wedding. Forever was a long time, after all. It almost comforted her to know he was having doubts too. She once told Matt that her motto was to live life without regrets. Although she claimed to live by this motto, she regretted almost everything she had ever done and was scared that her marriage might fall into the same category. The "what ifs" were torture.

"Zuriel, parents aren't all that bad. Every once in a while they're right. The cost of not listening can sometimes be beyond what a person should have to handle. I'll probably try to visit your father this week. There's a lot I need to talk with him about."

"You have a lot you need to talk with him about?" She wondered what was going on. His answer was not at all what she expected. Why was he acting to so weird? She found it strange that he suddenly cared about her dad's feelings; however, Matt had always been old-fashioned. They had only slept together a few times, and he refused to let her move in with him until after they were married. She didn't understand why he felt that way, but she was willing to honor his wishes on the matter. Most guys only had one thing on their mind, and he had always seemed to be less concerned about that than he was about her self-worth. At least she knew she could trust him. He really did love her for who she was, instead of merely wanting her body.

"Yes, and I need to talk to you too. Are we still on for Applebee's tomorrow? It's my only day off this week."

She felt nervous. Why couldn't he talk to her now? She also felt disappointed and guessed he was going to have to go soon. She didn't want to be left to her own thoughts and fears. She didn't like what she found when she was left alone with herself.

"Of course we are. Are you okay, Matt? Did something happen?"

"Yeah; I mean, no. I'm fine; there's nothing wrong. In fact, life is better than it's been in many years." He sounded confused, but so was she. Life had really been difficult before Matt came into the picture. They had both been through a lot together, so she could only assume his odd behavior was the result of the same fear she was experiencing. They wanted to be right for each other, but there was only one way to find out. At least life was the best it had ever been. They had each other for now, and that was worth being content.

"I'm glad," Zuriel said, hoping to make sense of her sentiments. "Things have never been better for me either. I love you."

"I love you too, baby," he said softly. It was unusual for him to be talking this way, and she wondered if he was hung over or if he was just tired. He exhaled loudly before finally speaking again. "Well, I'll let you go. I'll pick you up at noon tomorrow."

"Okay. Text me tonight. I'll see ya!"

He said good-bye and hung up, and she was shaken by his abruptness. What was wrong with him?

Zuriel rolled out of bed, intending to get her mind off things. She wanted everything to be perfect but had come to terms with the fact that nothing ever would be. She expected Matt to be back to normal after a good night's sleep. She didn't like these feelings of insecurity.

❧

Matt Lowell stared out the window, wondering how he would survive the day. He'd be leaving shortly to pick Zuriel up for lunch. He wasn't sure how soon that would actually be since he had so much on his mind. He didn't want to face the task at hand. He needed a few more hours to reflect on this and figure out exactly how the words were going to come out. He had made so many mistakes in life. Were they regrets? He wasn't sure what to think of them. His mistakes had led him to Zuriel, and he had never loved anyone like this before, so in some ways he was thankful, but he questioned whether everything had really been worth it. What would she say if she knew?

She would probably understand his mistakes. She might even open up about her own past, and it could become a good part of their relationship. However, he recognized that this next part of his story would be hard to explain. He hoped she would somehow understand. He hoped she would believe.

But what if she wanted to break up with him? What if the truth was too much for either of them to bear? He didn't know, but he knew what he had to do. This was about more than just himself and his own desires. As much as he loved Zuriel, there were things he was willing to put above her if he had to, and he knew it wouldn't be pretty. This was about doing something right for the first time in his life.

Grabbing his keys, Matt walked out the door. As he shut it, he whispered, "God help me!"

 *Chapter 2*

Zuriel watched out the window of her apartment where she had a good view of the parking lot below. It was June 1, and the flower plots were blooming. Cars zoomed past, and people were everywhere. The sight usually put her at ease, but today it brought concern. What was taking Matt so long? He was already half an hour late, and he wasn't answering any calls or texts. Matt was probably just fine, but she couldn't stop feeling anxious. She would be sure to reprimand him for not answering her messages.

She was anxious to talk to him. What did he want to talk with her about anyway? She thought she knew Matt and was sure there were no secrets between them. Still, there was a haunting question about trust. Some days she was so excited to be getting married, but other times she felt like maybe six months was too soon to get engaged. Her thoughts tortured her. She knew she couldn't live without Matt, but she also wondered if she could live with him.

Zuriel checked her phone again. It was now 12:40. Matt was very late and it wasn't like him. It was a sunny day, so there was no wind, snow, or rain to slow him down. Whispers of fear plagued her mind. Was Matt with another woman? Did he get drunk last night and sleep in? Was he angry with Zuriel? Was he hurt?

Each minute seemed like an eternity, and her foot swung impatiently back and forth. She struggled to text him again because her fingers weren't hitting the buttons very well. She reread her last text: "Matt, I'm really worried. Please reply." Zuriel hoped he could sense her urgency. All she needed was a quick text letting her know he would be late. Was that too much to ask for?

She pushed her brown love seat over by the window, continuing to study the parking lot and check the rows of cars over and over again. Each car that drove by brought a quick wave of relief and then despair. Matt was nowhere to be seen. She wished she'd known he was going to be this late. Then surely she would have put more effort into her deflated hair.

She smoothed the wrinkles out of her black pencil skirt and tried to straighten her silky blue top. Zuriel was aware of her outfit's flattering affects and was hoping Matt would take notice. Maybe he would finally decide to move in with her, now that they were engaged. She hated living alone, especially now. If they were living together, she wouldn't be waiting to hear from him.

Zuriel checked her phone every few seconds. Who could she call? Matt didn't have any family and he lived alone. Who on earth would know his whereabouts? What if he was ignoring her on purpose? Knowing her luck with people, it wouldn't be too surprising. Everyone she ever cared about eventually left her. She tried to shake the thought from her mind. Matt wasn't like that. He was *different*. He could have forgotten about their lunch date.

She thought about it and felt silly. Maybe she was being impractical? If he had really just forgotten about it and fallen asleep, she was wasting a lot of time fretting. Her stomach grumbled, and she wondered if waiting to eat was worth it. If Matt forgot, he would have already eaten by now. Tossing off her three-inch heels, she headed for the kitchen.

It was almost two o'clock when she sat down for lunch. Zuriel didn't find the food overly appetizing. She impatiently gulped down the ham sandwich, but her nerves were none the better.

"Everything will be fine," she told herself. It had to be fine. Soon this horrible waiting would be over and she would be in his arms again.

She tried to write a shopping list. Her eyes wandered back to the window again. She glanced at her phone, stunned to find her inbox empty. Her bare foot swung faster, and her eyes burned from forgetting to blink. Perhaps she could busy herself with laundry?

Time quickly passed, and Zuriel desperately tried to ignore it. There was nothing she could do. If she had a car she would drive to his place and get to the bottom of it right now, and if she knew someone willing to drive her she would have called hours ago. She had to be strong. She didn't want to be one of those whiny and nagging girlfriends. She was tempted to send yet another message and try calling again, but if he hadn't answered the others, why would one more help?

Her clenched fists were sweating as she read the time once more. It was already four. Zuriel didn't care about the date anymore. She just wanted to know that Matt was okay. Was he hurt? Was he angry with her? Hot tears streamed down her cheek. "Oh, God. Oh, God! What's going on?" she whispered.

She went to the love seat and curled up, pulling her knees against her chest. The tears dripped down her face and made her lips taste salty. There went her makeup. She wanted to impress him, but it didn't matter now. Matt wasn't coming for her.

More time passed and Zuriel felt numb. She went back and forth between feeling stupid for worrying and then freaking out. She stared at her phone and watched the time tick away. She had to call someone!

She frantically dialed Drew's number. Drew Jacobs had been friends with Matt for several years, and they always hung out. If

Drew didn't know, at least she would have someone else to worry with. She focused on calming her breathing. She didn't want to freak poor Drew out. But his phone kept ringing and ringing, and Zuriel started to cry. She reached his voice mail.

"Ah, Drew. I can't get hold of Matt. It's been like six hours since he was supposed to come over. Just call me back." Zuriel abruptly hung up and put her phone beside the love seat. She needed her fiancé but had no idea where he was. She lay down and closed her eyes, trying to stop the tears. She was such a mess! Why was she so insecure? She finally drifted off to sleep.

Zuriel opened her eyes to the sound of her phone vibrating. For a moment she forgot yesterday's troubles, but realizing she was still wearing her blouse and skirt, she was thrown back into reality. *Dear God, please let it be Matt!* She glanced at her phone and saw that it was Drew. Heart pounding, she answered.

"Drew?"

"Hey, I got your message." He sounded shaky.

"Well, have you heard from him?" Emotion flooded into her voice. A good night's sleep had done nothing for her fragile nerves.

"I haven't heard from him. I …" He cleared his throat.

She felt her heart stop. What happened to Matt?

"Zuriel, I just got a call from the police."

Zuriel couldn't breathe. "What is it?" Her voice was stern and low. Her throat hurt from suppressing tears.

"I don't know how to say this. A semi driver fell asleep at the wheel and ran a red light. He hit someone, and both drivers were instantly killed."

She couldn't believe what she was hearing. Was he saying Matt was dead? It couldn't be possible! Matt was her lover, her future husband, and her only hope.

"What are you saying, Drew?" she managed to ask, despite the fact that her cheeks were drenched with tears.

"He's dead." He let out a soft sob. After a brief silence he said, "Matt's dead, Zuriel. He's gone."

Zuriel began to shake. She couldn't answer Drew. Her throat had completely closed up, and suddenly she couldn't cry. Her hands felt cold and clammy. Why would God do this to her? If there was a God, he was cruel.

She tried to speak, but all she could do was whisper, "Bye." She hung up and stood and then started pacing. After a while, she went to her bed and tried to lie down, but she had to stand up again.

She needed a drink of water. Zuriel walked to the kitchen and filled a glass. She took two sips and felt intense grief rocket through her blood. She hurled the glass as hard as she could into the sink. It shattered loudly.

She ran full speed toward her room and jumped into bed. Pounding her fists into the pillows, she let out a blood-curdling scream. Then, at last, came the sobs.

Did she deserve this? Did Matt deserve this? How could this be fair? What kind of stupid jerk falls asleep at the wheel? This could not possibly be happening! She had everything and now she had nothing, absolutely nothing! The only one who had ever truly loved or understood her was gone. There was nothing left in the world but hurt and death. There could be no such thing as a happy ending.

Zuriel's mind went back to the night of their engagement. She could almost smell him and feel his strong arms surrounding her body. He was so handsome. His brown eyes were so inviting. She had lived for his love like it was a drug. She breathed for each time she saw him. His kisses, his touch, and everything else about him had completely captivated her heart.

She hugged herself tightly, trying to remember what it felt like to be in his arms. She didn't want to lose that feeling. She didn't want to lose Matt. She needed him in every way, and now God had taken him away. Her only treasure and hope was dead. Dead! There was no one to love her now. She would be lonely forever!

The pain was unbearable. Grief suffocated her. Zuriel screamed again. Sitting up, she pounded her fists into the pillows again.

"Why? Oh God, why?" She screamed and let out a string of curses. She didn't care what God thought about her now. She was mad. She was hurt. She might as well be dead! Why couldn't God have taken her instead? Matt would have found someone else to love, but she had no other chances. Her life was over.

So now she would have to plan the funeral and do everything herself. Matt didn't have any family, and she wasn't going to let him be buried without dignity. She cringed at the thought of what he must look like. Zuriel cried out, feeling more sorrowful than at any other time in her entire life. Everything about the situation was horrible. She wanted it all to go away. She wanted to be free. Oh, how she wished she could go back in time and see him again.

Memories flashed through her mind. They pulled at her soul, causing a longing. She just wanted to be held. She just wanted to be cared for. All she wanted was a little bit more of Matt. Couldn't she have held him one more time before they had to say good-bye forever? How could God be so heartless?

She grabbed a blanket and went back to the love seat by the window. So many times she had sat here waiting for Matt to come over. So many times she had stared out the window to think and daydream about him. It was only fitting that she sit here to grieve. It was only right that she should cry here. Perhaps she could die here?

She knew she was too much of chicken to kill herself. She also knew Matt needed a good funeral. He deserved that much at least. Maybe after that she could run into another sleeping truck driver. If she died too, then all this pain would die with her.

Zuriel's shoulders shook as she wept. Her throat ached as she cried and cussed into the air. If this was how love ended, she would never love again.

Her phone vibrated against the metal vent in the floor. It must be the police or hospital. They probably wanted to set up plans for the funeral. Not that she was in any condition to do that. It would be a miserable and extremely stressful event. There was no way she could do any of this herself.

She made her way to the phone. She practiced saying hello a few times before answering.

"Hi, this is Rick Vanderson. I'm with the city police. Is Zuriel Rawson there?"

"Yeah, this is her."

"I'm calling with some unfortunate news, regarding Matt Lowell. He was involved in a car accident yesterday afternoon." He paused, and then continued. "I'm so sorry ma'am, but he didn't make it."

"I heard the news. I guess you want to me to get the funeral stuff taken care of?" She hated the way he was speaking, so calm and collected. Didn't he know death was bad news?

"Oh, no. His family is taking care of all that. His parent's are here at the station taking care of those details now."

Zuriel suddenly felt queasiness begin to build in her stomach. Family? What family? This didn't make any sense at all. "I'm sorry, Officer, but I don't understand. I was under the impression Matt didn't have any family. His mom died of cancer a few years ago."

"I wonder if I have the right number. You are Zuriel Rawson, aren't you? We're talking about Matthew Lowell?"

She wished he had the wrong number. "Yeah, this is she. I'm Matt's fiancé. I think I would know about his family." She couldn't hide her irritation. How could he be so insensitive? Her fiancé just died, and nobody had even taken the time to check over the story before calling? What a jerk!

"Ma'am, I don't doubt you knew him well. Believe me, I don't understand the story either. I just know that I spent the last hour talking with various members of his family. His parents said they hadn't heard from him in five years. His brother had made some contact with him, but for the most part he's been a stranger."

She felt overwhelmed. None of this could be true! Had Matt lied to her? Why would he do that? "Matt told me he grew up with a single mom who died a few years ago. I just don't see why he would lie to me." Zuriel was experiencing way too much stress for one day. She didn't like this Officer Rick.

"Apparently he has two living parents, an older brother, and two younger sisters. They live in Toledo, and they're planning to have the funeral there."

"I don't believe this. Do you have their phone number? This feels more like a bad dream. What do you suggest I do?" She wondered what this guy expected from her. Her fiancé was dead, and it turns out he was a liar. Perfect!

"The family offered to let you stay at their house this week. They want to know what Matt was like these last few years, and they want to meet you. I can hand the phone right over to his mother if you want. She's in the next room."

"I guess …" was all Zuriel could say. She really wanted to crawl into a corner and cry, but she couldn't. She felt numb. She would just have to suck it up a little longer.

Zuriel wondered what visiting Matt's family would be like; that is, if he really had one. She was still not convinced this guy was right in the head. She knew Matt, and Matt wasn't a liar. At least she didn't think he was.

"Hello?" The voice sounded sweet and sorrowful.

"Ah, hi."

"I'm Anne Lowell, Matt's mother. I'm so sorry about all this. Are you hanging in there?" The question hit an emotional cord. No one had asked her yet how she was doing. She started to cry. The embarrassment of crying to a complete stranger only made things worse.

"Oh, honey, I know. I feel the same way. Listen, I'm praying for you, and I would love to meet you. I'm sure you're a wonderful woman if Matt was going to marry you. You're more than welcome to come stay with us during this mess." Her words were sincere and undeniably inviting.

Even if Matt was a liar, Zuriel didn't care. She loved him and now he was dead. She would do anything to find out the truth about his past. "That's nice of you, but I don't want to intrude. I didn't even know Matt had a family." Her tears made it hard to speak.

"You won't be intruding! I already talked to Drew Jacobs. He said he would drive you down here. Does that sound good to you?"

"Yeah, that sounds okay." She had already talked to Drew?

"All right, dear. Drew will pick you up at two tomorrow."

"Thank you. I guess I'll meet you then."

"Okay, sweetie. Now you go get some rest."

"Bye." Zuriel hung up and felt sick. Matt was dead. Matt had a family. Matt had lied to her. What did all this mean? She would find out tomorrow, but first she would have a good cry.

 Chapter 3

Samuel Lowell stood outside his apartment building. He had just taken a trip to hell and back. He wasn't in the mood for sitting in his room alone. One option sounded remotely bearable—he would run. Surely a nice jog would at least give him time to think. He needed air.

He started off at an even pace. It felt good. The sun was starting to set—a scene that was so symbolic of all that had recently transpired. Matt was dead. His only brother, the guy he had prayed for constantly, was now gone forever. His prayers had never been answered.

"God, where are you?" he whispered under his breath. His mind flashed back to late last night. A normal family dinner had turned into a crying session in mere seconds. His parents had wept openly and his sisters cried in each other's arms. And what had he done? He felt a cold numbness creep into his soul. He felt nothing except anger. Samuel felt sorry for his family. They weren't just mourning the loss of a life; they were mourning the loss of a soul.

It had all started when Pastor Carter left. His betrayal had been hard on everyone, especially Matt. At least Samuel had God to get him through it all. At the time, Matt had been going through a phase where he wasn't sure whether to believe in God or in the philosophies of his atheist friends. Matt had debated with them for hours and had slowly begun to doubt the credibility of God. Still, though, he continued going to church and had been a good kid. He was Samuel's best friend. Everything changed when their youth pastor, John Carter, had been caught stealing money from the church.

It hit Matt hard, and he brought his troubles to his friends instead of God. It was the excuse he needed to stop going to youth group and to justify his drug use. He rebelled against his parents and became a different kid. Samuel was the only one Matt trusted, but he didn't trust him enough to listen to his advice.

The betrayals of both John and Matt had ripped Samuel's heart to shreds. Samuel had planned to study medicine, but dropped out to become a youth pastor. He wasn't going to let his brother or anyone else down. He felt he had to make things better and rebuild the reputation of pastors too.

He tried and tried to reach out to Matt during this time, but it was hard. Samuel lived on campus and worked a lot, watching as his brother slipped completely away from church, his family, and God. It hurt, but things only got worse. When Matt turned eighteen, he left his home in Toledo and moved to Detroit. He didn't keep in contact with anyone from back home. He lived his own life and completely ignored everyone else.

Their parents were heartbroken. The whole family grieved. They all prayed for the Prodigal Son to return home. He almost did, once upon a time, but in the end he chose his life in Detroit.

In the meantime, Samuel had finished school and become the youth pastor of their church. He had made something of himself, but in the end it still wasn't enough to save Matt. Matt was dead.

A cool breeze blew against Samuel as he ran. It was getting dark, and he was almost glad. It matched the darkness he felt closing in around his heart. His brother was dead and gone, probably in hell. Why hadn't Samuel been able to stop it? Why couldn't he have led Matt back to God? Why did God let this happen? How could Matt do this to his family?

He felt so angry, but at whom? Matt? Himself? God? It was all just a big mass of pain. Who was to blame? Maybe if Pastor Carter hadn't betrayed them, everything would be different. Maybe if Matt hadn't listened to his stupid friends. Maybe if his parents had stepped in earlier. Maybe if Matt had trusted in God more. Samuel didn't know who to blame, but the worst part was that now he could never have peace with the past.

Samuel ran faster. Sweat dripped down his face as he breathed in the night air. He didn't feel like going home yet. Samuel felt if he were to stop running, the earth would stop spinning. He didn't want to pause and think about what was going on. How could Matt be dead? Why had God ignored their prayers?

Matt was such a pigheaded jerk to leave like that. He had left home and enjoyed every pleasure imaginable. The drug problem didn't last too long; he had apparently gotten help. But how was Samuel supposed to know what to believe about Matt? Matt had been a wasted loser who spent time with one girl after the next. Samuel wondered what had become of that poor woman Matt had fallen for. He had probably used her just like the rest. Why did girls seem to cling to that train wreck?

Samuel had been in love once too. He knew he hadn't been the most fun guy to be around after Matt left. It was understandable considering he had just lost his two best friends. However, his girlfriend didn't even try to understand his pain. She had no sympathy and broke up with him at the worst time possible.

He tried to think of something else. He knew full well his heart was still bitter from his past relationship. That bitterness had made it even more difficult to watch Matt treat his girlfriends so cavalierly.

Apparently, Matt had gotten over his first love and gotten engaged. Shocking! Was the boy really going to settle down with one woman? Samuel wondered what she would be like. She was probably a drop-dead gorgeous airhead who flirted constantly and showed too much skin. He wondered how much she had given of herself in order to keep Matt in the relationship. Samuel shook the thought from his mind. He was a youth pastor; he wasn't supposed to struggle with things like this.

He wished he could be free, but his vices were suffocating him. Was he any better than John Carter after all? Samuel knew the bitterness he held on to was not pleasing to God. The Scriptures said to forgive. Had he really been forgiving? He thought he had forgiven John, but now he was angry again. Matt was dead.

The thought echoed through his brain. *Matt is dead. Matt is dead.* His only beloved brother was dead. Samuel was now in a full-out sprint. His legs cramped up. Only God knew how long he had been running, and only God knew the internal pain he felt. He kept running faster and faster until suddenly, his muscles cramped again and his joints locked up. He yelped in pain and tumbled on to the grass.

As he lay there with his muscles aching and sweat pouring down his face, the floodgates of his heart finally broke loose. He wept shamelessly. His tears soaked his face, mixing with the sweat. How could God allow this? The God he had studied and trusted his entire life now seemed so distant.

Samuel had gone to school to prevent people from turning out like his brother. He had prayed night and day for Matt. He had waited patiently for the day when Matt would finally come back to Jesus. Everything Samuel had worked for suddenly seemed pointless. What was the purpose of his life now?

Samuel slowly stood and headed home. It appeared he had a good hour or more of walking ahead of him. It would be lonely and long. He wiped the tears and sweat off his face with his shirt.

Staring out into the night, he began to pray. "Oh God, I have no idea what to do. I don't know why you allowed this. I don't understand why Matt had to die, or even run away to begin with. My family is heartbroken and my heart died with Matt's. Please bring something good out of this mess. Help my family. Help me. Please get us through this." Samuel sighed as he looked around. This would be a tough walk and a long, long night.

 *Chapter 4*

The hour-long ride to visit the Lowells was silent. Zuriel didn't want to talk. She knew most psychiatrists recommended conversation, but that would only cause unbearable anguish. She was about to go visit the family of her dead fiancé. There was nothing to talk about, only inexpressible feelings of darkness. She might as well enjoy an hour without weeping.

She stared outside as the road dragged on, pulling her into her lover's past. Who knew what she would find there?

Drew slowed the vehicle and turned into what appeared to be a wealthy neighborhood. As they wound through the placid streets, Zuriel felt instantly confused. The houses were immense, brick, and well-maintained. Old ladies were power-walking, children rode bikes, and teenagers were walking their dogs. She was far from home. Matt had always made it sound like his life had been difficult. She believed him when he told her about his single mother dying of cancer. She had imagined that he had grown up in Detroit just like she had, yet this suburb was anything but low-income. This was the kind of upbringing that Suzy, her drug-addict friend, had been part of. Everyone always wanted to be Suzy's friend, but Zuriel was the one who'd managed to become her best friend. She had always been jealous of Suzy's family's status and collection of stuff. Zuriel never understood why Suzy didn't like it there. Zuriel would have done anything to be part of that crowd. She never dreamed her fiancé had been a part of this foreign world as well.

Matt's childhood home was a beautiful brick house with a cream-painted porch encircling the front half. There was an abundance of grass out front, plots of lilies planted in dark mulch, and a small wooded area in the backyard. The breathtaking sight reminded her of visits to the park. The last time she had seen that much nature was when Matt proposed.

Zuriel tired to maintain control of her emotions. The memories were sweet and sour, like mixing pickle juice with punch. No matter how sweet the punch tasted, the pickle juice just ruined the whole thing.

It was impossible for Zuriel to comprehend that the person she thought she knew so well could be so opposite of what he had portrayed. Why had Matt kept such a secret? Matt was a good person; he wouldn't leave something good behind. Maybe his family was as dysfunctional as her own. Perhaps that's why he understood her so well. If that was the case, then why would he keep the truth from her? It made absolutely no sense. Who was Matt Lowell?

"Drew, did you know about Matt's family?"

"I didn't know much. I just knew he had left a crazy life behind. He wanted nothing to do with them for a long time, but I think he regretted it later on. He never really liked to talk about it. His family seems nice on the outside, but they're all pretty heavily into all that religion stuff," Drew explained as he put the car in park.

The family spilled out the front door to meet them. The situation seemed so awkward to Zuriel.

"Well, I guess that makes sense," she said. "I hated my family too, but sometimes I feel bad about it. I've seen too many movies with happy families in them. I don't really think a happy family even exists. Maybe Matt and I wouldn't have been very happy after all." As she spoke, she felt a deep sense of despair. Was there ever a chance of having true happiness with a guy?

As Matt's family came running toward her with arms open for hugs, she closed her eyes, shoving the thoughts far away. She got out of the car, carefully making sure that every emotional guard was in place.

A short, plump woman approached her first. The older woman's dark hair was in a tight bun with chopsticks poking out. Her brown eyes were a haunting copy of Matt's.

"God bless you, dear. I'm glad to see you! We'll have to comfort each other through this somehow. Oh, you are so beautiful! Of course Matthew would love you." Tears streamed down her face.

Zuriel felt oddly comfortable when the woman hugged her tightly. She didn't have much experience with warm embraces, but this little woman obviously had practice.

"My name is Anne; Anne Lowell." She finished her hug.

"It's nice to meet you," Zuriel managed to say. She stepped back, putting comfortable space between herself and Anne. Surveying the group in front of her confirmed her worst fear: Matt really did have a family. They all looked like him. He really had deceived her and couldn't defend himself now. It was too late for reconciliation. The horrid truth overwhelmed her, and tears trickled out of her glassy green eyes. The introductions continued, forcing her to gather her strength once again.

"This is my husband, Will Lowell," Anne said, introducing her to a tall man whose eyes were as dark as his hair was white.

He stepped forward and clasped her hands between his. "It's good to meet you. I know this is a tough time, but let us not forget that God is watching out for us all. I'm so glad you've come."

Zuriel only smiled and nodded. She knew her mascara was streaking down her face by now.

"These are my daughters." Will said, gesturing to two young women. "This is Christina, and this is Elizabeth."

The two girls waiting behind Will and Anne rushed forward and hugged Zuriel. They were beautiful.

The older one, Christina, was tall and dark like her father. She was slender but not lacking in feminine form. She whispered in Zuriel's ear, "The end is not the end." Her words were confusing, but she guessed it was probably some religious quote meant to make people feel better.

Elizabeth, the younger one, probably in her mid teens, came next. She was also gorgeous in face and form, but she was not tall like her sister. She was small and petite, just barely taller than five feet. She hugged Zuriel shyly and dabbed her eyes with a rose-colored tissue.

Then they all shook Drew's hand, except for Anne, who abruptly wrapped her arms around his wiry body. She seemed to have no pretenses whatsoever. "Well, shall we go in?" Will asked, taking his wife's hand and leading the family inside.

Zuriel and Drew followed. She had never been so formally greeted in her entire life.

The front room was breathtaking. The staircase, the chandelier, and the family photos all screamed that this was a picture-perfect home. It made Zuriel wonder even more what had happened. Why would Matt want to leave this? She noticed a cross hanging on the wall and remembered that this was a religious family. You would only be accepted here if you were good—that's how it had been at the little church from her childhood, so she assumed it was the same here, and maybe it had been too much for Matt to take.

Anne spoke in a steady cadence as she handed Zuriel a glass of pink lemonade. "You're very welcome here! I'm sure you're tired.

We will have dinner in a few hours. You'll probably want to get settled. We have a couple different rooms you could stay in. How would you feel about having Matt's old room? Some people are comforted by that and others aren't. We have other rooms if that would make you feel uncomfortable."

Zuriel was more than happy to hear she could have Matt's room. She would do anything to get a glimpse of who he really was. "I think I would like staying in Matt's room. Thank you."

Mrs. Lowell smiled and gestured toward the large staircase.

The oak railing felt smooth on Zuriel's hand. She noticed how well decorated and coordinated the house was. She knew Anne had put a lot into making this house a home. Maybe it was a "mother thing"? But how was she supposed to know, considering she never had one!

Anne led her into a small white room. It was dark because thick, navy curtains hung from the windows. The twin bed was neatly made, and the mahogany dresser was clean without a single thing on top of it. Posters of various rock bands hung above it. Zuriel recognized some of the bands from Matt's CD collection.

In the corner was a small, messy desk. Pencils and pens were strewn everywhere. Gum wrappers, books, and a Bible were buried in dust. How strange that everything else in the room was clean except for this.

"I haven't had the heart to go through or change this desk," Anne said, noticing Zuriel spying the dusty mound. "This is where Matt did most of his homework and where he was always writing. It's also where we found his letter, the day he left." Anne paused, clearly trying to hold back the emotion in her voice. The tears triggered Zuriel's own sorrow. "I just wanted him to come back to us, but more importantly back to God. Oh, Zuriel, do you know if he believed in God?"

Zuriel felt sick. She didn't have the heart to tell this woman that her son was an atheist. However, she couldn't lie. She would have to tell the truth. "I'm sorry, but I don't think he cared much for religion." Zuriel felt her tears falling faster, but she didn't understand why. She didn't really believe in God, but Anne's intense concern made her wish Matt had at least believed in God's existence. Anne was the first one she had ever met who seemed sincere about her beliefs. What a shame some people sank into religion so deeply.

"Well, I believe deep down, Matt knew." Anne wiped her eyes and forced a plastic smile. "I'll let you rest now. I'll send someone up to get you for dinner. Feel free to look at anything on his desk. There are tissues in the closet. You'll probably need them."

"Thank you so much, Mrs. Lowell."

"Please call me Anne." She smiled sincerely this time before leaving.

The moment she was gone, Zuriel jumped into the bed and curled up under the covers. This was where Matt grew up and had slept for most of his life. As angry as she was because he kept this secret, she almost didn't care. She missed him. She missed him intensely. Zuriel hugged herself tightly and tried to imagine his arms around her. Closing her eyes, she began to weep softly. Her Matt was dead.

 Chapter 5

Samuel sat on the leather living room couch next to his father. He felt slightly guilty for not going out to meet the guests with the family, but he just couldn't bring himself to. He knew he would meet his brother's fiancée soon enough. He was having a hard time dealing with the whole situation. It wasn't just the fact that Matt was dead. It was the fact that Matt had died without believing in God. It was the fact that Samuel's own bitterness had driven him into becoming a youth pastor for all the wrong reasons, yet as hard as he had tried, he could never convert his brother. It was all a sick, twisted mess of regret, bitterness, and anger.

Did his actions please God? Certainly not, but Samuel wasn't even sure how to do that anymore. God had seemed so distant lately. Maybe in a few years this would make a great sermon, but right now talking about God's goodness didn't seem that appealing. His poor mother had actually hoped and believed Matt had never left the faith to begin with. As if the drugs and defiance weren't a clear enough sign. She asked Zuriel when she arrived and was, of course, disappointed.

Samuel was pretty sure he knew what kind of woman Zuriel must be. He could imagine her being beautiful, but only in that artificial, seductive way. She would probably be unpleasant and dry-eyed. Her makeup would be perfect, and she would delight in purposely making his mother cry. What kind of name was "Zuriel" anyway? It made him think of Ariel the mermaid and *The Prince of Egypt* all at the same time. It was going to be difficult to hide his reluctance to meet her.

Samuel felt sudden disgust with himself. He was acting like one of the high school girls in youth group. He was judging Zuriel and assuming he was so much more worthy than she was. Samuel felt tortured inside. He knew better than to act this way, but he was so tempted to not even care. Samuel had spent years trying to become this godly man, yet he was still no better than his dead brother! Was he going to throw his faith away because of one more trial? That's what Matt had done.

Samuel knew his father meant well as he sat composed and strong on the couch across from him. He wore his usual attire: black slacks, a short–sleeve, button-up shirt, and a pair of old loafers. His snowy hair was combed, and his shaven face brought awkward attention to the hair growing out of his ears. Samuel used to think his father was too young to have a white head, but today the haggard appearance suited him. Will Lowell looked concerned, not grieved. He seemed to have an uncanny ability to deal with just one issue at a time. It was as if his father had forgotten about Matt and was only concerned with his living son for the moment. His eyes were closed and Samuel knew he was praying. He was probably praying for Samuel. It was humbling.

"Samuel," his dad said, breaking the silence, "I know you're hurting. You used to believe it was your calling to bring Matt back to God." He paused and softened his expression. "Don't be too hard on yourself, son. God has always had so much more in store for you."

"I know, Dad. I just don't feel God's presence with me anymore. When Matt first left, I became so close to God. I studied the Bible every day and prayed for Matt. I had a purpose and a mission to help teens stay on the right path. I thought God had chosen me for something." He exhaled heavily. "I failed. We all failed. What point is there in moving on and pretending God is always good?"

Samuel hated the sound of his own voice. He clenched his fists. What was he even saying? "The kids at youth group have been through some pretty horrible things, and I kept telling them God would always be there to take care of them."

"And do you believe that?" Will's voice was low and steady, as if his words were a rolling train.

"Of course I do! If I didn't, my whole life would be one big waste. God is in control, but I can't pretend to understand him, or that I like what he's doing."

"No one is asking you to pretend, Samuel. You know that forgiving Matt and God is the only way to get yourself out of this mess."

"Yes, I know." Samuel knew God was real and good. He knew salvation was only found through Christ. He still believed, but his confidence was shaken. The slow-growing cancer of anger and bitterness was ruining his ability to be used for God's glory. He was a Christian, but his heart hated accepting the circumstances. He did not want to forgive himself or anyone else, and the worst part was that he knew it was keeping him from experiencing peace.

"Dad, it's just not fair, though, is it?" Samuel lamented. "I have counseled so many people on how to trust God, even through trials. I thought having a lost brother helped me to understand, but this is beyond anything I ever wanted to understand."

"But this isn't heaven yet, son. Bad things happen to people."

"I know." He hated the truths battling inside himself.

"The best part of Christianity is that we have a loving God who is always there to comfort us when things get bad," Will said, continuing his lecture.

"True, but that sounds so ironic. It's like saying, 'Let's give God control so we can run to him for Band-Aids every time he lets us get hurt.'" Samuel felt sick in the pit of his stomach at his own sarcasm. Everything he felt was challenging what he knew to be true. He knew he would survive this. He knew God would work things out for his good, he just didn't know when. Samuel had a deep, dark feeling that the process was going to be painful.

"Dad, I don't mean to say stuff like this. I just don't feel in my heart what I know in my head. The idol of saving Matt has been destroyed, but I miss the idol. I miss my bitterness … I miss Matt."

The silence was sudden—peaceful yet painful. Samuel looked up at his dad, unprepared for the emotion that waited. Their dark eyes mirrored each other for a mere second before the tears began to fester. He wondered why this had to happen to him, and if he deserved this pain. He was the one who had been angry with God and Matt. His father was a whole different story, though. His dad had never doubted or wavered and had always prayed. This was cruelty at its finest.

They heard the call for dinner and slowly stood. Samuel's father gently put a hand on his shoulder. Samuel wanted to make eye contact again but couldn't bring himself to look up. He felt like such a failure. His father bowed his head once more.

"I know it hurts, son, but you have to let go of your need to see Matt saved and start letting Jesus save you instead," Will said, raising his head.

Samuel wasn't prepared for what he had just heard. Getting over Matt's rebellion wasn't a comforting suggestion. How could he ever forget that Matt was in hell? Samuel wished he hadn't revealed his struggles.

Together they walked into the dining room, Will's words still ringing in Samuel's ears: "Start letting Jesus save you." He was letting Jesus save him, wasn't he? He tried to let go of his hurt for a moment and focus on the end of his father's statement. Samuel knew he needed to go to God with this, but he felt distant, as though he had to figure it out on his own.

His mind wandered back to a conversation he'd had with Matt shortly before his brother left.

"Sam, I don't understand why this has to be so confusing. I keep trying to figure this God stuff out and it's not working!" Matt snapped, throwing his finished cigarette butt to the ground.

"You know you can't expect to figure it out alone, Matt. Remember what John taught us at the winter retreat: 'Apart from Christ you can do nothing.'"

"Yeah, and why would you bring John into this? He's been gone for months. He's a liar and his words mean nothing," Matt snapped.

"Even if John was lying, it doesn't make God's Word any less true. I've forgiven him and so should you."

Samuel's own words had burned in his heart. He had meant them when he'd said them, but after Matt left, he had looked for someone to blame. He'd wished his youth pastor and good friend hadn't fallen.

Samuel knew he had a choice. He could respond like Matt and run away from the truth, or he could follow his own advice and forgive. Apart from Christ he could do nothing, though. How could he let Jesus save him from his own bitterness? He didn't really know how to go about this.

Samuel took note of the delicious spread as he sat at the dining room table. The mashed potatoes, greens, and ham all looked appetizing. He looked forward to it as much for the noise and conversation as for the consumption of the food itself. Maybe they could talk about something normal and he could get his mind off his own thoughts. That would be nice.

Suddenly Samuel remembered the guest in the house as he saw the extra place setting. He would be meeting his dead brother's fiancée. Dinner no longer seemed so appealing. She was most likely an immodest slut, who only missed Matt for the physical benefits of their relationship. Samuel winced at his own thoughts. Once again he felt his bitterness and judgmental nature suffocating him. He was ready to throw stones. What did Jesus think about this?

Then Samuel saw her. A smallish woman with messy blonde hair walked shyly into the room. He was taken aback by her appearance. He had been expecting Matt's fiancée to be completely covered in makeup and fake smiles, but this woman was different than any of his imaginings. She was certainly beautiful but obviously sorrowful and exhausted from crying. Her green eyes were glossy and bloodshot, and she wore jeans and a crumpled, light-blue sweatshirt. She was certainly not trying to put up a front. Samuel felt a pang of guilt. No one could doubt her heart was broken.

She quickly sat at the table and looked down at her plate. It was apparent she was uncomfortable.

"I believe I'm the last to meet you. I'm Sam, Matt's older brother." Samuel extended a hand, feeling self-conscious. Why had he introduced himself as Sam? Only Matt had called him that. He met her teary-eyed look and felt her weak handshake. Once again, he felt guilty for passing judgment.

"Hi, I'm Zuriel." She looked at her plate again as soon as she finished talking. She seemed scared—really scared.

Everyone slowly found a seat at the table. Samuel could sense their sorrow. This meal wasn't going to be normal because there was no escaping the harsh reality that Matt was gone.

 *Chapter 6*

Zuriel stared at the square glass plate in front of her, afraid to look up at the family. They all looked just like Matt, and she felt their eyes intently making a study of her. To speak or even make eye contact was a sure recipe for tears and more unwanted embarrassment. She had never displayed this much emotion to anyone before, not even her own family. Being around strangers in a mess of sorrow was less than appealing. Zuriel had been so lost in grief that she completely forgot about looking in the mirror before trudging into the dining room. She realized she was still wearing her sweatshirt and jeans, and as she felt her hair with her fingers, she knew it was a mess. She lifted up her silver spoon and tried to see her reflection. The image wasn't clear enough to inspect her mascara. She felt her cheeks warm and concluded she was an eyesore.

Why did she care? She knew she was fully justified; her fiancé had just died. Still, she didn't know if she could be herself around the Lowells because she feared their judgment. Just the fact that they were all familiar with one another, and she was the only outsider, made her feel victimized. She wondered if Matt had felt the same way. She knew he was a good guy; therefore, she had to conclude that anything he didn't like was bad. Even if Matt wasn't there to coach her through this, she could at least try to do what he would have wanted. Matt's love and trust was the only thing she had ever been sure of, and she feared what accepting his betrayal would mean. So Zuriel secretly decided that Matt had good reasons for leaving and that he could be trusted. It was the only thing she could hold on to.

Zuriel covertly examined the people around her. The family was attractive; that was obvious. Even plump little Anne was captivating and graceful. Zuriel looked across the table and noticed Sam. He'd shaken her hand earlier, but she'd been too scared to really look at him. Now she noticed his broad shoulders, square jaw, and deeply inviting eyes. He looked so much like Matt she could hardly look away. His red polo complemented his olive skin, and the short sleeves revealed his defined biceps. Zuriel remembered staring at Matt's muscles, and comparing her own pale skin with his, telling him how lucky he was not to have to tan. Zuriel looked at her plate again, hoping Sam wouldn't catch her staring. He just looked so much like Matt that she couldn't ignore it. She had to look, but she couldn't, because looking made her soul ache with emptiness. She knew he wasn't Matt; Sam was taller, lankier, and had a few different facial features. Still, she felt vulnerable around him and wondered if she should stay away. Using Sam to fantasize about Matt summoned more heartache than she could take.

Zuriel needed to be around someone safe. She couldn't wait to see Drew again; at least he could join her as an outcast. As everyone found their place, she was dismayed not to see him. She knew he wasn't a fan of the family from the expression on his face after Anne had hugged him, clearly invading his privacy. However, she hadn't expected him to boycott the family altogether.

"Is Drew not coming to dinner this evening?" she asked nervously, feeling awkward using such formal language. She felt somewhat pressured to use upper-class words in this house.

"Oh, he left not long after you fell asleep," Anne said. "Didn't you know he planned on leaving? He said he would be back for the ..." Her voice trailed off. She looked at her husband and received a soft, compassionate smile. She smiled back through her tears. "He's planning on coming back for the funeral."

"Oh, I didn't know that," Zuriel mumbled, slightly aggravated that Drew had not told her his plans. She was fascinated though, by the exchange between Mr. and Mrs. Lowell. There were only a few couples she had seen interact—her grandparents mainly; however, their interactions were rare, especially ones involving smiles. The Lowells seemed to find comfort in each other, and Zuriel could not imagine her family responding to each other that way. The silence that followed felt awkward, but it seemed normal to the rest of them. She stared at the food, wondering what to do. Where they waiting for her to serve herself? She was the guest, after all.

"I think it is time for us all to pray," Will softly announced. He smiled lovingly at his wife once again and then glanced around the table. He took the hands of his daughter and son on either side. Zuriel felt Christina reach for her hand and then saw Anne reaching out to her as well. Zuriel felt afraid suddenly. She wasn't a Christian. She didn't know what she was supposed to say and do. For several of her younger years she remembered her grandmother reciting a few fancy prayers, but that was the extent of it. She held on to Anne and Christina, hoping they didn't notice her hands beginning to sweat. Zuriel was thankful she wasn't sitting next to Sam. She looked across the table and caught his eye. She looked away quickly, feeling embarrassed. She couldn't wait for this dinner to end.

Finally Will began to pray. "Dear Lord, we come together today in need of you. We are grieved by the loss of a dear son, brother, and fiancé. We do not understand your will, but we trust in you during this time of tragedy. Please bring comfort to us and help us get through this together. Thank you for your precious son, Jesus Christ, and the price he paid. Bless the food and my lovely wife, who prepared it. And we especially thank you for our guest today, Zuriel. Thank you for bringing her to us safely. In your name we pray, amen." He lifted his head as he finished.

Anne squeezed Zuriel's hand and smiled before letting go. The dishes were passed around and the clatter of silverware began. Zuriel felt like an alien in another world. The prayer had not been rehearsed but simply said. What did they mean by thanking God for her? Didn't they know she wasn't even a Christian? They all treated her like she was someone very important to them and to God. Was this really the kind of life Matt had grown up with?

❦

Will Lowell looked around the table at his family as they began to eat, and he felt burdened for them all. How were they going to be able to let go of Matthew? Most of the funerals that his children had been to were for people who were obviously Christians. It was easy to celebrate their lives and grieve because they could have peace in the fact that the deceased had gone on to heaven to be with the Lord. There were no comforting words or thoughts of heaven for his son, though. The Matthew they knew had lived a life of rebellion against God. Will knew all too well the result of that kind of disobedience.

Still, he also knew his family needed him to be strong. He had faithfully prayed for his family and for Matthew, and he had not received the answer he was looking for. How could comfort his family? How could he lead them in faith? He knew God was in control, but he didn't understand why God would allow such suffering.

He thought of Samuel, his firstborn son. Samuel would have a difficult road ahead if he never forgave himself for the last five years.

And now they had Zuriel, his son's fiancée, in their midst. Perhaps she would come to know Christ as her savior. Will hoped it was part of God's plan and prayed that God would show him how to love her instead of judge her. Was one soul more valuable than another? He knew God loved everyone the same, and he did not want to think of trading his son's salvation for Zuriel's. Nevertheless, he knew God wanted to save her, and Will wanted desperately to find some meaning and purpose in this trial.

He didn't know what to say or how to begin, but he was curious about what kind of person his son had become. He hoped Zuriel would be able to comfort the family with some positive stories about Matthew. He knew his wife needed to hear them more than anyone else. She was trying hard to be strong, but Will knew she was dying inside. She loved Matthew as much as he did, and she had always believed he had never actually walked away from God. She seemed to punish herself for not getting counseling for him. The long arguments they'd had over their son often lasted into the night. And now that he was gone, they both gave up trying to figure out who was at fault. He knew they both just wanted what was best for Matthew, but that somehow it wasn't good enough. There was nothing either of them could do to change things.

He looked up again at the family and caught sight of Zuriel. She shied away from his gaze, looking to her plate for comfort instead. Will felt helpless. He couldn't rely on his wife to make everyone feel comfortable this time. It may have been too late to counsel Matthew, but it wasn't too late to counsel and show compassion to the people he now sat with. No one was comfortable, and no one wanted to break the silence with the harsh reality that hung in the air. Will was starting to understand what leading his family was really about, and he was surprised by how afraid he was. He would have to proceed with God's help.

"Well, Zuriel, we are all so glad you're here. We've been looking forward to getting to know you and finding out what our dear boy was up to the last few years." Will said, breaking the icy silence.

"Oh, well, that's nice of you. I only met Matt about six months ago. Drew actually knows more about his life before that." Her voice was shaky.

Will felt sick to his stomach. Only six months? He was aching to know what had gone on for the last five years, and now he wondered if he really wanted to. He saw his wife lean eagerly over the table. He could tell she didn't care what kind of life Matt had lived, she just wanted to know.

"Well, he did propose to you, so you must know him better than most," Christina said, smiling. Will smiled back, thankful for his daughter's apparent cheerfulness. She would be engaged soon, so he knew she would be a great help in comforting Zuriel.

"He was a very good guy. I had never met anyone who treated me like he did. He always helped me into the car, paid for the food, and told me I was pretty and stuff." Zuriel blushed and looked around. It was clear that she felt out of place but was happy to share about the love she had for Matthew. "I had dated some real losers in my life, but then he came along and made it obvious that he was perfect for me. Even though we only dated for six months I just had to marry him. I couldn't stand the thought of losing him …" Zuriel stopped abruptly and tears collected in her eyes.

Will smiled again at his wife, relieved that Zuriel was sincere. He silently thanked God. Zuriel would be a huge blessing to the family during this time.

Anne said, "That's wonderful. He was always such a sweet boy. When he was little he would pick dandelions for me. He cried the day he found out they were weeds, but I told him that I loved every single one he had given me." She beamed with joy.

"Yeah, Matt always was a lady's man!" Samuel added sarcastically.

Will tried to scold his son across the table with a sharp look, but it was no use.

"Did you guys live together in Detroit?" Samuel asked, causing Will to cringe. Why did Samuel have to bring up Matthew's fallen lifestyle?

"Oh, no. Matt wouldn't. He wanted to wait until we were married. I don't know why he was so old-fashioned. I suppose that's why I was so attracted to him, because he was different and romantic."

"I'm glad to hear it, Zuriel. It's always more romantic that way!" Christiana's relentless joy was overwhelmingly obvious, especially compared to Samuel's bitterness.

"Well, it's great that he managed to do that. I wonder what changed him," Samuel said condescendingly.

Will finally caught Samuel's eyes and shot his son a glance that told him he'd better stop his negativity. Will knew Samuel's statement was valid, but it was entirely inappropriate for the occasion.

"I'm not ignorant of Matt's past," Zuriel shot back indignantly. "His friends always joked around about how he used to be more fun. I know that he made mistakes back then, but so did I. I never felt a need to know about all the details. He said he changed, and I fell in the love with that person. I don't care who he used to be."

Will smiled. He knew it was naïve for a girl to enter a relationship without knowing who she was marrying. However, he couldn't help but recognize the truth in what she was saying. She understood forgiveness and grace better than most of the Christians he knew.

"I'm glad you were able to know him and see all of the good things about him. He was wonderful child," Anne said as she stood. She began to clear the dinner plates for dessert.

Will felt relief, knowing that dinner was almost over. It was clear God had something special planned. He wondered what his good friend was up to.

 Chapter 7

Zuriel was relieved when she could finally escape and be alone in Matt's room, even if it was only for a few minutes. She needed to collect her thoughts. They were all sad that Matt had died, but they weren't grieving normally. There was something she could not explain about them. It fascinated her yet made her angry at the same time. They acted as though comfort really did come from God. She found that hard to swallow because she was pretty sure the whole thing was God's fault. Zuriel knew they were heartbroken, but she was insulted by their trust in God. Why didn't they just let themselves be sad? The only explanation that seemed possible was that they were faking. They had to be! Matt must have known and left in search of reality. And now he had found it.

Even still, they all seemed to care for each other, and for some reason they acted like they cared for her too. They truly gave the impression of sincerity, which made her feel guilty for her indifference toward them. Zuriel had never seen a family go so long without screaming at each other, and the serene atmosphere made her critique her own family. She wondered what kind of person she would have become if she had lived here. Matt had lived with them for eighteen years and still turned out to be just like her. Maybe it didn't matter what family you grew up in.

She had been surprised by her own father's sympathy after she called him with the news. Considering how he'd responded to her engagement, what comfort he offered was shocking. And now, after examining the inappropriately joyous family dinner, she was glad her dad at least was in touch with reality. He knew death was a bad thing, and generally it wasn't something that could be comforted with Bible stories. Zuriel was surprised at her own discovery. She had viewed herself as white trash for most of her life, but now she thought she would rather be white trash and be real, rather than be rich and important with fake smiles.

She shuddered to think what the viewing tomorrow would be like. She wasn't ready to face it, much less face the smiles from hundreds of people she didn't know. Every time she remembered that her precious Matt was gone, the panic came back, along with uncontrollable sobs. Thinking about hugging strangers for hours brought on a similar affect.

"Zuriel!" Her thoughts were interrupted when Christiana called her name.

"Yes; I'm here," Zuriel answered, sliding her fingers under her eyes, hoping to remove the leftover tears. She opened the bedroom door and peered down the oak staircase, to find the source of the voice.

"Oh, hello! Mom, Elizabeth, and I are going through pictures and making a slideshow for the viewing and funeral. I understand you brought some pictures we can add to it. Would you care to join us?" Christina was smiling again. It confused Zuriel so much. Why wasn't she depressed?

"Sure. Yeah, I brought my flash drive and I have some pictures on there. Drew e-mailed me a bunch from their good times too. I don't know if you guys will want to use them though. He's drinking in most of those pictures." Zuriel felt almost triumphant, telling her that Matt drank. She wasn't sure why, but Christina's joy made her feel angry.

"Oh. Well, I'm sure they'll be fine. I can't wait to see who he grew up to be."

Zuriel was astounded again. Christina didn't even seem fazed. She had half-expected Christina to ask her if Zuriel drank. Either Christina wasn't as judgmental as most Christians or Christina had a drinking problem herself. The thought amused Zuriel and made her smile.

Zuriel followed Christina into the kitchen. The dimmed lights shined on the granite countertops, and the dishwasher was making a whooshing sound, which instantly annoyed Zuriel. There where piles of pictures lying across the black breakfast table, and a laptop was plugged into a large scanner. Elizabeth was sitting Indian style on one of the chairs, leafing through a photo album. When she noticed their presence, Elizabeth looked up at them with tear-stained cheeks. Zuriel felt her stomach squirm; maybe she should have just gone to bed.

"Remember when Matt buried me in the sand when we went to Florida?" Elizabeth recalled thoughtfully.

"Oh my goodness, I do!" Christina pulled the picture from the photo album and showed her. Zuriel saw a boy in his early teens smiling beside a sand mound where a little girl's head was poking out. Matt looked so adorable as a boy, and Elizabeth's smile exposed her glee.

The girls pulled out multiple albums and began reminiscing about Matt's life. Zuriel watched in awe as the sisters cried and laughed together. Zuriel felt dissolute in their presence, fully aware of her own misjudgment of them. Their sorrow was cavernous, only because they had experienced such euphoria. They had an abundance of terrific memories, and twice as many reasons as she to miss him.

Zuriel was enthralled at what a full life in which Matt had partaken. She saw Matt as a baby, a boy scout, and a baseball player. She saw him camping, biking, swimming, canoeing, hanging out, and even sleeping. She recognized his goofy side in picture after picture, where he stuck out his tongue or gave his sisters bunny ears. He seemed happy. Everyone seemed happy.

"I don't understand!" Zuriel blurted, immediately regretting it.

"What don't you understand?" Christina asked, apparently startled by Zuriel's outburst.

"I just don't understand why he would keep all this a secret from me. Why would he leave all this behind? What did you guys do to him?" Zuriel asked.

The two sisters were silent for several seconds. Their eyes watered, and they looked at each other sympathetically.

Zuriel's hands shook out of anger and complete mortification at her own behavior.

"Well, I never understood it all myself," Christina began. "Matt had some problems in his late teens, and we tried to help him. He just didn't want help and he didn't want God. Matt felt like Christians were hypocrites and that religion was made up to control people. He felt like he was being controlled by his family, so he left." Christina's shoulders shook with grief, which was answer enough.

Zuriel understood in that moment that the family wasn't only mourning Matt's death but the five years they'd missed. Christina couldn't be faking. Zuriel's shaking started to subside and was replaced with silent weeping.

She didn't understand God or who Matt really was, but she did feel sorry for this family. She wished so badly that Matt were still here to explain himself. She wanted to hear his side and know for sure what had happened.

Elizabeth studied the pictures in an obvious attempt to hide her own tears. Zuriel could only watch and wonder. It was evident they loved each other and had loved Matt. She wished she could change things for their sake. She wondered what it would have been like to meet Matt while he'd lived here. The unfortunate truths remained, though, that Matt was dead and the mystery he left behind was unsolvable.

They continued to work in silence, afraid of spoiling the pensive mood. Zuriel felt like a robot, looking at each picture, becoming more aware of all that he had never told her. The betrayal was a knife in her back, but now it was going in deeper. She didn't feel like trusting Matt anymore.

Anne brought out an assortment of chocolate truffles, which brightened the vibe considerably. They could at the very least comment on the supernatural powers of chocolate. Zuriel plugged in her flash drive, causing a role reversal. They had never seen him as a twenty-three-year-old adult, and that familiar feeling of betrayal was all over their faces.

Zuriel painfully clicked through the pictures, struggling to keep her sorrow from exploding. She landed on the picture right after the engagement and finally allowed herself to gasp for air.

"He was so handsome! Oh my goodness, I can't believe that's my son!" Anne exclaimed merrily. "And Zuriel, you look absolutely beautiful."

"Thank you. He *was* handsome," Zuriel said, sniffling a few times before continuing. "He proposed that day. He took me on a night walk through the park, and everything was so beautiful. He held me and told me he loved me. When he asked me to marry him, it was so easy to say yes."

"That is so romantic," Christina said, almost whispering.

Zuriel smiled thinking about the romance but suddenly felt sick. He was so handsome, sweet, and kind, but he had lied to her. Still he had pretended that his childhood had been difficult like hers. She felt deceived and lonely all at once.

Anne hugged her tightly. Zuriel was dumbfounded by how quickly they could read her emotions. "Why? Why did he lie to me?" she confessed again, feeling like a broken record.

"Oh, Zuriel, I don't know. I don't know why he lied to you or to the rest of us. I just know he must have loved you very much, because I can't help but love you!" Anne cried, mourning along with her.

"But why did he leave? Didn't you ever find out?" Zuriel suddenly remembered the note Anne had mentioned. "What about the note? Did he tell you why he left?"

Anne released her embrace. Anne tried to say something, but her grief overwhelmed her. She looked at Zuriel apologetically and left the kitchen.

Zuriel felt horrible for bringing it up. She guessed it was a terribly painful thing for a mother to go through.

"It's okay, Zuriel; it's just a difficult subject. I'll go check on her," Christina said before going after her mother.

Zuriel hoped Christina was right and that it would be okay. She glanced at Elizabeth, delighted that at least someone would stay in the room. Zuriel didn't want to be alone right now, even if her companion was only sixteen.

"I remember the day he left," Elizabeth said softly.

Zuriel stared at her, not completely knowing what to expect. Elizabeth was so much quieter than the others in the family, and Zuriel guessed that it must have taken a lot of courage to say even those few words.

"Zuriel, I was eleven, and I remember waking up and hearing them all crying. Mom and Dad were sitting on his bed crying together. Christina was in her room for most of the day. Samuel was …" Elizabeth stopped to suppress the oncoming wave of emotion.

Zuriel felt herself involuntarily putting her arm around Elizabeth's shoulders.

"Samuel was so angry. He blamed himself for Matt leaving. He'd wanted to lead Matt back to God. Samuel became a different person after that day, and he dedicated his life to helping kids like Matt. He was going to be a doctor, you know. He switched majors and schools. That's when he and his roomate started to go to downtown Detroit on a regular basis to witness. Although I think Samuel went just because he wanted to see Matt."

Zuriel wasn't sure what witnessing meant, but it sounded horrendous. She felt sorry for Samuel, and for the whole family. She had loved Matt, but she had no idea that someone so wonderful could be the cause of so much pain. It almost didn't seem to matter what kind of family you were born into, something always came up to ruin things.

"And Zuriel, you should have seen my parents. My dad kept saying Matt would come back, like in the story of the Prodigal Son. He promised us that one day Matt would realize he needed God and needed us." She paused, trying to recompose herself. "I wish it were true. I wish he would have come back. I wish he would never have gotten so angry and left ..."

"I'm so sorry, Elizabeth. I wish he were alive so that you could talk to him," Zuriel said, but she felt silly trying to calm Matt's sister. She didn't know what to say. Zuriel wasn't a Christian and neither was Matt. Although she didn't plan on becoming one, she wished Matt had stayed one just for the sake of his family. However, most of all she wished Matt was still alive. She wanted the deceiver to explain himself.

"It's hard to know who to blame. I wrestle with it all the time," Elizabeth said calmly.

"What do you mean?"

"Well, before all this trouble, our church hired a new youth pastor. His name was John Carter. I wasn't old enough at the time, but Matt and Samuel went to youth group. John had become good friends with Samuel. I remember they would go out to eat and for Bible studies and things like that all the time. Samuel was even helping out at youth group after he graduated. Then it happened."

"What happened?"

"I don't think Matt had truly given his life to Jesus. He was still unsure about how much of his life he wanted to let God have. That is a pretty common stage for most teenagers to go through, but Matt didn't handle it well. When Matt was seventeen, the youth pastor was caught stealing money from the church. John Carter had to resign, and the youth group was unstable for a little while. Matt started doubting everything John had ever taught. He started to hang out with a bad group of kids at school, and he stopped going to youth group."

"Oh, so that's why," Zuriel pondered, coming to a better understanding of her lover's past. She could at least understand that Matt had been betrayed by the hypocritical and unfeeling world of religion. She could still remember how reluctant her grandmother was to go to church when they all found out her father wasn't a believer. Zuriel was supposed to have had her first communion, but it never happened because she refused to go without her father there. Zuriel wondered if she had escaped something disastrous, or if she and Matt had been too stubborn to see the good parts. The rest of the Lowells seemed okay.

"Yeah, things got pretty crazy. He ended up tapping into drugs. He didn't see the point in getting out of them or making himself better. He argued that God didn't exist after all. When he turned eighteen, he left and moved somewhere in Detroit. We didn't hear from him for a long time."

"But you did end up hearing from him?"

"Samuel got a call from him once, about a year later. Samuel went to Detroit to meet him and came back pretty discouraged and depressed. He was really angry because of what Matt had done but then later regretted what he told him and tried to find Matt again. Unfortunately, he never did."

"Did you ever find out why Matt called Samuel or what he did that made him so angry?" Zuriel asked, dying to know the answers.

"I don't know if I should tell you. It might be better just left in the past."

Zuriel was disappointed. She wasn't about to give up though; she had to uncover the mystery.

"It's okay, Elizabeth. I found out that my fiancé had been lying to me the whole time I knew him. There's nothing you can say that could be worse." She tried to force at smile at Elizabeth to reassure her.

Elizabeth nodded and took a deep breath before beginning. "I don't know the whole story, but Samuel said Matt had gotten a girl pregnant. I guess the girl had an abortion and Matt was angry about it. Samuel tried to convince Matt to come home, but they got into an argument. Samuel won't forgive himself for it."

Zuriel wanted to cry all over again. She had never liked talking about or knowing of past relationships her boyfriends had been in, especially ones that involved getting girls pregnant. Zuriel remembered how Matt had told her he wanted to do things the old-fashioned way and didn't want to move in together. Zuriel wondered if he had loved this other woman more than her.

"I'm sorry, Elizabeth …" Zuriel lamented. Her voice seemed lost in her tears. She felt bad for crying so much, but she couldn't hold any of it in. She needed to escape and figure some things out. "I'm really tired. I think I'll go to bed early."

"I understand. We all have a busy day tomorrow anyway."

Zuriel nodded and stood. After an awkward hug with Elizabeth, she was relieved when she made it up to Matt's old room. Collapsing on the bed, still wearing her jeans and sweatshirt, she wept again.

 *Chapter 8*

Samuel jerked awake, breathing hard and sweating. He glanced at the alarm clock beside his bed. It was barely five am. He had just dreamed that his brother was in hell calling his name, and he could only watch Matt be engulfed in flames. Samuel lay still, catching his breath, trying to become reacquainted with time, place, and person. He didn't feel like trying to go back to sleep and combating the nightmares that had plagued him so far. Even in his sleep Samuel couldn't escape the emotional agony. He groaned, stretched, and rolled on to the floor. It was the day of the viewing, and tomorrow would be the funeral, neither of which he was looking forward to. He prayed God would make him forget his dream and protect him from having anymore.

He made his way to the kitchen. Maybe some cold water and some time with the Lord would be a good idea. It was going to be a long couple of days, and he would need every bit of strength he could get. Entering the kitchen, he was startled. There was a man sitting at his table, texting. Samuel rubbed his eyes and looked closer; it was Michael, his roommate.

"Michael! When in the world did you get here?"

His friend turned slowly and smiled. "Oh, hey! Yeah, I just walked in, but I didn't bother calling. I knew you needed your beauty sleep." Michael raised his eyebrows and pointed at him.

Samuel knew his friend was referring to his sloppy sweatpants and bare chest. Michael always teased him about fashion, especially when he was in his pajamas.

"As you can see, I havn't been getting much. What on earth brought you back at this hour?" Samuel asked, glad to see his friend.

"It wasn't easy getting a flight here. I picked the first one available and here I am." He'd gone with his parents to South Carolina on vacation and had hoped to share his faith with them. His vacation was cut short when Samuel called with the news of Matt's death. Samuel expected him to arrive in Toledo later that evening but was glad he came earlier.

"I really appreciate your coming back up here, Michael," Samuel said, taking a glass from the cupboard. He filled it and sat at the small kitchen table.

"Of course I came. I knew this would be tough." He looked at Samuel warily. "You all right?"

"No." Samuel knew his friend deserved more of an answer, but that's all he could say. At least he was being honest. "It's been like hell. I can't believe it."

"I'm sorry, man. I've been praying for you." He stood up to initiate a hug.

"Thanks. Hopefully God will hear you, 'cause my prayers haven't done much lately." Samuel hated the sound of his own words. They were brutally honest but as sour as lemons.

"Sam, you can't blame yourself for this; you don't know the whole story. And because of what happened with Matt, God has used you to reach all sorts of kids. Don't pretend God abandoned you like some lost puppy."

His words stung. Why was Michael always right? "I just feel like I failed, you know?" Samuel tensed his muscles, feeling his fury build. "Why couldn't I bring Matt back?"

"You can't do anything on your own and you couldn't make choices for him. He was *your* brother, but he made his own mistakes. There are people everywhere who choose the path he chose. Don't blame yourself for his decisions."

"I can't help it. I was the only one who had a chance to bring him back … I saw him a year later in Detroit. He told me he was angry with his girlfriend for getting an abortion. I laughed because it seemed strange that he felt guilty for that, when he had done all sorts of other terrible things. He felt so guilty that he broke up with Lena and refused to talk to her." Samuel shook his head in disgust; he remembered the look on his brother's face and the anxiety in his eyes. "I asked him about the drugs, and he claimed he had left them a long time ago. He had apparently seen what they did to others. I guess Lena had a problem with his addiction too and helped him quit. I asked him to come home, but he said he was still angry with God. He told me I was the only one he was ready to talk to."

"He had a conscience, Samuel. His guilt is a sign he still knew that some things were wrong."

"I wish I would have seen it like that. I felt like he was just judging his ex-girlfriend when he had acted just as badly as she had. I should have used that day as an opportunity to rebuild our relationship; instead, I vented my own anger. I told him he had ripped the family apart." Samuel fumed. The last four years he had lived with the tortured memories and regret. He strongly wished he could go back and make things right.

"You can't change the past, Samuel." Michael shook his head.

"I know. I still wish it were different though. I wish John hadn't left like that. None of this would have happened if he hadn't stolen the money."

"You don't know that," Michael fired back. "Matt could have still turned away even if John hadn't done what he did. If Matt was leaning that direction anyway, then he just needed the right excuse. If it hadn't been John, it would've been someone else."

"Maybe so, but then I would have at least had a friend and mentor to help me through this. Matt wasn't the only one hurt by John's actions." Samuel clenched his fists, furious that he never got the comfort everyone seemed so willing to offer Matt. Suddenly his thoughts were interrupted by an object hitting his head. A pen hit the floor near his feet. "What was that for?"

Michael stood nearby, grinning. "So you needed a friend to help you through this, huh? I guess I must mean nothing to you!"

Chuckling despite himself, Samuel picked up the pen and hurled it back at Michael. "Obviously you're a great friend," he exclaimed sarcastically.

"Come on, Samuel. I've heard you teach this hundreds of times. You can't directly change most of the circumstances that happen to you in life, but you always have a choice to do the right thing. When God judges you, he isn't going to let you use Matt or John as an excuse. I know it's tough, Sammy, but you have to get over it. You loved Matt and you still do. It's okay to mourn him."

Samuel felt a strange emotion overtake him as Michael spoke. It wasn't the familiar feeling of anger, it was just plain sadness. He knew his friend was telling the truth, but he wasn't ready to get emotional in front of him.

"You're probably just mourning the fact that you have to wait longer to propose to my sister!" Samuel said mockingly, trying to lighten the mood. Michael had been dating Christina for a while now and already had permission to propose.

"Baloney! You're my best friend and I live here. I could have gone to see Christina before coming here if I'd wanted to!" Michael contested.

"At five in the morning?"

"Oh, whatever! You need help, Sam." Michael threw the pen at him again.

"I know," he said almost solemnly. And he was completely serious.

Samuel got up from the table and made his way to the bathroom. He would shower and head over to his folks' house early. He always liked meeting with God in the woods at their place. There was something about the serene setting and being surrounded by nature that made him feel closer to God. Samuel desperately needed to feel him, and before the funeral. It was supposed to be a beautiful June day, after all.

Samuel pulled into his parents' driveway at 6:32 a.m. He knew his father wouldn't be getting up for another hour, which would give him the privacy he desired. He stepped out of his car and started walking around the brick house, toward the backyard. Seeing the white picket fence, Samuel gave himself a running start before clearing it. He landed firmly on his feet and smiled. It felt good to do that, even as a twenty-five-year-old adult. He quickly strode across the lawn toward the line of green trees. Eyeing the path his father had made so long ago, he began his hike through the familiar territory.

The early birds were out, singing their songs of praise, and the rest of creatures seemed to be moving to their tune. The trees were full, except of course for the few rotting ones here and there. His father had plans of chopping those up for fuel after putting in a wood-burning stove. It had never happened, and now that his parents were getting older, he doubted it would ever would. Samuel could now start to hear the little stream up ahead. It was his favorite place, the place he felt nearest to God. He slowed his pace and began to pray out loud, thankful that the God of the universe was listening.

"Dear God, I can't forgive him! I know you want me to, but I can't. I need you to change me so I can, because I don't feel like moving on is possible." Samuel shouted. He stepped closer to the stream, watching the waters swoosh through the muddy canal, driving leaves and pollen with it. It seemed like God was the water and he was one of the withered plants, pushed against his will. "I'm mad, God. I'm really mad, and I don't understand why you let this happen! I thought you were good!" He moaned, unloading his honest rage.

He heard a rustling and noticed movement out of the corner of his eye. He stopped and turned just in time to see Zuriel walking away from him. Samuel guessed she'd probably heard everything. What was she doing out here so early, and how dare she invade his time with God? He decided to ignore her and walk back the other way. He didn't like the idea of being in the woods alone with his dead brother's fiancée. It sounded like a women's Lifetime movie special. He had come out here to be alone with God and find forgiveness. What had she come out here for? He almost wanted to ask her. At least Samuel had God to comfort him and help him through this. What did Zuriel have? He picked up the pace, ready to return to the yard. Maybe he could sit on the deck for a while? His ideas were thwarted when he heard the crunching sound of footsteps behind him.

"Sam! Sam, wait!" Zuriel called. He stopped and slowly turned to face her direction.

"You're up early," Samuel managed to say when she caught up.

She smiled shyly and looked at the ground.

He noticed she was still wearing the same blue sweatshirt and jeans and wondered if this girl had any other clothes. Her blonde hair was pulled back, and her large eyes were glossy. He knew they were green, but next to the green foliage, they were stunning. She was a beautiful woman.

"I suppose I should say the same thing to you. I thought you went home last night," she shot back seamlessly.

"I did, I just needed some time alone. I always used to come back here to think and pray." He immediately regretted mentioning time alone. He could tell she was sensitive and probably felt bad for bugging him.

"I'm sorry for interrupting your time. I was going back to the house anyway." She apologized and started to walk past him.

Samuel knew it was selfish to send her away. He felt obligated to at least talk to her. "Please don't worry about it. What brings you out here?" he asked, trying to make conversation.

"I was just having trouble sleeping. I saw the woods and wanted to come out here. It makes me feel closer to Matt. He proposed in the woods, you know."

"I didn't know that. I'm sorry," he said, detecting sorrow in her voice. Maybe she had actually fallen in love with Matt. He was mesmerized when he met her gaze, and he honestly felt sorry for her. She looked so small and helpless yet completely innocent. He knew better though than to believe that.

"It's okay. You guys have all been so sweet. I'm not used to it." Sweet? Samuel knew he hadn't been the sweetest of guys, especially to her.

"Well, I have a great family," he conceded.

"I can see that. Your parents seem very happy with each other. It must be nice growing up with all this," Zuriel said, making a sweeping gesture as she spoke.

"Yeah. We moved into this place when I was in the middle of high school, so it wasn't always this nice."

"I wasn't talking about the house." Zuriel smiled again with her shy grin.

Samuel was once again caught off guard.

"I thought families like this were only on TV. That's why it's so hard to understand why Matt would leave this for the life we had in Detroit," she wondered out loud.

He saw her countenance fall and was surprised. Even though she had Matt's engagement ring on her finger, she was still just as puzzled as he was.

"He must have made us sound horrible."

"No, actually, he never mentioned any of you. He told me he was raised by a single mother who had died of cancer. He convinced me he'd had a tough childhood." She crossed her arms and leaned against a large oak tree.

Samuel wasn't sure how to respond. He hadn't realized Matt had fooled her. He sat on a stump, trying to understand. "I didn't know that. That makes things even more difficult for you, I'm sure."

"Yes it does. I keep trying to understand who he was and why he left. You know, you really shouldn't blame yourself."

Samuel winced at her words. Was it obvious that he felt somewhat responsible, or did someone tell her? "What makes you think I blame myself?"

"You just seem really hard on yourself. I heard you basically dedicated your life to helping Matt come back."

Now it was Samuel's turn to avoid eye contact. He didn't feel comfortable with her knowing so much about him. "Yeah, did my dad tell you that?" He couldn't keep his annoyance out of his voice. "Matt had some real problems, and I guess I was no match for them."

"Everyone has problems, but Matt only had a few," Zuriel said sternly. She moved to a tree a little farther from him and resumed leaning before continuing her lecture. "Matt was the best person I've ever met."

Samuel pitied her ignorance but knew it had to be clarified. Didn't she know who she had almost married? "I'm sure he was nice to you. It sounds like he was attempting to be a good guy, but you didn't know him back when he was a pothead."

"You're right, I didn't, but he wasn't a pothead anymore when I met him. Why do you keep thinking of him as the same rebellious teenager? He wasn't eighteen anymore."

Samuel didn't understand why Zuriel was so focused on defending Matt. He'd lied to her, so why was she still on his side? She didn't seem to care about his past, but Samuel felt she needed to know the truth.

"Drugs completely took over Matt's life for a long time. He let them completely separate him from his whole family and all his friends at church who cared about him. If you had ever been close to someone who became a drug addict, you would know what that kind of stuff does to a family." He fumed, trying to clear things up for her.

Zuriel eyed him fearlessly. She tilted her head and gave him that smile and death-glare combo that only an angry woman can produce. "Sam," she began, much too sweetly, "I understand that you have been to inner-city Detroit. What I don't think you know about me is that I actually grew up there! My best friend, Suzy, was living with me when she began her drug addiction."

Samuel suddenly felt very stupid for his condescension.

Zuriel smiled again, enjoying his discomfort, and spoke again like she was speaking to a child. "You must be one of the only people I've met who hasn't at least tried the stuff. Oops, I'm sorry; I almost forgot I was talking to a youth pastor."

"What's that supposed to mean?" Samuel realized he had dug himself into a hole. "Help me, Lord," he silently prayed.

"You churchy people always think you're better than everyone else. You guys always talk about forgiveness, but you never actually forgive anyone. I'm so sick of being judged by people like you. I can't take it anymore!"

Samuel had heard those words many times. It seemed everyone who didn't like God blamed the church because the people in it were so judgmental. Samuel hated being part of that reputation but knew he had been guilty of judging others too. "You know, Sam, you really have a wonderful family," she said, walking toward him. "It's a pity you aren't more like them."

"I'm sorry you think that. I guess I've just become a bit bitter, that's all. Please don't let my attitude keep you away from God's love," he coolly responded.

"God's love? Is that what you call your pastor friend stealing money? God's love?"

Samuel wondered who had told her about that. She had clearly been thinking about it for a while.

She began pacing. "Or maybe you think Matt's death is all part of God's love?"

"No, God never wanted those things to happen."

"How do you know? Don't you believe God is in control?" Zuriel challenged.

He felt like he was talking to Matt again. Everything was a question and every question was a test.

He quickly defended his faith. "God is in control and he is good. There is evil in the world, so sometimes bad things happen. God is still good though, and he always wants what's best. Humans, on the other hand, are a different story. John Carter had a choice, and so did Matt. They didn't have to do the wrong thing, but they chose to anyway."

She stopped pacing and crossed her arms. "And what about you, Sam? You don't have to do the wrong thing, do you?"

Samuel almost laughed. She was bent on ruining any pride he had left. "No, I don't. I know I'm not good at doing the right thing; you have made that quite clear. If I have any power to do the right thing it's only because of what Jesus did for me," Samuel snapped, feeling insulted.

"Then why won't you choose to forgive Matt and John like your family has?"

As much as Samuel despised what she was saying, he knew she was right. Hadn't he prayed just this morning that God would help him forgive them? And now God was using a godless woman to speak the truth to him.

"Isn't that what you church people are supposed to do—forgive people?"

Samuel felt like a deer caught in headlights. He knew forgiveness was the only escape from the bitterness he felt. It should be so simple to forgive, yet his pride fought hard against it. He suddenly realized the opportunity was right before him. Yes, this would be difficult, and yes, Matt's story was tragic, but that's why it could be such a testimony. He remembered the words of the Apostle Paul: "While we were yet sinners, Christ died for us." It wasn't about Samuel getting his act together and deserving forgiveness. Forgiveness was offered to everyone despite their obvious lack of worthiness. If he really valued Christ's forgiveness, there was really only one response Samuel could make. The time for him to choose had come.

He knew Zuriel had seen his bitterness, and she had told him he thought he was better than everyone else. He was ready to admit his own sin and forgive the ones who had hurt him. Samuel would have to throw away his pride and humble himself before God. He understood now why God had made things work out this way. Zuriel needed to see what the true Church of Jesus was meant to be. It wasn't designed to be a collection of judgmental Bible readers. It was a collection of broken souls, saved by God's grace as a result of Christ's sacrifice.

"You're right, Zuriel. We are supposed to forgive." Samuel hesitated, not sure how to explain this. "You see, that's why I need Jesus to forgive me too, because I'm so far from being perfect.

I'm not better than Matt or John, but like you said, I do have an opportunity to choose."

He smiled, feeling his faith returning. "I have chosen to live with my anger for a long time, and the last five years have been very difficult because of it. I need to forgive them because I also need forgiveness."

Zuriel looked surprised and confused. "I don't understand. What are you saying?"

"I'm saying I was wrong, really wrong. I'm one of the reasons people don't believe in God's forgiveness." Samuel stopped, realizing the weight of his own words. He had dedicated his life to leading people to God, yet in the process, he himself had pushed people away. He thought he had failed by not saving Matt, but he had actually failed by not forgiving him.

"I'm sorry, Zuriel. I really am. You're right; I do need to forgive Matt and John."

Zuriel looked down at the ground and shuffled her feet awkwardly. Samuel could see she was being affected by what he said. She slid down the trunk of the tree without saying a word and sat in the dirt.

He wasn't sure what he should do. He wanted the truth of his words to sink in, but he also wanted to keep walking in the woods and talk with God. He had been hiding from God for the last five years, and it was time for him to go back home. A few tears of joy slid down his freshly shaven face. He finally felt free, as if a burden had been lifted from his shoulders. Forgiveness was sweet.

Samuel walked over to Zuriel and then kneeled to face her. She avoided his gaze, but he could still see her green eyes, lost and lustrous. "Thank you, Zuriel. Whether you believe in God or not, he just used you to help me. The truth … well, the truth is that forgiveness is free. God offers it to you, just as much as he offers it to me. I'll give you some time alone." Samuel stood and headed further into the army of trees. He had a new prayer to pray now.

 *Chapter 9*

Zuriel stepped through the sliding glass doors into the house. She was baffled by her conversation with Sam, and didn't know what to make of it. She had always been a firm believer that people could change if they wanted to. However, she found that changing herself was nearly impossible. She gave a lot of credit to people who began their lives badly and turned out well. She had even comforted herself last night as she slept by thinking of how much Matt had overcome. Even if he hadn't been the best or most honest person, he had conquered a world of addiction and anger. Zuriel had known Matt as a sober, mild-tempered person and was thankful she had those kinds of memories, instead of the broken memories the rest of the family had.

What she couldn't get her mind around, though, was the sudden change in Matt's older brother. Sam was clearly the one who struggled with Matt's death the most. She hadn't really seen him grieve, but she had heard his sarcastic and bitter remarks. Yet in the middle of their simple conversation, this proud and unshakable man had admitted he was wrong. He talked about forgiveness and did not deny the damage he had done. Sam had made Christianity appear to be a group of sinful people. He was a youth pastor but admitted he was just like everyone else. As much as Zuriel's mind wanted to use that as proof that Christianity wasn't worth anyone's time, she had to admit his honesty was refreshing. Not only that, Sam seemed like he had really found healing from the bitterness. She wondered how long it would last.

Zuriel slipped back into Matt's room and quietly closed the door. Today was going to be difficult. The visitation hours would begin at eleven and would drag on for most of the day. There would be an hour break in the late afternoon, but then they would continue until eight. It seemed like a lot of time for only a few people to show up. Zuriel was glad they were not showing the body of her beloved. The accident had nearly destroyed any evidence of his identity. She felt better knowing that her last memories of Matt were of when he had been in one piece. The slideshow and photo albums would be the only things for the visitors to see; she still wasn't sure if she even wanted to be part of that.

Zuriel took a long, hot shower. She wanted to relax and avoid the upcoming emotional havoc. She took her time choosing an outfit and doing her hair. She wasn't planning on wearing much makeup, so everything else had to look good. She wore her favorite black skirt with a dressy cranberry shirt. Cranberry always looked good next to her lighter hair and green eyes. As she finished the last touches, she heard the rest of the family out and about. It was comforting to have people around, but she didn't want to see Sam. She wasn't angry with him, but the thought of seeing him again after their early morning encounter made her feel awkward and embarrassed.

She reluctantly made her way to the kitchen table. Will was sitting there drinking his coffee and reading from a large Bible. She decided not to interrupt him, but he noticed her before she could escape.

"Good morning!"

"Morning," she bashfully replied.

"There is a wonderful egg casserole on the stove. You're welcome to it. A good breakfast will be important on a day like today." He smiled gently, motioning toward the stove.

Zuriel didn't feel hungry but thought it would be rude to refuse. She smiled and placed a small square of casserole on a plate. She wasn't sure where to eat it but noticed that Will was still smiling at her. She sat at the table, hoping he would return to his reading.

"It looks delicious," Zuriel lied, hoping her comment would keep Will from watching her slowly eat.

"It was! You're the second person to dig in. I wouldn't be surprised if it's gone in the next hour, especially since Samuel is here."

Zuriel almost blushed at the mention of Sam. She hoped he wouldn't come in until after she was finished eating.

"Have you seen him? I need to talk to him before we go."

"Ah, yeah. He was walking outside this morning. We were both up pretty early."

"Oh, so you got a chance to talk? Good. How is he doing?"

Zuriel wished he hadn't brought it up, but she was glad she could give an answer that would make him happy for once. She felt guilty that she hadn't been able to offer the family any indication of Matt's faith. Now she could at least tell Will that Sam was still strong. She wondered if Will ever feared losing Sam.

"Yeah, we talked about Matt for a while. Sam talked a lot about the things he was angry about, but then he started talking about how much he needed to forgive people." Zuriel didn't see any significant indication that Will was happy or sad. He merely closed his eyes and then slowly opened them again.

"I'm glad to hear it. Where you able to talk with him about the Matt that you knew?" he asked, eyes full of anticipation.

"Yes, I talked to him about it." Zuriel didn't know how to expound upon that. She felt strange talking about a man she barely knew with his father, whom she knew even less. Zuriel shoveled another bite of egg casserole, hoping Will would change the direction of the conversation.

"I'm really glad you were both able to talk. I've been concerned about him," he admitted, placidly smiling.

Zuriel felt sure she would never understand people. Why was he smiling? "Yeah, he seemed pretty bitter."

Will looked intrigued.

Zuriel saw that he wanted her to go on. She suddenly felt like she was still in elementary school tattling on another kid. "He talked about forgiveness and how he needed it more than Matt or John did. I don't know exactly what happened, but he seemed like a different person all of a sudden."

"Thank you, Lord," Will said softly. He remained silent for a few seconds. "Zuriel, that's the power of God. Christians are just as human as everyone else; the only difference is when they let Christ inside."

Zuriel tried to smile and then finished the last bite of her breakfast. She was glad Will was proud of his son, but she didn't want to hear a sermon. The Lowells certainly had a different view of religion than she had ever seen. However, Christianity was still a religion and it still didn't make sense.

"Good morning!" Christina said as she entered. Zuriel was thankful to be saved from more interrogation. Christina scrambled around the kitchen until she found her purse. She quickly applied lipstick and pinched her pale cheeks.

"I take it Michael arrived?" Will asked, smiling playfully at his daughter.

"Yes, he just pulled in." She smoothed her black dress and walked to the front room.

Zuriel smiled. She wasn't the only woman who got nervous when her man arrived. Zuriel heard the sounds of the door opening and the murmur of voices. She remembered many times waiting in her apartment for Matt to arrive. Her heart would tense to a stop and then suddenly release when she saw his face. Zuriel would nervously watch as he examined her. She loved the wide-eyed look he had when he told her she was beautiful and gathered her into his arms.

She thought of how she had waited for him just a few days ago, when he was coming to pick her up for lunch. She'd been so excited to spend time with him and there were no words to describe the disappointment when he didn't show up. The pain in her heart as she watched the time pass without the sweet release of seeing his face was unbearable. Now she would never see his face again and her heart would forever be tied in knots. That was why she was here in this strange house, and that was why she would spend the day talking to people she didn't know about a person they barely knew. Her smile turned into a grimace of pain as a tear slipped out of the corner of her eye.

"Zuriel, Drew's here," Elizabeth said, entering the kitchen for breakfast. Zuriel felt a little relieved. At least Drew had recently known Matt. She was thankful that someone else would be there to feel awkward and strange with her. Zuriel walked into the living room and saw Christina sitting next to a very handsome brown-haired guy.

"Zuriel, this is my boyfriend, Michael George. He's Samuel's roommate too." Christiana seemed happy to introduce him, although her face still showed evidence of grief.

"It's nice to meet you." She shook his hand. "I heard Drew's here?"

"Yes, I think I heard him. He might still be talking to Mom in the front room," Christiana suggested.

"Thank you." Zuriel made her way to the front room, unprepared for what she saw. Drew had told her their friends would be meeting them at the funeral home, but the woman

Zuriel saw in front of walkway was all too familiar. Drew had not come alone, like she'd expected. It had only been nine months since the last time they'd spoken, and this was last place she would've wanted to reunite. Zuriel knew the shocked look on her face must have communicated the raw emotions that she could not hide.

Drew slowly walked up and hugged her. "Suzy begged me to come," he explained as he walked into the other room, leaving the ex-roommates alone.

Suzy Baker still hadn't moved, but her tears fell quickly. Zuriel felt sorry for her but wondered what was going through her mind. Suzy had been Zuriel's best friend for years but went off the deep end after her boyfriend broke up with her. She hit depression and began to party a little harder. It wasn't long before her occasional fun became a drug addiction. Zuriel could still remember the nights when Suzy came home high and lost in another world. After failing a mandatory drug test, Suzy lost her job and couldn't pay her part of the rent. Zuriel was kind at first, but after a few months, she gave Suzy an ultimatum to get things straight. It had ended badly, and Suzy left their apartment for life on the streets.

The final picture Zuriel had of her friend was of Suzy throwing up in the parking lot as she carried her belongings into the truck of some guy she had met and slept with the night before. That image was drastically different from the clean and sober woman who stood before her now. Her curly red hair was framed around her face, instead of wild and unkempt. Her brown eyes were clear and peaceful, instead of bloodshot and full of fear. Zuriel didn't know what to say or how to proceed. She looked around and wished they hadn't all left the room.

"You have every right to be angry with me," Suzy began, wiping her eyes. "I was a slave to getting high. You saw me, Zuriel. I was a mess." She paused again, and was somehow smiling through her crying. "I finally found freedom from it all. Not just from the drugs, Zuriel, from everything."

Zuriel didn't know what to think of what her old friend was saying, but she knew something had changed. She needed a friend right now and had genuinely missed her. Still, she never would have chosen to be reunited with Suzy, but she didn't have the energy to remind herself of the hurtful words they had last exchanged.

"I don't …" Zuriel hesitated. She didn't want to cry, but the subject was sensitive. She gulped hard and tried again. "I don't understand what happened to you, but I'm glad you came. I don't know what I'm going to do now that Matt's gone." She felt her composure slip away as she was reminded of why they were here. Zuriel felt Suzy's arms wrap around her and she fought the urge to turn away. It felt wrong to welcome Suzy back into her life so easily, but Zuriel didn't feel strong enough to make anything right. In fact, she wasn't sure what truly was right anymore. All she could do was surrender to her sadness. So they cried alone together in the front room. Zuriel could not understand why losing Matt continued to bring other people together. God was cruel if he created the world to need tragedy.

They pulled apart just as Sam entered the room. At the sight of him, Zuriel couldn't help but let out another loud cry. She felt so vulnerable.

He stopped and offered a condoling smile. As he walked past, he gently squeezed her shoulder. She was thankful he understood the situation enough not say anything or ask. There was nothing worse than being asked what was wrong, especially when there were so many things wrong at the same time.

"I heard the news and just had to come," Suzy explained, pulling several tissues from her purse.

"Thanks," Zuriel managed to say. She glanced at the large clock on the wall beside her and knew it was time to go. She wasn't ready for this; everything was moving so quickly. If this meeting had taken place under different circumstances, she would have spent the whole day trying to understand what had happened to her friend. But this meeting, of course, was not under different circumstances. This particular circumstance meant going to grieve the loss of the most wonderful person she had ever known.

Will said as he helped Anne into her sweater, "We're going to leave now. Elizabeth is riding over there with Samuel, Christina and Michael are riding together, and the three of you can follow us over, if that would make you feel more comfortable."

Zuriel solemnly nodded. As the family began to round up, Anne went to the closet and pulled out several stacks of small tissue packets. The women stuffed as many into their purses as possible before making their way out to the cars.

Zuriel silently stared out her window, thankful the other two passengers were not saying anything. She had discovered so much about the past of the man she loved within the last couple of days. It was ironic that both Suzy and Matt had struggled with drugs at one point. She felt silly comparing Suzy with Matt, but she felt the weight of all sorts of pain bearing down on her. She knew her dad and grandparents would be coming. She didn't feel ready for any of this.

It would take a long time to heal from the trauma of losing the person she loved the most and the realization that he had lied to her. It would also take a while to heal from the pain that Suzy had caused her, all in the name of addiction. She wondered if it were possible to ever truly heal. Her heart was in tatters. She had grown up with her bitter father and crazy grandparents. She had tried to survive high school but hadn't left completely uninjured.

She thought of Nick, their friendship, and the day they broke each other's hearts, never to see each other again. There was always something that hurt, always something to make things difficult.

They arrived at the funeral home, and Zuriel wished she didn't have to go in. It didn't feel right going into a house dedicated to the dead. She wished so badly that she had never said yes to meeting him for lunch. Maybe if she had asked Matt to come an hour later or earlier he would still be alive. She wished she had a car because then maybe she would have gotten in the accident instead. Most of all she was angry that he hadn't moved in with her. Why didn't he love her enough to want that? This never would have happened if he wasn't so stubborn.

The agony of her thoughts was terrible yet impossible to stop. She wanted Matt back, and she certainly wasn't ready to say good-bye and accept what had happened.

Everyone entered the large room and began setting up. Zuriel walked across the burgundy carpet, trying to look busy by inspecting the art work. She was sure the paintings were meant to bring comfort, but she felt flowers, sunrises, and rainbows were salt in an open wound. She was glad they had brought their own decorations. Everything from Matt's Cub Scout uniform to his first baseball glove were there to bring memories alive. The picture albums were arranged and the slideshow disk was put on repeat. It didn't take Anne long to rearrange the flowers and gifts. It all looked surprisingly beautiful.

Zuriel admired what Anne had done and figured she'd made herself busy in an effort to escape her grief. Everyone seemed to have their own way of coping, but Zuriel felt like she didn't have a method for herself. She sat in a floral-patterned chair in the back of the room, needing time to be alone, to think and clear her mind. She didn't want to sob every time someone offered condolences.

"Hey, you hanging in there?" Zuriel turned her head to see Sam standing there.

"Well, that depends on how you define 'hanging in there.'"

"You're a strong woman; I hope you know that. I'll be praying for you."

Zuriel was happy for some sympathy but was trying to wrap her head around his kindness. "What if I say I don't believe in prayer?" she asked, feeling too bitter for his comfort.

"Well, then I'll pray anyway, and I'll forgive you for not believing it." He smiled and winked.

She couldn't help but feel somewhat amused. He was trying to remind her that he forgave Matt. She was thankful that he had; that made it easier for her to forgive him too.

Will called Sam over to help move something for Anne, and Zuriel was once again left alone to think. She heard voices in the hall outside and knew that the craziness was about to begin. She hoped that if there was a God, he was listening to Sam's prayers.

 *Chapter 10*

Samuel Lowell poured a few mints into his mouth and quickly chewed them up. He wanted his breath to smell halfway decent as he talked to the crowds. He was the youth pastor of Living Grace Church, so everyone would be there. He knew he would have to see many members of the youth group, and they were all going to be watching him. This would be a test in the minds of many of the teens, a test to see if their leader walked what he taught. They would want to know his faith was still solid and that God was good even in terrible times like these.

He had hung out in the woods for quite a while that morning. There was so much that needed confessing. Samuel had kept the anger bottled in his soul, and it was finally being rooted out. It was humbling and pretty much sucked, but at the same time it was what he needed. Finally he had forgiven his brother, but there wasn't a sudden warm and fuzzy feeling. Deciding to let go unleashed a part of him he had never known before. He was surprised by the scars and grief that were now unmasked. He missed his brother, and that was difficult to face. Samuel had cried most of his tears in the woods and was glad to be done with them for now; however, the crying had just begun for everyone else.

Familiar faces filled the room. Samuel stood near the entrance because he thought it might be useful if the first person the mourners saw wasn't crying. He knew if anyone could stay strong in the midst of weepy faces, it was him. It made him happy to see Zuriel standing between Elizabeth and his mother. She would have a lot to deal with today. He understood that she would only know a few people, and he prayed everyone would show love to her. He hoped people wouldn't bother her with too many questions, especially about Matt's spiritual condition.

When Samuel caught Zuriel in the front room crying and staring at the woman in the doorway that morning, he had wondered what was going on. It was clear these women had gone through something incredibly difficult together. He remembered the odd feeling in his gut when Drew told him the woman's name was Suzy. He figured it was the same woman Zuriel had watched fall into the world of drugs. It didn't seem fair that she should show up at a time like this. Samuel knew God had a plan for Zuriel, but he didn't understand God's method for winning her over. She had been hit with one heartache after another. Samuel tried not to daydream while the many people came up to him with hugs and condolences. He felt like a robot saying the same things over and over again. It would be all too easy to remove himself from the commotion that he was surrounded by. He spotted a middle-aged man walking toward him, followed by an elderly couple. He was sure he had never seen them before.

"Hello, thank you for coming. I don't think we've met before." Samuel extended his hand.

"Oh, I'm not from around here. I'm Zuriel's father; Pete Rawson is the name," the man in the faded suit explained, giving Samuel a weak handshake. He looked nervous and his eyes seemed distant, as though his mind was in another place.

Samuel had seen that same look in Zuriel's eyes before. "Nice to meet you. I'm Samuel, Matt's brother."

"Matt?" he asked, seeming genuinely unfamiliar with the name.

Samuel could hardly believe they didn't know whose funeral this was. Did he really have to explain this? "Zuriel's fiancé, the deceased." he said, trying to avoid sounding annoyed.

Pete turned red, undoubtedly embarrassed.

Samuel wondered if Zuriel was as much a stranger to them as Matt had been to him.

"I'm sorry … we never met the guy."

"I understand."

Pete stepped aside to introduce the tagalongs. "These are my parents, James and Mary."

The older man looked even more lost, like he was half-asleep. The crease on his forehead was deep, and it didn't appear to change with each quizzical expression he made. His wife, Mary, was thin and alert. Her beady eyes surveyed him up and down.

"So it's your little brother who went through all this?" Mary asked, frowning as if she were an investigating cop.

"Yes, Matt was three years younger."

"Was he a good kid? Maybe it was for the best. He was going to marry my granddaughter, you know? I don't like the idea of her getting hooked up with some hooligan."

Samuel suppressed a laugh. It was clear that tact and politeness were not among their better qualities.

"Mom, I'm sure he was fine. You shouldn't say things like that," Pete reprimanded looking at Sam with shame. "I'm sorry. She meant no disrespect to your brother. She's still recovering from the engagement news."

"That's fine. It's not always easy to accept the choices the people we love make," Samuel conceded, saving face. He remembered what he had thought when he heard Zuriel was coming for a visit. His own thoughts had hardly been courteous. At least he had been taught some manners growing up. These people didn't appear very bright.

"Where's Zuriel?" Mary asked, still frowning.

He wondered how he had gotten on her bad side so quickly. "She's down the line. I think she's with my mom and sister."

"Well, thanks. I really am sorry for your loss. I truly am," Pete said, nodding shyly as he led his parents further into the room.

Samuel prayed they wouldn't say anything insensitive when his mother was listening. Hopefully his dad would meet them at the same time, and then he could act as a buffer so the things they said wouldn't seem so offensive.

Samuel turned back to the funeral home entrance just in time to witness a little kid wipe out. He saw Ben Rice, the senior pastor, run to his grandson's rescue. Samuel chuckled, glad to see Ben. Samuel had been busy helping everyone else cope and was looking forward to hearing encouraging words from someone else for a change. The elderly man smiled at him across the hall while placing the shaken little boy in his mother's arms. He kissed his daughter on the cheek and strode toward Samuel.

"That kid spends most of his time recovering from falls! I guess he takes after me." Ben laughed, patting Samuel on the back. "I'm so sorry, Samuel. You're in our prayers."

"Thanks, Pastor."

"Sometimes it's hard to understand what God does or doesn't allow. We can't always understand or know the answers. He will reveal his good purposes in his own time."

Samuel appreciated the encouragement, even though it was difficult to hear. There was no way he could explain or justify what had happened to Matt, but he could have faith that God was still in control and still cared. Samuel knew he would be tempted to doubt and would be tempted to get angry all over again. He felt peaceful, but he had no earthly reason for that peace. He knew his trust in God's sovereignty was the only reason.

"It is more difficult for me accept that than I would like to admit," Samuel acknowledged solemnly. "I spent so much of my life being concerned about him. You know how many times I talked to you about Matt, and how I wanted to help the youth."

"You had a lot of zeal back then, Samuel. You were ready to explode with the Gospel."

"I only wish I had wanted to serve God for the right reasons. I think I fooled even myself." He paused, not sure if this was the time or place for a confession. "I believed my anger and hurt were zeal for God's calling, but I finally came to the truth this morning. I'm free from that bitterness now, but I can't deny my selfish reasons for all I have done. I'm sorry ..."

He felt strange. He didn't have to confess anything; he could have just accepted his pastor's condolences. However, he felt like he had deceived the church when he became their youth pastor. Not that his work wasn't good, and not that people hadn't come to know Jesus as a result, it was just that his reasons were all for himself. He cared more about ridding the world of all the "Matts" in it than about loving each Matt that he encountered. This wasn't the best place to confess all that, but he felt good to get it off his chest.

"The flesh is an interesting thing, isn't it, Samuel?" he asked rhetorically before clearing his throat and rubbing his chin. Ben always did that before advising anyone. "We're supposed to selflessly do good without expecting a reward. We try not to think too much about a reward, but we know God will reward us for selfless acts. We can get caught up in thinking, *If I'm expecting a reward from God, how am I really being selfless?* That kind of thinking leaves us feeling useless. We can't always make the human part of us cooperate; all you can do is act on what you know. Paul even talked about that in the context of preaching the

Gospel. The amazing thing about the Gospel is that it's powerful by itself. It doesn't matter what your original intention was. Those who were ready received the good news when they heard it."

Samuel paused, taking in the counsel. God had used even his own anger for good. His bitterness had been a bad thing, but Christ had the power to make all things good. Now that the bitterness was gone, Samuel knew God would do even more, because Samuel was finally willing to be used for the right reasons. He would have real joy in serving God, instead of doing things out of a sense of obligation.

"I'm glad he's so merciful. Whatever the reasons were that got me here, I'm here now and I'm ready and willing to do whatever he wants me to do," Samuel said.

"Amen, brother. In a week or so, I'll give you a call. We can grab some burgers."

"Sounds great."

"Good. Hey, is your dad around? How's he doing?" Ben asked. He looked concerned.

"He's always strong and always praying." Samuel could never really tell with his dad. He was always stoic and strong, but those did little against the grief of losing a son.

"I'll go talk to him. You'll be in my prayers, Samuel."

"Thank you."

After speaking with Ben, Samuel greeted the oncoming visitors with more gusto. He felt more at peace with himself. At least all of this wasn't for nothing. He could still be a youth pastor for God's glory, even if he had selfish motives in the beginning. Losing Matt was painful, and he hated admitting Matt was gone. It was just that his anger and bitterness had been so shackling that even under the circumstances he felt freer than ever before.

He was happy when the crowd died down and it was time for a break. He smelled the delicious food the church ladies had prepared. He was hungry and ready to breathe. He wondered how his family had fared during the event, and how the meeting with Zuriel's parents had gone over.

He made his way to the hospitality room and found most of his relatives eating. The room was large, with several forest-green couches and a number of coffee tables. To the back of the room was a foldout table holding every kind of food imaginable. He made his way to the spread, trying to give condoling looks as he passed each person. He grabbed a paper plate and didn't hold back as he piled the food on it. He found a spot on the couch next to his sister, Elizabeth.

His family ate in nearly complete silence. Samuel guessed the visitation had been more difficult than they anticipated. The worst thing about the meal was knowing they all had to go back out there and do it again. Samuel knew that if he was dreading it, his mother and sisters definitely were.

Zuriel shuffled into the room. She grabbed a few muffins and sat on the only empty couch. She checked her cell phone before staring at her plate. The atmosphere was heartbreaking and pensive.

Samuel put his arm around Elizabeth and broke the silence. "Dad, did you get a chance to talk to Pastor Ben? I talked with him for a while."

"Yes, I did. It was good to see him. He prayed with me and gave me a few encouraging words." His father talked normally, but the look in his eyes was unfamiliar. His father had begun to show outward signs of grief. The realization affected Samuel a little more than he anticipated. His father was always the emotionally sturdy one. His strength had been comforting to the family, but Samuel felt sorry to see him this way. He decided he would try to switch spots with Will for the next visitation hours. Maybe the separation from the family would make his father feel more comfortable with grieving. Samuel could tend to his mother and sisters.

"Did you get to meet Zuriel's family?" Anne asked, trying to appear happy and inquisitive.

"Yes, I did. I met her father and grandparents." Samuel glanced at Zuriel and saw fresh tears forming. Suzy noticed them too and changed couches to sit by her.

"I tried to convince them to stay and eat. They plan on coming tomorrow," Anne said.

Samuel loved how his mother always acted like everyone was wonderful. She seemed sincere, even though everyone in the room was well aware of their ill manners.

Christina entered the room and tossed her used plate in the trash. It sparked Samuel's thoughts, and he wondered where his Sister's boyfriend was. He wanted to talk to Michael.

Samuel left the room and made his way through the tiled hall. He found Michael sitting on a pink loveseat in the lobby, eyes fixed on the open laptop.

"Doing some last-minute Facebook stalking?"

Michael looked up. Samuel was expecting a playful look in response. Instead, Michael looked forlorn.

"I was just e-mailing my parents. They said they're missing me on vacation. I was just taking some time to reply before we had to go back in there."

"I don't want to go back in their either."

"It's been hard watching Christina cry for hours. I didn't even know Matt, and I was crying like a baby."

Samuel nodded; there was nothing fun about funerals. "Are you holding up okay?"

Michael nodded. "Only by God's grace."

Samuel sat down beside him. "I've forgiven him, Michael, just like you said. The only problem is that for the first time, I'm actually missing him."

"I really wish I could have known the guy. I almost feel like I do. Your sister keeps telling me all about him."

"Yeah, I wish I could have known him when Zuriel did. It almost sounded like he was trying to turn his life around. He may have still been a jerk, but I might have been able to get along with him."

Michael closed his laptop and stood. "Well, if he was anything like Christina, then I'm sure he was wonderful. If he was anything like you ... well, I don't know if I could stand him." Michael grinned and embraced Samuel. A little humor was refreshing, but it probably wouldn't be enough to make the next visitation shift any better.

They walked back into the main reception room. The family had already assembled, and they all looked exhausted. Samuel had a strong feeling the next half of the day was going to be a bit more emotional.

As the sound of voices alerted them to the beginning of the next session, Samuel took a few deep breaths and began to pray. He would need God's help if he was going to endure this.

 *Chapter 11*

Zuriel stood on the green June lawn and felt the sun shining on her face. For a moment she felt that things would be okay, like maybe God was making the sun shine just to warm her. That's what the pastor had said earlier that morning. He told all those gathered for the funeral that God had shown his love through sending his son. He said the sun should be a reminder of the love of God shining down. Zuriel wanted to be comforted like the rest of the people attending the service, but she just couldn't. She could not escape the feelings of hurt and confusion that surrounded her. Her life felt cold and empty. This "love" that God was supposed to be shining on her was nowhere to be found. She knew the sunshine could not reach Matt's cold, dead body as it rested in the casket nearby.

The large group began to break up as they made their way back to their cars. Zuriel wasn't ready to leave. She didn't think she would be ready for a long time. There was too much to think about, and there were too many people waiting to talk with her. What did she really have to say? She had nothing to offer them, and no comfort for the mourners. She wanted someone to say Matt had gone to a better place, but if God was real, Matt was in hell. So when they asked her what kind of man he had become, she had nothing to say. He was a good man, but she knew no one else thought so. If they all thought so ill of him, they would never accept her. She wasn't made for a world like this. Zuriel was from a low-income, no-good, white-trash world. She knew she would have been happy with Matt. Finally she had convinced herself that they were meant to be. Meant to be, but separated by death. The thought made her sick.

Zuriel heard loud weeping and saw Matt's parents kneeling by the coffin. She saw Will's shoulders shaking with grief. It was the first time she had seen him cry. The sight brought her to tears. She hated the mess Matt had left behind. She hated the pain and the emptiness. The worst feeling of all, though, was the loneliness. She was so very lonely.

Suzy came up to her and placed a hand on her shoulders. Zuriel was quick to shrug it off. She had accepted Suzy's comforting touch earlier but wasn't in the mood for her sympathy anymore. Suzy was just another person who had let her down and left her alone when she had so desperately needed a friend. But why had she come back at a time like this? Zuriel couldn't help wondering what had happened to her, but at the same time, it didn't matter. Everyone would fail her, so why should she bother trying to understand?

Zuriel saw Drew standing nearby. She again felt a strong pang of loneliness. Even her best friends were pathetic. When would she know what it truly meant to be loved? When would she feel the warmth of the sun as it shined upon her?

The visitation hours had been torture. She had met many people, most of whom hugged her and told her they were praying for her. She guessed the statement was supposed to be comforting, but she felt guilty every time she heard it. Zuriel wondered what they were thinking and what exactly they were praying for. She wanted comfort, not a sermon. Her father and grandparents had come, and as much she could barely tolerate them, she was so glad they were there. She could tell her dad really did grieve for her. He had lost his partner and never recovered from it. Would her fate be the same? She didn't want to turn out like him, but part of her was tempted to live the rest of her life in bitter survival mode. She didn't want to heal. She never wanted to let go of Matt.

The night before the funeral had been long and broken. As Zuriel lay in her bed, she tried to imagine Matt lying beside her, holding her and telling her he loved her. She had tried to remember the feeling of his kisses, and she wished so much that they could have had one more moment together. She wrestled with questions about how much he had truly loved her—how he had gotten his ex-girlfriend pregnant, but been careful to avoid any such circumstances with her. She wished that they had moved in together so she could have gotten to know him better. Then she would have had more to remember, and more evidence to prove that he really loved her; that he really would have been perfect for her. Those thoughts only brought more distress to her already tortured soul. In tears, she decided to give him the benefit of the doubt. She remembered him telling her that he had never before loved a woman as much as he loved her. Zuriel remembered him telling her over and over again that he didn't ever want to take advantage of her, that she deserved respect. She decided to believe that this respect was a deeper expression of his love. Matt had loved her deeply, and Zuriel would never stop loving him.

Zuriel's thoughts returned to the funeral, and she was so thankful that it was over. They had asked her if she wanted to share anything during the service, but she had easily refused. She couldn't stand up there and talk to these people about Matt. She was perfectly content to sit and simply wait for it to end. They sang songs about God and his love, but Zuriel felt like it was all a bad joke. Why were these people thanking God when someone had just died and gone to hell? It seemed like they must have been brainwashed or something.

Will gave the eulogy after the music ended. He spoke well and, of course, talked a lot about the importance of faith. Sam also said a few words, while pictures from Matt's childhood were projected overhead. The pastor ended by talking about God using tragedy to lead people to Jesus. Zuriel wanted to laugh. How was this leading her closer to Jesus? If anything, it made her want to run away and hate God for all of eternity. She would never understand these people. How could they call themselves human?

Her dad came up and embraced her after the funeral. She could hardly believe it, but there were tears in his eyes. His voice was shaky and cold. "Zuriel, I'm sorry."

"I know. Thanks, Dad."

"When I lost your mother …" His voice faded out as he got choked up with emotion. She had never heard her father bring up her mother of his own free will, and to do so with tears was a surprise. She wondered if he might still love her after all. "When I lost your mother, I felt like my life was over. Zuriel, I wish I could tell you it gets better." His words brought Zuriel more tears. She allowed her father to hold her, breathing in his strong cologne. Zuriel had never understood him or felt sympathy toward him, but now she felt strangely close. Perhaps he was the only one who really knew what she was going through.

After they parted, it was time to begin the procession to the burial grounds. Zuriel was, once again, thankful for the silence of the car. She liked staring out the window and allowing her mind to wander. She didn't want the car to ever arrive at the cemetery, but it did.

Once they arrived time had flown by, but now it was already time to go. She couldn't bring herself to leave, so she sat on the grass, not caring about her black dress getting ruined. She wanted to stubbornly protest that it wasn't time to leave yet. Zuriel wanted to be with her Matt. She wanted him to come back to life. She wanted this all to go away. Surviving would be difficult, and letting go would never happen. She was sure of that.

Zuriel watched as they lowered the coffin into the grave and began to fill it. She looked behind her and saw that Suzy and Drew were waiting in the car. Everyone else was clearing out. She felt hurt. Did no one care that she was left behind with her grief and sorrow? Zuriel knew it was her own choice to stay, but she hated that her choices so often left her alone. She thought of Matt and how lonely she would be without him. She began to cry even harder.

The sun shined brighter, and its heat felt good against her face. The grass seemed more inviting now, and she laid her head on it. Even with her eyes shut she could see the sunlight. She felt peaceful and happy for a moment. She wished with all her heart that Matt could somehow come back to life. Maybe when she opened her eyes she would see his face leaning over her. He would laugh and tell her she was silly for lying on the grass in such a pretty dress. He would help her up and then carry her to the car, all the while planting kisses on her face and neck. She wanted it so much, but all she could do was cry because Matt was not coming back. Matt was dead.

❧

Samuel glanced at the time as he drove away from the reception. It had been a good forty-five minutes since the family departed from the burial grounds. Zuriel had lingered by the gravesite and he almost went over to talk to her, but then decided she probably needed some space. He talked with Drew, who said they would hang around and give her a few minutes. Apparently those few minutes had stretched on for a long time, and half the reception attendees had already gotten their food. Samuel asked around, but no one had Drew or Suzy's cell phone number on hand. He finally made an executive decision to go back and see what was going on. He had a feeling they would stay out there for a long time if someone didn't fetch them.

He was concerned for Zuriel and didn't trust her friends. He'd glanced at her a few times during the funeral service and knew she felt like a fish out of water. Samuel was hoping and praying that she would step forward when the pastor gave the invitation, but Zuriel was staring at the coffin, twisting the program in her hand. He wished he could make her understand but knew it wasn't his place to give her a sermon. His goal for right now would be to break her of the idea that Christians were unloving and judgmental.

He neared the gravesite and saw Drew's car, the front seats still full. He looked for Zuriel and didn't see her. He felt slightly panicked. He didn't know why, but he felt like her salvation was his responsibility.

As he parked the car, he realized how hard it would be for his old habits to die. He felt like it was his responsibility? This seemed all too familiar. He needed to let God take care of her salvation and not allow himself to become the same person he had been when Matt left. He got out of the car and walked to the front window.

Drew opened the door and stepped out sheepishly. "Forget something?" he asked, acting like he didn't know why Samuel was there.

"No, I just getting concerned. You guys have been here for a while. Where's Zuriel?"

"Oh, she's still out there." Drew pointed, and Samuel saw the small woman lying on the ground with her palms facing up.

He looked at Drew in disbelief. "Is she okay? Have you guys talked to her?"

"Suzy tried to talk to her earlier, while people were here. She didn't want any comfort, so we thought it would be best to leave her alone."

Suzy chimed in. "We didn't want to make it worse."

Samuel felt annoyed; Zuriel had been out there alone for almost an hour past the time everyone else had left. Why hadn't they tried harder to talk with her? He headed toward her.

Samuel didn't want to scare her, so he began calculating the best way to let his presence become known. He slowed his steps as he approached and caught his breath when he saw her. She looked beautiful. Her hair was falling over her shoulders and spilling onto the grass. She looked radiant and almost happy. Samuel stepped beside her, blocking the sun and causing a shadow over her face. Zuriel opened her eyes and smiled. Samuel smiled back, surprised by how attractive she was. She slowly sat up and then her countenance changed. She held her head in her hands and began to cry. Samuel felt horrible. She had probably been thinking about her fiancé, and he interrupted her reverie. Samuel wasn't sure what to do now.

"Zuriel, I'm sorry." He knelt beside her, praying that God would give him the words. "I know it's hard to leave him here, but everyone else left a long time ago. You can always come back later."

She nodded and looked up at him mournfully. He helped her to her feet.

"I'm sorry." Zuriel said through her blubbering. "I just … I …" She tried several times to talk, but her throat would not let her.

He felt for her and wished he had brought one of his sisters along. She would have known what to do.

"It's all right, Zuriel." He hoped he didn't sound like a complete fool.

Her black mascara had left rings of gray under her eyes, which only added to her heartbreaking appearance.

"No, I really am sorry." She gulped, and glanced at his brother's grave. "It's so hard to leave."

Samuel nodded and wrapped his arms around her for a hug. He felt awkward because he never knew how to comfort girls, especially pretty ones who had been previously engaged to his brother. He was more attracted to her in this moment than he wanted to admit, which made him feel insecure. Today was his brother's funeral, and what was he thinking? He pulled away gently and led her to Drew's car. Without a word, she climbed into the backseat and began fixing her makeup with a small compact. As Drew started the car, Samuel waved good-bye and walked back to his own car. It was hard enough to leave his brother the first time, and now it seemed impossible. He understood why Zuriel wanted to stay, but he knew no one was coming after him.

Samuel watched a robin land on Matt's gravestone, before flying away. The cemetery seemed empty, like the giant whole in his gut. He could hear Zuriel's words in his head: "It's so hard to leave." The realization that his brother was under the dirt forever hit him abruptly. He prayed silently for strength. His old anger with himself and John was building up once again. He started the car but wasn't sure if he could drive.

"God, I have to forgive them again. You know what happened, so please help me. And please help Zuriel. She needs you." He wiped his eyes and put the car into drive. He would pray all the way back to the reception. His family needed him, but he felt just as needy as the rest of them. He told the pastor that he would be ready to teach Sunday school again, but that was only a few days away. He hoped he really would be ready. There was an abundance of things he wanted to talk to them about, and he knew Elizabeth would be in the class. It would mean a lot to her to see her brother teaching again. She, above all, needed to see that he was going to stay faithful.

Samuel finally arrived at the church. He got out of the car and saw Zuriel and the others enter. He wondered how long they would stay at his parents' house after the reception. Strangely, he hoped Zuriel would stay a while. Maybe his family could find a Christian counselor or something for her. He didn't know why, but he was afraid for her. She didn't seem ready to return to the real world yet. He knew she was used to Detroit, but it didn't seem like she should be going back there.

Samuel reentered the church and was immediately met by a few of the ladies. Samuel didn't feel like talking. The thing about church that he hated the most was gossip; he had been burdened from hearing gossip about his brother for most of his life. Not surprisingly, they were full of questions about where Samuel had been and how Zuriel was doing. They heard she'd had a "Rough life." He wanted to shake them off and tell them to leave him alone, but he knew better.

"Yes, she's been through a lot, but Jesus loves her just as much as He loves the rest of us. She has put up with quite a bit of sorrow, especially recently." Samuel excused himself and was hoping to find Zuriel, but there were people everywhere. He was glad so many people had come to show their love and support, but he wished more of them had actually known his brother. He hated thinking that most of the people would be whispering about the question of Matt's salvation at the next who-knew-how-many church potlucks.

Samuel rounded a corner, heading toward the main sanctuary. He wondered if Zuriel had gone in there to eat. He stopped abruptly when he noticed Elizabeth sitting on a couch in the lobby. Samuel wanted to make sure Zuriel was all right, but he knew it was just as important to make sure Elizabeth was okay. Realizing he hadn't really gotten a chance to talk with her about how she felt, he sat beside her and put his arm around her shoulders. His little sister was almost ten years younger, but he knew her heart was breaking just as much as his.

"You doing okay, sis?"

She glanced at him and quickly turned away to hide her tears.

He hugged her closer. "I know; it's so hard to say good-bye."

"Yeah, but I feel like I barely even got to say hello." Her shoulders shook, and he felt sorry for her.

She was only ten when Matt first got into all that trouble and just barely eleven when he left. She had spent some of the most significant years of her childhood watching her family worry about their lost son. Life's hardships were revealed to her at a young age, and she was a very mature sixteen-year-old because of it.

"Aw, sweetie, you feel like you never really got to know him?"

"I don't know who I'm grieving for. I just want everyone to be okay. I feel so bad for Mom and Dad. They're good parents; I just don't understand why Matt would do that to them."

Samuel understood how she felt, and he wondered if he wasn't the only one who had been struggling with bitterness and anger. "The most difficult part of these types of situations is that so often our desire is to blame someone. I blamed Matt for a long time. I was so angry with John Carter and so angry that I couldn't make Matt stay. It's not easy to forgive, but it is the only way to come to peace with everything."

"I just wish I could have a reason to grieve for him!" she exclaimed.

"Oh, it seems like you're grieving for him enough as it is. Don't feel bad because you think other people have more reasons to be sad. Elizabeth, Matt was your older brother." Samuel wondered what was really going through her mind. He wished he had taken the time to have more conversations like this with her over the last several years.

She frowned and shook her head in annoyance before explaining. "No, it's just that I feel bad for not knowing him and loving him more. When I think about him, I mainly just think about everyone's worry and sorrow. Everyone was so concerned that I would end up like him … I heard so much about him … I can't even say it out loud."

"What is it, honey? It's okay."

"Sam, when I found that he was dead, I was sad for Mom and Dad, but I felt relieved. Isn't that horrible?" She burst into another episode of weeping, and Samuel felt a deep sense of grief for his little sister. She had spent her whole life being compared to an older brother she didn't even know. So many things that should have been happy for her were not, because there was so much emphasis on Matt. Christmas should have been the best day of the year for an eleven-year-old girl, but instead her parents and family were solemn—hoping and praying that, by some miracle, Matt would come home. Elizabeth had lived with this burden for years, but now that he was dead, there would be no more unspoken questions. There was no more nagging hope he might come back.

"No, it's not horrible. I understand how you could feel that way. Matt was the source of a lot of pain for you, and he wasn't even here. I wish I could tell you it would go away, but Mom and Dad will probably talk about him for a long time to come. We have to help each other forgive him."

She nodded, and large teardrops dripped from her chin.

He understood how she felt: that feeling of knowing what God wants you to do yet knowing it means giving up emotions you've held on to for years. It was a true sacrifice.

Samuel held her close and prayed. He saw Zuriel leaving but decided he could check on her tomorrow. His sister needed comfort right now, and he knew she had been left to deal with the pain on her own for far too long. Elizabeth had always reminded him of Matt: quiet but inquisitive, and always concerned about what other people were thinking. Samuel prayed God would give him the strength to be there for her and help her find her strength in him too. He couldn't stand the idea of losing another sibling the way he'd lost Matt.

❦

Samuel turned his car into the neighborhood in which his parents lived. It had been a rough day, but God had been faithful. He smiled at his sister beside him. He had decided to take her out for some coffee after they left the church. She had opened up about a lot of things, and Samuel was able to share some of the positive similarities between her and Matt. It had been a really good time for closure and healing. He felt better about being a youth pastor too. It was different counseling teens when the pain was still so fresh in his mind. He didn't like the pain, but it did make his conversation with Elizabeth feel a lot more real. It kept him from using all of the usual Christian clichés, because he knew all too well how meaningless they were.

He saw his parents' house coming into view, but something was missing. He didn't see Drew's car.

They pulled into the driveway and went inside. It was quiet. Samuel made his way to the kitchen where his mother was warming up leftovers from their funeral lunch.

"Hey, Mom, where is everyone?"

"Oh, hello, sweetie. Your father's in his office and Christina went out to dinner with Michael."

"What about Zuriel?"

"She went home."

Samuel could hardly believe it. The funeral was today and she already went home?

His mother saw his reaction, and he could see that she was sad as well. "I tried to convince her to stay, but she said she needed to get home and go back to work."

"Oh, I guess I'm just surprised that she left so suddenly, and without saying good-bye." Samuel was disappointed. He wanted to talk with her again. The last time they had really spoken was yesterday morning. He wanted to talk to her about God again, but he wondered if there were more reasons than just that. Samuel felt silly even admitting to himself that he was attracted to her. Whatever the reasons for his disappointment, he would still pray for her. She would have a long road of healing ahead, and she would need God's help.

 *Chapter 12*

Zuriel opened her eyes and stretched her arms above her head. It felt good to be home in her own bed. Anne had offered to let her stay longer, but she just couldn't. Zuriel needed to get back to her normal life and get away from all the memories. She had almost decided to stay in Toledo, but she didn't know when she would have a ride home next. It was difficult leaving without saying good-bye to the whole family, but it did spare her a lot of pain. Zuriel had quickly come to love the family but didn't feel worthy to be with them. Anne begged her to stay in touch and visit sometimes, but Zuriel had no intention of initiating either option. She needed to be free from the past and start over.

She rolled out of bed and went into the kitchen to get herself something to drink. She pulled on her favorite slippers—orange with lime-green stripes—and strolled to the small living room. She was ready to spend the day alone, to rest and grieve. She went to sit on the couch but stopped herself abruptly. Suzy was sprawled out across it, sound asleep.

Zuriel groaned loudly and went back to bed. *Why is Suzy still in my apartment?* She wondered, hoping her prodigal friend didn't think she had the right to just move in. Zuriel was angry, knowing full well that her peaceful day of rest would be ruined. She was annoyed but curious.

It would have been a huge deal for Suzy to come back into the picture whether Matt had died or not. Showing up the day of the viewing did seem rather insane, though. Zuriel wondered how the meeting with Suzy would have gone if Matt had been alive. She wouldn't have accepted her so easily, or offered her forgiveness. She wouldn't have needed a friend because she had Matt. However, Suzy had walked into the picture at Zuriel's weakest moment. And now Suzy was taking advantage of her generosity and insecurity by camping out.

She heard the toilet flush and knew her old friend was now awake.

Zuriel hated confrontation, so she decided to stay put. Maybe Suzy would think she was still sleeping and leave?

The face that appeared in the doorway confirmed leaving wasn't part of Suzy's plan. "Are you awake?" she asked in a half-whisper.

"Yes, unfortunately."

Suzy walked toward her and sat on the edge of her bed. Her hair was pulled back into a bun, and her freckled face showed signs of leftover makeup. "How's it going?"

"Well, my fiancé is dead," Zuriel snapped. She couldn't understand why so many people didn't just assume that when someone you love more than anything else in the world dies, life is bad. It doesn't suddenly get better the next week, so why keep asking the same question?

"Yeah …" Suzy was silent for several seconds. She traced her finger down the stripes of her pajama pants. She looked tense. "At least he's in a better place, though."

"A better place? What's that supposed to mean?" Zuriel asked softly, but she took no pains to hide her irritation.

"Heaven. He went to heaven."

Zuriel laughed softly. "Suzy, if there is a God, then Matt's in hell." She sniffed and wiped her eyes. She didn't want to start the day off crying. "When did you start believing in heaven anyway?"

Suzy looked surprised. "Why do you ask that? His whole family is clearly devoted to God. After the funeral I was amazed that you were going to marry a church guy. It made me think that maybe you had found faith too. I—"

Zuriel interrupted. "No, it's not like that. Matt wasn't like his family." She didn't want to talk about this. She had come home to get away from these kinds of conversations.

"But everyone who talked about him just seemed so peaceful about everything …"

"Matt ran away from home when he was eighteen. I'm surprised that you weren't able to pick that up." Zuriel was done listening and was ready to let her know how things really were. "You didn't hear anyone say anything about a better place. Do you know why? Because his own family thinks their son is burning in hell for turning away from God. What kind of God does that? Matt was smart to get away from that kind of judgment."

"Zuriel, I didn't mean to make you upset. Don't listen to them; only God knows if he's in hell or not. Just because he ran away doesn't mean he lost his faith."

"I'm not upset, I'm just angry that everyone seems to have such a grand interest in where he is spending eternity. And I know he lost his faith! He didn't want anything to do with God, and it's no wonder, when he was living with those goody-goods his whole life!" Zuriel realized her heart was beating faster. She didn't understand why the topic upset her so much.

"Oh? I thought you liked his family." Suzy's words were like darts.

It was true that Zuriel liked Matt's family. She had always wanted to live in a big house full of people with exciting lives.

One of the most painful parts about being there was knowing what her fiancé had willingly left behind. She tried and tried but couldn't wrap her head around it.

"I do." Zuriel paused, trying to figure out what to say. "I like them, but if Matt left, then there must be something about them that I don't know."

"I liked them too. They all seemed happy to meet you and spend time with you."

"That's what I don't understand."

"What don't you understand?" Suzy asked. She was nosier than Zuriel remembered.

"It's just that Matt was such a good person. If they didn't accept him and if they think he's in hell, why were they being so nice to me? It just doesn't add up. They have to be faking or something, because it's clear that we don't measure up to their standards." She didn't understand it. She felt like a bad person around them, but she didn't know why. They tried to appear to be perfect, yet there were still plenty of problems in the family.

"I don't think they were faking. I really think they love you," Suzy stated matter-of-factly.

"Well that's great, but your opinion doesn't mean much anymore." She could hardly believe she had said the words out loud. She wasn't the type to be so blunt.

Suzy looked at her solemnly and nodded.

Zuriel felt terrible. "I'm sorry. I didn't mean to say that. It's just that, well, you know, you left and you were a mess. You lied, you rarely paid rent, you came home high, and you hurled insults everywhere. It just seems strange that you're suddenly back."

Suzy pulled her knees up to her chest. She looked thoughtful and unsure of what to say. "I was trying to figure out how to talk to you again, after everything that's happened to me. When I found out about your fiancé I just felt like I needed to come."

"You keep acting like you're here to help me. I think we both know better than that."

"Do we?" Suzy's words were nonchalant, but her eyes were focused. What comfort could Suzy possibly have to offer her?

"Well, yeah! For the last several years you've needed major help. If anything, I should be helping you! Do you expect me to think the person I've known my whole life just suddenly changed in the last six months?"

"I know it's hard to believe, but that's exactly it, Zuriel. I hit rock bottom. I was wandering the streets, using what money I had for drugs. My parents weren't giving me any help because I refused to go to rehab. No one could talk any sense into me. You know that, 'cause even you tried."

"Yeah, you were really stubborn." She could remember when things got really bad. She was afraid for her friend's life and begged her to get help.

"I was more than stubborn—I was lost."

"So then what happened?" Zuriel asked impatiently. Judging by her friend's body language, the story was going to be a long one. Zuriel fluffed a few pillows behind her back as she leaned against the white headboard. She wasn't sure what to expect, but she was curious enough about her friend to sit through the explanation.

"I was trying to sell myself to a guy on the street," Suzy began, already surprising Zuriel with her story. "He was wasted and standing there smoking while leaning against the side of a building. I was sitting next to him on the ground, trying to convince him to take me home. Then a man came up to him and started talking. He asked if we wanted some free food, so we followed him to a bus and rode it to a rundown building a few blocks over. It was crazy how packed the place was. There were so many people swearing and yelling. The desire for food and a chance to get out of the neighborhood kept us all behaving pretty well, though. We got there and got to pig out on pizza. We all found a seat and then that same man stood up on top of a chair and started talking."

"So some random guy inspired you to get sober?" Zuriel was trying to understand her friend. Suzy had always been an easy girl, but she never expected her to turn to prostitution. Things must have gotten a whole lot worse for her after she left.

"No," Suzy said, her eyes getting glossy. "He said, 'Imagine if your life could be everything you ever dreamed it would be. Imagine if you could fulfill a purpose and be rewarded for it. Imagine if you could be loved the way you were supposed to be. If I told you about a way to get that, would you want it?' Of course most of us were nodding and looking at each other, wondering who this guy was. Then he started talking about this amazing place where there wasn't any pain or sorrow. He described perfect happiness and freedom."

"Yeah, so what was it? Did he tell you to quit using dope so you could start following your dreams? Sounds real promising for a bunch of thugs," Zuriel bitterly commented. She didn't believe that a "just say no" campaign had gotten through to her friend.

"Yeah, it seems like something tacky and elementary, but this guy had our complete attention. He started talking about how, in order for us to go to a place of perfection, we had to be perfect. He told us the guilt that was bothering us, guilt from all the bad things we did, was holding us back. He said we could become perfect if the penalty was paid."

Zuriel felt sick thinking about it. Was the guy drunk? It sounded like some sort of cult. "What a crack head!" Zuriel laughed bitterly. She looked at Suzy, trying to figure out if she was actually serious.

Suzy just smiled back, before calmly continuing. "He asked us who was willing to receive forgiveness and become clean. Most of us felt like our while lives were a punishment, so a few people cursed, but a lot of people stood. Everyone was so beaten down they were willing to try anything to start over."

"I can't believe they actually responded. Did you? Was he doing some kind of magic spell to make you stop craving a hit?" Zuriel was disturbed but strongly intrigued.

"No, I didn't move. I was scared, not only for myself but for the people who went up there. I knew some of them were just drunk and bored. They didn't really know what they were doing. The man talking had them all stand in a line and then announced that he had some good news. He said someone had decided to take the punishment for us all. He said that our past mistakes had been taken care of, and we could go to that place of perfection someday if we wanted to."

Zuriel was sure this con artist must have been looting their pockets or something. The story sounded oddly familiar, and she wondered if the guy teaching was trying to become the next Gandhi. It was ridiculous. A story like that could only fascinate someone who wasn't right in the head.

"That's just plain weird." She said, rolling her eyes.

"I was pretty creeped out too. Especially when he told us the punishment for our mistakes was death. We were all supposed to die, but someone else died for us instead. The room erupted with yelling and threats. Some of the guys in the front started calling the man a liar and telling him he was a fool if he thought he was going kill them. The man whistled really loudly and said he deserved to die too. He told us he was just like us, that we all deserve to pay for what we have done. The man who had died for us, the man who took our punishment came back to life. He's alive and wants to save each of us from eternal death."

"Who does this guy think he is, Jesus?"

"Exactly! He was telling us the story of Jesus—the true story."

Zuriel could hardly believe what she was hearing. Her friend was talking about God? Had Suzy become a Christian? She wasn't a churchy girl, so she didn't understand how Suzy could become one. The story seemed crazy. How could anyone believe that?

"The whole time he was just setting up the story of Jesus?" Zuriel asked, feeling uncomfortable.

"Yes, and I knew I deserved to die. I knew I didn't stand a chance."

"Suzy, don't tell me you bought into all that garbage?"

"I did, Zuriel. I couldn't get rid of my guilt and sins alone. I wanted to escape from all the suffering on earth. When I die I want to go to heaven."

"Heaven …?"

"Yes," Suzy confidently answered.

Zuriel had been curious about Suzy's story but never would have guessed that her old friend would become a Christ follower. She could remember all the late-night talks they'd had about their beliefs. They both felt strongly that religion was a waste of time. Now, after all of their talks, Suzy was choosing to be part of the very thing that had so disgusted her before.

"I just don't get it, though. If God was real, then he wouldn't let so many bad things happen in the world. How can you say there's a God when Matt is dead?"

"The best part of following him is knowing that we get to leave this place of suffering behind. I don't understand God. I don't know very much about him yet, but I do know He loves me and has helped me very much. Zuriel, I haven't even taken a single drug trip since that night." Suzy was crying and smiling at the same time. Zuriel felt like she was talking to a completely different person than the woman she had known. She was honestly happy that Suzy had gotten sober, even if it took religion to do it, but there was no way she was going to embrace this religion as her own.

"Well, I'm happy for you then. I hope it lasts," Zuriel commented dryly. She stood up and started getting ready for the day. She wasn't in the mood for talking anymore. She put on her jeans and a white tank top. Then she slipped on her flip flops and headed for the door. A walk would do her good right now, and she was glad when Suzy didn't try to stop her. She didn't want to hear about Suzy and her God anymore. She wanted God to bring Matt back from the dead. If Matt was truly in hell, then she didn't want to go to heaven.

 *Chapter 13*

Zuriel put on her gray polo and pulled her hair back. She wasn't looking forward to her first day back to work. She used to like the fact that the small grocery store where she worked was only a block away. Now she wished the Corner Mart was in another city. Her employer had been understanding and had given her a couple weeks off; she was thankful for that, but she wasn't looking forward to all the questions about how she was doing. She hoped there wouldn't be any questions or conversations; all she wanted to do was survive.

Zuriel could barely say hello when she saw Brenda, the store manager. She hadn't expected coming back to be so difficult. She felt like she needed more time to grieve. Zuriel clocked in and found her place behind a register. She had a feeling that today was going to be a long day.

As much as she didn't want to be at work, she wasn't really looking forward to going home either. Suzy had been staying with her for a few weeks now, and Zuriel still had a hard time understanding how her friend could have changed so much. They had spent a lot of time talking about the reasons, but Zuriel didn't feel like talking anymore. She was sick of hearing about God. Wasn't it God who had killed her fiancé?

There were many times when she was glad she wasn't alone though. The last several weeks had worked out okay, and Suzy hadn't really done anything wrong. In fact, Zuriel was impressed. She had expected her friend to return to her old ways, but instead, it felt as though Suzy had become *different*. Zuriel had a feeling that whatever went on at church must have been the cause. She couldn't help but admit that religion had made Suzy a better person. It was an unusual realization, but Zuriel wondered if maybe religion actually did work for some people and just not for others. She thought of Matt and his family. Some people were good at the church thing and others weren't. Zuriel was sure she would never be.

The big decision before her now was whether to let Suzy move back in permanently. Suzy had asked many times, but Zuriel just couldn't give her an answer. She felt like she needed more time. She had promised Suzy she would make a final decision by tonight. Even though she had been trying to decide for the last two weeks, she still didn't feel confident about her answer. She was still heartbroken over Matt. It wasn't easy trying to forgive so many people at the same time. She wasn't sure if she could trust Suzy again. It was going to be tough. Suzy had hurt her, but Suzy had also been a better friend than anyone else had. Suzy had brought her chocolate and tissues many times throughout the last few weeks and had listened to her talk about Matt day after day. The only thing Zuriel wasn't sure about was Suzy's constant references to God. Suzy was always offering to pray for her, or bring her to church.

It seemed like everyone she knew just wanted to talk with her about God all the time. Zuriel had many voicemails on her phone from the Lowell family, and the messages were always about how much they missed her and were praying for her. She started to feel guilty for not answering, so she had finally worked up the courage to call Anne a few days ago. Zuriel was still fascinated and confused by her attitude.

Anne had begun the conversation by saying, "Zuriel, it was so nice to meet you. I'm so glad you came to stay with us."

"Well, it was really nice of you to let me stay, even with everything else going on."

"Of course! I couldn't stand the thought of your being alone during that time. We all miss Matt so much, but you knew him the best. I've been praying for you. We all have."

"Thank you. I'm glad I was able to stay with you. I hope we can all heal soon," Zuriel agreed, feeling like she didn't have any comfort to offer the woman.

"It's such a sad thing that he passed away, but I'm really starting to believe more and more that God has a plan for all this," she proposed, causing Zuriel's blood to boil. She was sick of hearing this. "You know, Samuel is practically a different person, and through his influence, the whole family is beginning to change for the better. Even the youth group is growing in their faith and in numbers too."

Zuriel heard her words and felt growing frustration. She knew she was part of the reason Sam had been able to get over the death of his brother. She wasn't sure how she felt about that. Sam had been so angry, but then all of a sudden he was apologizing to her and talking about forgiveness.

"Well, I'm glad things are working out," Zuriel said. She was irritated that Matt's death was being looked at in a positive light. There wasn't a single thing that could make what happened a good thing. Death was always bad. A few people growing stronger in their religion didn't justify what had happened.

Zuriel's mind was pulled away from the past when the first customers got in line to check out. Zuriel tried to be positive, but she couldn't smile. She wanted the day to be over, and she wished she didn't have to make the decision about Suzy staying with her quite yet. Besides that, Drew had asked if he could stop by tonight. Zuriel couldn't say no, even though it was the worst possible time for her to have more company. She had a feeling Drew liked her and wanted to date her once she got over Matt. Zuriel was annoyed that he would show signs of interest so soon after Matt's death. This was not going to be an easy road to healing, and this was not going to be an easy day.

The clock slowly ticked on. The moment it was five o'clock, Zuriel headed home. The city was decorated for the upcoming holiday, but Zuriel didn't feel very festive. She had been looking forward to seeing the July Fourth fireworks with Matt. She tried not to think about all the dates that would never happen as she made her way back to her apartment. She saw Drew's car in the parking lot and groaned. She wasn't going to get a chance to talk to Suzy until later.

Zuriel climbed the stairs and opened her door. She smelled pizza and felt her stomach growl. She entered the kitchen and was met by her two friends.

"Hey, how was work?" Suzy enquired with an unnecessary amount of cheerfulness.

"Take a wild guess," Zuriel answered sarcastically as she placed a slice of pizza on her paper plate.

"Not good, huh? Maybe it's too soon to go back to work?"

Zuriel shrugged and took a seat. She guessed Suzy was hinting about moving in. If Zuriel didn't go back to work, she wouldn't be able to pay her rent. If Suzy was paying half the rent, going back to work wouldn't be as urgent.

"Three weeks does seem a little soon," Drew chimed in.

"I know, but I've got to move on sometime," Zuriel explained, hoping to get them off her case.

"It's okay to take your time." Suzy's words were sympathetic, but Zuriel still wondered about her motives.

"So, Drew," Zuriel began, changing the subject, "what have you been up to?"

"You know, the usual. I've been worried sick about you, though." He switched the topic back to her.

Their comfort was infuriating. "You don't need to worry about me. I'm pretty independent, so I'm sure I'll survive. Like Matt used to say: 'Take it one day at a time.'" Zuriel quickly took a bite of pizza. She was sick of answering questions about how she was doing. When would they drop the subject so she could move on?

"Zuriel, it's okay to be upset," Drew said.

"I know! Haven't I been upset enough, though? I think its okay for me to at least eat dinner without drinking my tears." She was aware of the edginess in her voice, but she didn't care. She didn't want this to become another crying session.

"I'm sorry. I'm not a psychologist; I just want to help," Drew whispered. He sounded sincere.

"I know. It's just hard because I loved Matt very much and I think I always will. I figure I should get used to always missing him …" Zuriel's voice trailed off and she began to cry. She wanted to slap Drew across the face for bringing up the subject of Matt's death again. Didn't they realize she wanted a break from sadness?

"Of course you'll always love him," Suzy said, putting her arm around Zuriel.

"You really think you'll love him forever?" Drew asked indignantly.

"Yes, I do. What's your problem with that?" Zuriel challenged, recognizing the source of his true concern.

"Come on. We all know Matt was a lady's man. I mean, no one stays in love with the same person forever anymore. You wouldn't have loved him forever, even if he had stayed alive. I understand missing him, but do you think he really would have made you happy? Why are the dead always remembered only for the good stuff they did?"

Zuriel could hardly believe what she was hearing. "How can you talk like that? He's only been dead for three weeks and you seem like you're already over it. What kind of friend are you? And what's so bad about believing he would make me happy? *You* could certainly never make me happy, if that's what you're alluding to!" Zuriel snapped. She unloaded her anger and was happy to see that her arrows had hit their mark.

Suzy sat in silence, clearly surprised by what was being said.

Zuriel just cried, frustrated that she couldn't go more than a few hours without losing it.

"Listen, Zuriel—" Drew began.

Suzy interrupted, defending Zuriel. "Drew, please, I think that's enough."

But Drew kept on. "You all think Matt was this amazing guy. I'll admit he was going the good-boy route when he started dating you, but that wasn't always the case. You're lucky you didn't have to face the heartbreak that he dished out to many other girls before you." Drew fumed. "I'm sorry to be the one to say this, Zuriel, but it wasn't like Matt to be steady. After he broke up with Lena, he was a basket case. He didn't even date girls for more than one night; he just flirted to get what he wanted."

"Drew, that's enough! Can't you see you're only making things worse?" Suzy cried.

Zuriel knew Suzy was loyal, but now she was curious. Zuriel had heard about this Lena girl before. It seemed like she had made quite an impact on Matt's life. Zuriel hated Drew for bringing her up, but now she had to know the whole story.

"What do you know about Lena?" Zuriel asked with a sudden calmness. Suzy and Drew both looked surprised.

"Didn't Matt ever mention her?" Drew scoffed, scooting his chair in and placing his elbows on the table. He looked amused.

Zuriel recanted what little she knew. "No, he didn't, but I did hear some things about her from his family. All I know is that Lena got pregnant and had an abortion. Apparently, Matt was pretty worked up about that and things didn't work out."

"You're right, he got her pregnant. See, when he came to Detroit we started hanging out and I introduced him to the party life. He met Lena at a party and started hanging around her a lot. He fell for her big time. I don't think he had ever been in love before, and he was so sure she was the one. She found out about his drugs, and he gave them up cold turkey after she asked him to stop. It was crazy.

"But then he started to act a little weird. He had been away from home for about six months and was starting to feel guilty. We had money troubles and I guess his brother Sam had tried to contact him. He even went to church one Sunday, but he came back even more depressed than before. He didn't party for a week. I was really concerned about him, especially when I found out Lena was pregnant. He was so scared because he didn't know how he was going to raise a kid. I mean, he was only eighteen."

Zuriel tried to take in all the information. It was difficult to hear about her man loving another woman.

"So is that when they had the abortion?" Suzy asked.

"No, it wasn't something they both wanted. Lena thought getting rid of the baby would make him happy again. The opposite happened, though. He was furious and accused her of murdering his child. He couldn't believe she would do something like that without talking to him first. They got into a huge fight and never spoke to each other again. He was depressed for a long time."

"Sam said he talked to Matt right around that time. What was the deal with that?" Zuriel wanted to know the whole story.

"Yeah, his brother was one of those guys who would walk through the streets and talk to random people about God. When he found

Matt, I guess that situation wasn't real pretty. Matt said Sam was angry with him for abandoning Lena. It didn't make sense, though, because those Jesus people hate abortion. Matt was furious with his brother. I don't think they ever spoke to each other again either."

Zuriel was bewildered. This didn't sound like the man she had dated. She couldn't imagine Matt holding a grudge like that toward his girlfriend or his brother. Matt was kind and forgiving, so it didn't make sense that he had been such a jerk. Zuriel tried as hard as she could to not start crying again. "That doesn't sound like Matt," she whimpered, trying to comfort herself.

"Oh, but it was." Drew snarled. "After he talked to his brother, it's like he snapped. He became the life of every party and refused to talk with anyone about his family or his ex-girlfriend. His personality went from being a lovesick, sheltered druggie to an angry, determined guy who would do whatever it took to have some fun. The only thing he kept from his relationship with Lena was never going back to drugs."

"That's not the man who put this ring on my finger," Zuriel insisted. "I know he changed, no matter what you or anyone in his family says. It feels like you're all trying to convince me things wouldn't have worked out between us, but how can you know that? The past is the past, and every person deserves the freedom to change." Zuriel was angered by the things she was hearing. She wondered if Drew thought telling her about all the bad things in Matt's past was going to help him build a relationship with her. It amazed her how stupid men could be at times.

Suzy joined the conversation. "Zuriel, you're right. Everyone deserves the chance to leave their past behind. I know what it's like to live that kind of life. I changed, and I believe you if you say that Matt was different."

Zuriel cheeks heated up. Here she was talking about people deserving a chance to change when all her friend was begging for was a chance to prove she had changed too. Zuriel knew without a doubt that Suzy would be here to stay. If she really loved Matt, and if she really believed her own words, she had to accept Suzy back into her life too.

"I know he changed," Drew said, standing. "One day he just told me he was tired of messing around. He kept saying he had wasted the last four years of his life, and that he had more important things to think about than just having a good time. We had some long talks, and he was certainly determined to become better, whatever that meant. He started working more and stopped picking up random girls. I thought he would go back to the other life, but he never did. Then he met you and, well, you know the rest."

"Even *you* admit he wasn't going back to his old life. It sounds to me like he would have been the best guy in the world to marry. You can't convince me we weren't meant for each other," Zuriel said firmly. She was crying silent tears of joy, thinking about how wonderful her fiancé had been.

"Yeah, the best guy in the world," Drew mocked dryly as he grabbed his keys off the kitchen counter. He nodded and headed for the door.

Zuriel was relieved when she heard it slam. She didn't want him to talk about Matt like that. She had been ready to marry Matt, but now Drew seemed to enjoy making his death appear like it was a good thing. She would never believe that, not in a hundred years!

Zuriel saw Suzy patiently sitting and waiting for Zuriel to speak first. She was thankful her friend wasn't pushing the subject of living space. She had to give Suzy the final verdict about sharing her apartment.

Zuriel picked up the paper plates and fit the pizza box in the refrigerator.

Suzy cleaned the glasses and wiped down the table. It wasn't like them to clean up right away; they usually left things at least overnight. She guessed neither of them wanted to bring up the subject, but they both wanted to get it over with.

"All right, Suzy, you can stay. So ... yeah." Zuriel stammered before practically running to her room. She didn't want to talk about it right now, but she was glad that at least she had gotten the words out. She decided to get ready for bed early and maybe watch a movie. Thinking about going to work the next day filled her with an overwhelming feeling of dread. She wasn't ready to move on yet, and she wondered if she ever would be.

 *Chapter 14*

Zuriel woke to her alarm clock buzzing. It was already midmorning, but she was glad she didn't have to work today. Today was July Fourth, so she finally had a holiday off. It was more than a month after the death of her fiancé, but she still felt as though she had heard the news just the day before. Tonight should have been a romantic date. They might have hung out with some friends for lunch, gone to a parade, and snuggled under the stars while they watched the fireworks. It would have been perfect, but another perfect moment was ruined. Instead of getting a night of romance, she was going to spend the evening with her grandparents. As a kid she loved seeing the fireworks from their backyard, so when her dad invited her, she had reluctantly said yes. It was better than sitting at home.

She made her way to Suzy's room, hoping they could do something fun this morning. She didn't want to think about what could and should have been. She was proud of herself for her new ability to wait to cry until she went to bed. It was nice not needing to keep tissues everywhere, because her pillow worked well as a tear-catcher. She could remember the last time she had cried at work—it had only been a few days ago. A customer had asked how she was doing on "this beautiful morning." Of course the morning didn't seem that beautiful, and she wasn't doing very well. Thankfully, Brenda let her go home early and get some rest.

She approached Suzy's door and knocked. "Hey, Suz, are you up?" Zuriel cracked the door open and walked in.

There she was, reading her Bible in the morning as had become her usual habit. "Good morning and happy Independence Day!" Suzy exclaimed with a smile.

"Well, good morning. You seem especially energetic today."

"It is a day symbolizing freedom, isn't it?"

"Yes, but what that has to do with your mood is beyond me," Zuriel said, rolling her eyes. "I told you I'm going to visit my family for the fireworks, right? I'm free until this evening, so what are we going to do to celebrate since you are so excited about freedom?"

"I didn't know about tonight, but yeah, we should do some celebrating today. I've already begun." Suzy nodded toward the Bible lying open on the nightstand.

Zuriel rolled her eyes again. Suzy found a way to bring God up all the time. Suzy was a new Christian, so she made it her aim to learn more about the Bible every day. For some reason, Suzy would often share what she learned, and Zuriel could never understand why that book was such a big deal to her roommate.

"Do you think God will punish you if you go a day without reading that thing?" Zuriel asked.

"No, I would be punishing myself! I want to read it, because I really want to know God. Like I told you before, I don't know very much about him. I keep finding out that I have been doing things all wrong. How am I supposed to do things the right way if I don't bother finding out what that way is?"

"Whatever, Suzy. You enjoy your celebrating; I'm going to make some coffee." With that, Zuriel left Suzy to her reading. She wondered what was so wonderful about the Bible anyway. What pleasure could anyone get from reading the Ten Commandments? Sure there were some pretty legendary stories in there, but they were just kids' stories.

She left the coffee brewing and got ready for the day. She was almost ready to leave the house with Suzy when she finally checked her phone. She wasn't surprised to find cheesy Fourth of July texts from all her friends. She scrolled through them and landed on an unknown number. She opened it, hoping to find a funny, random one that was meant for someone else. Instead, she found the text was certainly meant for her. It read:

Hey, Zuriel, I hope things are going okay. I know today will probably be tough. Matt always loved fireworks. I'll be praying for you. Hang in there. —Sam

Zuriel felt fresh tears come to her eyes, but it was more out of sentiment than sorrow. She sent him a simple thank you because that was the only way to sum it up. It was nice that someone else knew Matt and knew today was a big deal. They both knew he loved fireworks, but she had never gotten to see them with him.

She dried her eyes and met Suzy in the kitchen. They filled their travel mugs with coffee and split a package of pop tarts. Zuriel's friend Andy had texted her an invite to a cookout for the afternoon. They decided to celebrate there and maybe get to meet some new people. They hadn't originally planned to go to a party, but when the invitation came, they were both in the mood to get out of the house. Zuriel decided she could leave just before dinnertime to meet up with her folks.

Upon arriving, Zuriel felt her usual insecurity. The other girls seemed to be skinnier, prettier, and had clearly seen tanning beds recently. She felt out of place. At one point in her life, she thought she had matured enough to get past the insecurity and became comfortable with herself, but now she realized her confidence had only been the result of having Matt with her. She wondered if anyone would ever be attracted to her again. She wished so badly that Matt was with her, but she still wanted attention. For the first time she realized how much she missed being told she was beautiful and being held. It wasn't just Matt that she missed; it was the warmth of his arms around her, the sound of his voice in her ear, and the knowledge that no matter who looked prettier than she did, he was still choosing to be by her side. That comfort was gone, and she was left looking around and feeling slightly less hungry than she had been.

Zuriel saw a few of the guys eyeing her and felt uneasy. She liked their attention, but she thought of Matt and felt guilty. She found a good spot on the back deck and continued to analyze her surroundings. As she watched Suzy talking with everyone, laughing and smiling, Zuriel wondered if her friend would find a boyfriend soon. Suzy was beautiful and had always been popular with the guys. She wondered if her friend was staying out of relationships just for her sake. Suzy hadn't so much as gone on a date since the funeral. It didn't seem like her, especially knowing that she had been a prostitute. Zuriel smiled and thought of her friend's newfound faith. She guessed that when guys found out about her religion and unwillingness to have sex, they would turn away from her pretty quickly. Although thinking that way made Zuriel feel a little better about herself, she couldn't help trying to think of a match for her friend. She thought of Sam, Matt's brother.

It was almost too perfect. Zuriel had fallen in love with the younger brother who was a rebel and didn't care about God or religion. And now here was Suzy, the Jesus-loving ex-druggie. Maybe she would be a good match for Sam? Zuriel imagined them meeting and suddenly didn't like the idea. She couldn't explain why, but she didn't want anyone she knew to be somehow tied to her lover's family. She was hoping she wouldn't have to be reminded of them or of Matt. However, she had chatted a few times on the phone with them, and now she was texting Sam. She wondered if there would ever be a way for her to escape the past.

Zuriel saw one of the Andy's friends nod in her direction and then walk toward her. She wasn't sure what to do. She had already decided she wasn't going to flirt just for fun. She wanted to forget the pain she felt inside, but it was too soon after the accident for her to be trying to heal this way.

"Enjoying the party?" he asked as he sat in the lawn chair beside her. His short brown hair was slightly spiked in the front and his blue eyes were engaging.

"Yeah, it's nice."

"I was just really glad to get the day off. I'm ready to hang out and drink up."

"I needed a day off too. I feel like I haven't been able to enjoy the summer yet."

He smiled as he sipped his beer. She couldn't help but smile back and stare. They both turned their heads, hearing sudden cheering coming from the yard. Two of the guys were celebrating their victory at a game of Cornhole. They were laughing and defiantly calling out for the next competitors.

"Do you want to play?" Zuriel asked, surprised by her own forwardness. She suddenly wanted to join in and have some fun. Maybe it wasn't too early to try to move on.

"I would love too!" He smiled and took his last swig of beer.

Zuriel stood, feeling excited, and they headed down the deck steps.

He stopped suddenly, asking, "What was your name, by the way?"

"Zuriel. It's just like Ariel from *The Little Mermaid*, only different." She felt silly, realizing how ridiculous her flirting sounded.

"It's a beautiful name," he said, gently brushing her shoulder. "I'm Matt ..." His voice trailed off as he seemed to notice her countenance change.

Zuriel suddenly felt culpable and wished to God that his name had been anything but that. She had almost forgotten about Matt for a few minutes, but now he was fresh in her mind again. She could see his smile, his hair, and his voice in her head.

"Is something wrong?" the stranger asked, breaking her trance.

"Um, I don't know if I want to play anymore. I'm sorry." Zuriel could see that he was searching her face trying to figure out what he did wrong. She felt sorry for him but even sorrier for herself. What was she thinking? Matt was dead. Her soul mate and lover was gone forever, and no one could ever replace him.

"What is it?" He brushed her shoulder again, and she took a step back. He looked even more confused.

"I'm sorry, it's not your fault. My fiancé died about a month ago, and I wasn't thinking. His name was Matt too and I ... I just can't." She saw him frown and his eyebrows rise like he had made some kind of discovery.

"You were engaged to Matt Lowell, weren't you?"

Zuriel hated that he knew. She didn't want him to figure out that his name was the only obstacle keeping them from ever being friends. She nodded and looked down at her feet.

"I'm sorry. I didn't know. I knew he was engaged but I never heard a name. I'm really sorry for your loss. He was a lucky guy to spend his last days on earth with you as his girl."

Zuriel smiled, flattered by what he said, but slightly annoyed that he continued to pursue. At least she was still somewhat attractive.

"Well, thanks. Sorry." Zuriel apologized again, almost whispering. She turned and went back to her seat on the deck. This was going to be a more miserable day than she expected. She was surprised to see Matt sitting beside her again. She wasn't sure why he still wanted to talk.

"I really am sorry. Your Matt was a good guy. I had a lot of respect for him. He did what he wanted to do, and he wouldn't let anybody else's opinion shake him."

Zuriel was glad to hear someone talking about Matt in a positive way. She thought back to Drew trying to convince her that Matt was a player and a bad guy.

"Yeah, I'm really glad I knew him. He was the best person I have ever known," she said.

"I'm sure he was. It's hard to believe it's been a month already. How are you dealing with everything? Are you getting counseling or something?" His questions made Zuriel feel strangely calm. She wanted to open up.

"No, I'm just taking it one day at a time. I've been back to work and doing stuff. I guess getting used to my life without him is the closest thing to therapy."

"Of course, that's the best way to move on," he agreed, nodding. Their conversation was interrupted when someone called for Matt. Whoever was manning the grill needed another opinion on the state of the hamburgers.

Zuriel hated hearing them say his name out loud. She decided to go into the house and use the bathroom. Maybe she could have a few moments to organize her thoughts.

She passed one of the bedrooms and heard laughter. She stopped and turned, wondering who was in there. She looked in and saw the window open, and the grill was right outside. She kept walking, hoping to find the bathroom, but suddenly stopped and went back. Zuriel knew spying wasn't very nice, but she was curious. Maybe she could find out more about this other Matt. She stood beside the open window, just out of sight.

"Yo, Matt, what were you doing over there? I saw you hitting on Zuriel," she heard Andy say.

"Yeah, why didn't you tell me she was Matt Lowell's girl?"

"'Cause he's dead. Zuriel isn't anybody's girl anymore—that is, unless you have something you'd like to tell us." They all laughed, and Zuriel felt nauseated. They were talking about her like she was a used car.

One of the other guys said, "You're not going to get anything from her. Lowell died just a few weeks ago. Chicks don't recover that fast."

"Well, it just takes patience. It sucks that I have the same name as her ex, but if you get a girl confessing her deepest feelings, then you know you've won. It'll take some time, but have you seen her? She's worth a little waiting and manipulating."

Zuriel walked away from the window, disturbed by what she had heard. She certainly wasn't going to hang around him anymore. And what about Andy? She was surprised he would talk about her that way too. These guys seemed like mere fractions of the man her Matt had been. Didn't they have any respect for their dead friend—or her? Zuriel closed the bathroom door and sat on the floor. Hot tears ran down her face, and now she wished she had never come.

"God, why?" she whispered. She wondered why all this had to happen. She remembered Suzy telling her God made things work together for good for those people who followed Jesus. She didn't know if she wanted things to work out for good. She was tired of people trying to make her see Matt's death as a positive thing. She made a mental note to remind Suzy that since she was not a follower of Jesus, none of this was going to work out for her. "Matt, why did you have to die? Why was I left with the mystery of your family and your life? I wish you could be here. You were always so good at explaining things."

Zuriel dabbed her eyes with some toilet paper and tried to fix her makeup. She glanced at the clock and saw that it was only two in the afternoon. She wondered if she could leave early. She could use the excuse that she hadn't seen her dad since the funeral. Surely they would at least understand that.

Zuriel made her way back to the party and saw the guys from the grill. She quickly strolled past them and found Suzy talking to a group of people.

"Suz," Zuriel said softly from behind her.

Suzy turned and looked at her sympathetically. She could read Zuriel like a book. "What's going on? You okay?"

"Not really. Those guys are 'oh, so charming.' I overheard them talking. Andy's friend Matt was trying to use my vulnerable situation to get me into bed." She vented, thankful to have a female ally.

Suzy's face bunched up in frustration. "Lord, have mercy! What's wrong with them?"

Zuriel saw Suzy eye them and was suddenly concerned that her friend was going to confront them.

"Don't worry about it, Suz. I think I'm just going to leave early. I'll go hang out with my family tonight. It's weird, but I'm actually looking forward to seeing them. I guess I just need to feel like I belong somewhere."

"Are you sure? You've never wanted to go see your dad before," Suzy reminded her skeptically.

"I know, but I feel like we have a kind of understanding after all this. We both lost the person we loved the most."

Suzy nodded in understanding. They hugged, and Zuriel was more than ready to escape.

She walked around the house to the front yard to avoid seeing Andy and his friends. She texted her dad and walked to the bus stop. Her dad would pick her up when she got off at the next stop. She felt immense relief to be away from the party.

Zuriel could finally think freely as she stared out the bus window. She wondered what was happening to her. Had she changed because of Matt's death? Zuriel felt that she had, but she didn't know if she liked her new self. Would anything ever be the same? Would anything ever start to feel normal again?

 *Chapter 15*

Suzy fell to her knees, not caring what the other church members thought. Her heart was burdened and heavy. She was still a new a Christian, but she had come a long way very quickly. Her life before Christ had been full of pain, heartbreak, and hopelessness. Now she couldn't stop thanking God that things were so much different. Suzy wished so badly she had turned to God sooner. She thought about the drugs, sex, partying, insecurity, and her hatred of others. Tears trickled out of her eyes as she remembered it all. When she had first become a Christian, she was aware that she needed redemption and had done wrong things, mostly because the consequences were so painful. Now that she had taken time to read the Bible and discovered just how many things she had done wrong, she found herself repenting her sins daily. She begged God to help her change and be a light for him to shine in the darkness around her.

Suzy had been living with Zuriel for about five months now. She moved in after the funeral in an effort to lead Zuriel to the truth. She wanted her friend to see that God wasn't just a man in the sky who had fun ruining their lives. She wanted Zuriel to see that God loved her and desperately wanted to make things better.

Suzy prayed constantly and had every prayer group in the church praying as well. God had answered many of their prayers in small ways, but Zuriel still stubbornly resisted salvation.

Suzy had also prayed that Zuriel's relationship with her dad would improve and heal. Ever since she had watched the fireworks with him, their relationship had changed. Zuriel now met with him at least once a month to talk or just hang out. Suzy could hardly believe things had gotten so much better between them and hoped they would continue to move forward.

Even though everything else in her life kept getting better and better, the pain of losing Matt continued to be Zuriel's excuse for not coming to church or any Bible studies. Zuriel was afraid of never seeing Matt again and had convinced herself that if Matt was in hell, she wanted to go there too.

Suzy's shoulders shook as she wept. She begged God to draw Zuriel to Himself. She wanted her friend to be able to heal and be happy. Instead, Zuriel had spent the last five months simply getting used to the fact that Matt was gone but not allowing herself to have peace.

Suzy had invited Zuriel to church many times, and she had nearly come. Zuriel admitted that Suzy was a new person because of following Jesus. She had also told Suzy that she was the first Christian she had known who actually acted on what she said. Suzy was thankful for her friend's encouragement. She hadn't done things perfectly and had been very tempted to go back to her old ways many times. She knew which of her friends had drugs and where to go in order to get them. Suzy knew there were several guys who wanted to sleep with her, but she fought hard to stay away from them. She knew God didn't want her to just sleep around. It wasn't long after moving in with Zuriel that she felt convicted about going out dancing at the clubs downtown. It was hard to change, but Suzy knew that if she wanted to avoid getting back into her old lifestyle, she had to stay away from places that catered to her old sinful habits. Suzy was thankful that God continued to give her the strength to make the right choices.

Suzy was glad Zuriel had seen Christ in her. It had been a long and painful five months, and Suzy felt in her heart that Zuriel was close to the point of salvation. Zuriel had asked more questions about God recently and seemed to be making twice as many excuses for not believing. Zuriel stopped protesting when Suzy would pray over their food and had stopped making fun of her for reading the Bible. Still, Suzy had never been tested so much in her entire life. Knowing that a nonbeliever could see everything she did made her want to do what was right all the more. She wanted Zuriel to see that God was real and that He was powerful. Suzy felt that it wouldn't be long before Zuriel would finally trust in Jesus, so she decided she would pray now more than ever.

Dear God, I wish I was better at talking about you to Zuriel. I wish I could always do the right thing and say the right thing. I don't know what to do; I just know Zuriel needs you. Please help her to love you. Please help her to find you and turn away from her old life. I don't want her to go to hell. Please, Jesus, help me. I can't do this alone.

❧

Zuriel sat in her apartment, relaxing on the couch facing the large window. She looked out on the busy streets and parking lot, once again remembering the day she had waited so anxiously for Matt to arrive. It was painful to remember, but now she could finally think of him without crying. It had been a long five months, and the fall weather seemed to symbolize the direction her heart was going. It was an uncommonly cold October day, and Zuriel wondered if the winter would be as frozen as her own heart. Sure she had gotten used to life without Matt; in fact, she had almost been without him for as long as she had been with him. Now it seemed like the last year had been a total waste of time.

Zuriel had tried to move on. She had gone on a few dates but ended up dumping each guy pretty quickly. It usually took her about five minutes to see that Matt was better than each one of them in almost every way. Drew continued his attempts to tell her about the "true Matt." It drove her crazy, but she had begun to wonder if she was missing Matt or simply the idea of Matt. She couldn't help wondering if things would have worked out between them. Can people really change that much and stay changed?

Zuriel thought about her relationship with her dad. The change began when they were watching the fireworks in silence and Zuriel's tears streamed down her face. She remembered feeling her dad's arm suddenly around her. They stayed up late that night and ended up talking about the pain of losing the person you love. It was the most real conversation she had ever had with him. As a result of that night, she had been hanging out with him more in the last month than she had for the last several years.

The most proof she had seen that someone could change had been the miracle of what happened with Suzy. She had been waiting for Suzy to go back to her old self. Not that she ever wanted her friend to do that, but she expected it. Surprisingly, Suzy hadn't budged. Zuriel noticed that she had become kinder, more understanding, and much more willing to help other people. She acted a little bit strange though and had somewhat isolated herself from their other friends.

Over the last few months, Suzy had stopped going dancing on Friday nights. Zuriel asked if she thought it was a sin to dance. Suzy's honest reply surprised her. "No, Zuriel. Dancing isn't a sin, but some of the things that go on at the clubs are. It's hard enough for me to do what's right without going to a place where I know I'll be tempted to return to the drugs and be reminded of my life as a prostitute. I don't think you'll do those things just because you go; I just know that if I want to please God, I need to do everything I can to make sure I don't go back to my old life."

Zuriel had never forgotten her words.

It was interesting how she had always viewed Christians as people who believed they were better than everyone else. Zuriel had always thought they were people who were born without a desire to do "bad" things. Instead she was discovering that Christians were choosing not to do those things, even though they might still have a strong desire to. She recalled the day she found Sam while walking in the woods behind the Lowells' house. He had told her he needed forgiveness and that he had sinned by choosing to be bitter. It was so strange to hear a youth pastor admit that he struggled and that he wasn't perfect. Sam had even admitted that the things he had done wrong made Christians look bad, and he was sorry for that. Zuriel wasn't used to that kind of honesty. She was now sure that not everybody who went to church was bad; in fact, most of them were probably at least trying to do what was right.

Zuriel thought of her own life and wanted to cry. She was trying to do what was right, but it just wasn't working out. Matt had seemed like such a great guy and such a perfect husband for her, but he was killed, ending her chances of happiness. Zuriel wondered what it all meant. She wondered why God let bad things happen and she wondered why he made people go to hell. Zuriel felt just like the people in church. She was trying to be a good person and trying to be nice to other people. Zuriel figured that God wouldn't send people who meant well to hell, but Suzy believed it was easy to have good intentions but impossible to be good without God's help.

Zuriel was confused and full of questions. She didn't want to believe God was the only way. She wanted to believe people could change on their own—that she could change on her own. Watching Suzy made that harder and harder to believe.

Suzy didn't even know Zuriel had seen her, but Zuriel knew she would never forget what she saw. A few weeks ago, Zuriel had woken to the sound of crying. She heard the door close softly and went out to the living room just in time to see Suzy walking through the parking lot.

Zuriel quietly followed, concerned about what her friend was up to.

Suzy walked briskly down the street when she suddenly turned down an ally and pounded her fists on the side of the brick building. She slid to the ground. She was crying and praying out loud.

Her cries rang in Zuriel's ears. "God, help me! Why won't you take this desire away from me? It's so hard sometimes! I almost gave in. Oh, God, you saw me and I almost gave in! You know the evil I'm capable of."

As Suzy cried out, tears dribbled down her face, and she kept her fists tightly clenched. She shifted to her knees and rocked back and forth, hugging herself tightly. "I'm sorry, Jesus," she cried, "I'm so sorry. Please make me better. Don't let me ever give in. I want to be like you, but I can't do it on my own. I'm terrible at being good, but I won't give up. I promise."

Zuriel stood outside for a long time, watching Suzy cry. She couldn't believe what she was seeing, and she suddenly had a much greater respect for her friend. Zuriel knew at that moment that God was real, and that God had done something major to Suzy. It wasn't Suzy who was changing herself; there was something much bigger going on. Zuriel wished she could connect with God somehow too, but she was afraid of what it would cost her. She saw how much better Suzy was becoming, but she had also discovered how much pain was involved. Zuriel thought about Matt again, and how he was burning in hell. She had told herself over and over again that if God hated Matt, she might as well be hated too. But now she wondered if Matt might have had regrets. She wondered what would have happened if he had stayed with his faith. Would he still be alive? She had no way of knowing.

Zuriel brought her mind back to the present. She glanced at the clock and saw that Suzy would be coming home from church soon. Every Sunday morning and Wednesday night Zuriel would wonder what was going on at church. Why did Suzy like it so much? Why did she read the same verses in her Bible over and over again? Why did Zuriel feel jealous of Suzy without being able to explain what she was jealous of? Suzy seemed happier, but at the same time Suzy had to go through so much more pain and self-denial than anyone else she knew.

Zuriel's heart was tormented. She felt like she was missing something. For the longest time she thought the ache inside her was simply from missing Matt, but now she recognized the ache had been there long before she even knew him. It was the ache she felt whenever she wasn't being admired by guys, getting wasted, or the center of attention. She knew she was missing something, and for the first time she wondered if God might be the reason for that ache. God had fulfilled Suzy so completely that living without drugs, sex, partying, and clubbing was worth it. Maybe God was more than just the "Big Man Upstairs." Maybe God was the only reason Suzy had changed. Maybe God was the only reason Sam had changed. *Maybe God was the only way for Zuriel to change.*

Zuriel was nervous. Her own heart was realizing that she may have spent her life believing the wrong things and living for the wrong reasons. She didn't understand God, she didn't even like all the things she had heard about him, but she just knew she needed him. Zuriel felt angry with herself as she sat there, staring out the large living room window. God was bad, wasn't he? Hadn't he made her childhood difficult and allowed her mother to leave her as a baby? Hadn't he made high school a living hell? Hadn't he left her alone when Suzy went crazy with her drugs? Wasn't it God who had let her beloved Matt die? Yet despite all these things, Zuriel couldn't escape the feeling that God was *more* than that. She couldn't ignore her desire to be loved in the way that Suzy had described God's love to her. She wondered if it was actually God who had made her life miserable after all. Was it God, or was it a mixture of her own mistakes and the mistakes of others? She wasn't sure, but she almost didn't care.

Zuriel slipped onto the floor and was instantly on her knees. She looked out the window and stared as high into the sky as she could. Hopefully God would hear her.

"God, I never thought that I would say this, but I feel like I need you. I'm sorry I blamed you for everything and I'm sorry I cursed you for so long. I've seen what you can do in other people's lives. I've tried to be a good person for so long, but you know that I've failed so many times. I don't really know how to say this, or even what I'm asking, but I just want you to do for me what you did for Suzy and Sam. I want to become whatever they are. I want to be a better person and be ..." Zuriel stopped, overwhelmed with emotion, and could hardly say the next words out loud. Her hands shook. She was afraid of what she was asking, but even more afraid not to ask. "God please make me a Christian and please change me somehow."

Zuriel suddenly felt an unexplainable sense of peace wash over her body. She couldn't remember the last time she had felt this way, but she knew God had heard her. She knew that somehow she had become whatever Suzy, Sam, and the rest of the Lowells were. She remembered hearing about salvation at Matt's funeral.

She had heard that God sent his perfect son, Jesus, to die for her and that, by believing in him and accepting his sacrifice, she could be saved. She imagined Jesus on the cross and realized for the first time that he had done it for her out of love. Zuriel felt warm and free. She smiled, finally accepting the truth that she had denied for so long. God loved her, and now she wanted to love him back.

 *Chapter 16*

"I need to talk to you!" Zuriel demanded more harshly than she intended.

Suzy had just walked through the door, and Zuriel was ready to burst. She had been waiting for Suzy to get home for a couple of hours. Zuriel usually didn't care if Suzy stayed at church late or went out to lunch with friends, but today she was annoyed. She felt a pang of guilt, suddenly wondering if Christians were supposed to get annoyed. She wasn't sure, but she knew her patience was wearing thin.

Suzy looked surprised. Zuriel knew it was unusual for her to be sitting at the kitchen table staring at the door.

"You're home later than usual," Zuriel said, wondering why Suzy hadn't said anything yet.

"I'm sorry. I didn't know you cared." Suzy looked nervous as she set her stuff down and came to the kitchen table. "What's wrong?"

Zuriel wasn't sure what to say. She had thought of a hundred different ways to tell Suzy the news, but nothing was coming to her mind right now. She became keenly aware of how much it was going to hurt her own pride to tell Suzy.

"Nothing's wrong."

"Good." Suzy looked inquisitively at her.

Zuriel couldn't think of what to say next. She felt frozen and nervous. Several seconds passed.

"So what it is?" Suzy asked.

"Well, I just wanted to tell you something." Zuriel realized how dumb she sounded, but that was all she could say. She was sure Suzy thought she was crazy at this point.

"Obviously, but what do you want to tell me? You're scaring me a little."

"It's nothing scary." Zuriel planned to say more, but she was stopped by the tears forming in her eyes. This wasn't at all how she had planned it.

Suzy moved her chair closer and put a hand on Zuriel's arm. "It's okay. Did I do something to offend you?"

Zuriel's tears fell harder. She felt terrible for making her friend think she had done something wrong. It was actually quite the opposite, but Zuriel couldn't bring herself to say it.

"No, it's not that. This morning, I was just thinking and …" Zuriel stopped and caught her breath. She wasn't sure how to proceed. "I want to come to church with you." Zuriel was relieved that she had at least gotten some of it out.

"Oh, Zuriel, I'm so glad. Of course you can come to church with me." Suzy was definitely shocked and excited.

Zuriel was surprised to see tears welling up in her friend's eyes.

"What made you decide you want to go?"

"This morning I was just thinking about Matt and you. I was thinking about God, life, and all that kind of stuff." It was hard for Zuriel to talk through her tears. Her voice shook and her throat ached from trying to stop the crying. She let out a loud sob and thought it best to quickly say the rest. "I was thinking about God, and I realized I had been wrong. I guess I always thought he was against me and Matt, but I think I was wrong to think that. He really loved me the whole time, so this morning I told God I was sorry. I asked him to make me …" Zuriel inhaled deeply and coughed to soothe her sore throat. She attempted to finish. "I asked God to make me a Christian … or whatever you church people are."

Zuriel put her head in her hands and finally let herself cry. She wasn't sure if it was out of joy and relief or from the sorrow that came from knowing she had been wrong for so long. She felt Suzy hug her tightly, and felt her friend's hot tears dripping on to her forehead.

"Oh, thank you, God. Thank you, God!" Suzy cried through watery eyes. "I've been praying for you for so long, Zuriel. I'm so happy for you!"

"Me too! I'm just sorry it took me so long to see the truth. I'm sorry I said all those terrible things about you." Zuriel felt her conscience come to even more peace as they talked. Inwardly she thanked God that Suzy didn't say, "I told you so." She knew they would be friends for a long time to come and that she would need Suzy's help if she was going to do this whole God thing the right way.

Zuriel looked in the mirror one last time before meeting Suzy in the living room. She wasn't sure why she was so nervous about going to church. She hadn't been to any religious place of worship since she was very small, so she supposed it was only natural for her to feel this way. Suzy had explained that since tonight was Wednesday, it would be more of a small-group hangout environment. That scared her more than the thought of going

Sunday morning. She didn't know much about God, so she hoped no one would ask her any questions or expect her to lead a prayer.

Suzy had given her some spiritual instruction already, though. The last few evenings had been spent staying up late with coffee and talking about God. Zuriel knew God loved her but felt like he was still a stranger. She knew she had so much to learn and wished she could just skip ahead and instantly become more knowledgeable and full of faith. She thought back to the night she saw Suzy in the ally. Zuriel was horrified of what God might require of her, although Suzy had explained that God would always prepare her for what he wanted her to do.

She grabbed her purse and found Suzy waiting by the door; she was holding a gift bag.

"I'm ready, I guess."

"Oh, good! I have a present for you before we go too."

Zuriel looked at her friend and smiled. What could it possibly be? She took the bag and peered inside. "A Bible," Zuriel exclaimed, surprised by the gift. It was pink and brand new.

"I thought that since you're planning on following Christ, you might need a Bible of your own."

Zuriel put the bag on the ground and gave Suzy a tight hug. She felt a little more confident going to church now knowing she had a Bible of her own—one she could keep and read.

Zuriel felt strange as they made their way to the bus stop. She felt like she was beginning a whole new life. Instead of spending all her time wishing Matt hadn't died, she had been distracted by trying to develop her new relationship with God. She was asking him to help her move on instead of trying to do things on her own. Zuriel didn't feel like such a wretched person anymore. Instead, she felt like a woman with an important purpose. Life didn't seem so empty and lonely; even the air around her seemed thicker and more alive.

Zuriel felt more uncomfortable than she had expected as she sat in the padded blue chair in the church. The chairs where arranged in a circle—filled with confident, spiritual-looking people. All of them had their Bibles neatly placed under their chairs. They were chatting and full of smiles and laughter. She heard them talking and suddenly felt like a very new Christian.

"Thank you for praying for me, Janis. My doctor said things are looking much better!" one woman said.

"The concert downtown went off without a hitch! It was amazing to see how all those kids were so on-fire for God. I just pray that they continue to seek God's will and not give up," a younger guy explained excitedly to the middle-aged man beside him. She saw their heads turning as they noticed her presence. They smiled at her, and Zuriel felt her face growing hot. She wasn't sure whether she should've come after all.

"You must be Zuriel," the middle-aged man said, extending his hand.

Zuriel shook it nervously. She wasn't sure what to say. They knew who she was? She guessed Suzy must have told them she was coming.

"Yes, everyone, this is my best friend, Zuriel. She just received Christ on Sunday," Suzy said proudly.

Zuriel looked at her with wide eyes, unsure of what to say.

"That is wonderful!" a woman exclaimed.

"Thanks." Zuriel held the corners of her Bible tightly, trying to release her anxiety.

Zuriel sat and watched, amazed by what she saw and heard as the evening progressed. Many of them explained their various struggles, or people they knew who needed prayer. They prayed, and Zuriel felt a new level of belonging she had never experienced before. She had never prayed in a group setting and had never seen people care so much about each other's needs. Zuriel knew

God had to be good if the people who loved him could come together in such a way. This was so much different from the way she thought church would be.

She listened as one of the men began to teach from the Bible. He called out a reference to a Bible verse, but Zuriel had no idea what he was talking about. She was embarrassed when they all reached for their Bibles and turned to the same page at the same time. She just clutched her own Bible and listened. Zuriel was excited to hear the man read. She wanted to know what God wanted from her. She had no idea what it meant to be a Christian. Suzy had ensured her that everything she needed to know about her new life was inside the Bible. Zuriel hoped it would be simple for her to follow.

"Whoever wants to be my disciple must deny themselves and take up their cross daily and follow me," the man read.

Zuriel felt confused. What on earth did that mean? And what were disciples?

"If we want to be disciples—if we want to follow Jesus—we have to deny ourselves and take up our cross. Think about how Jesus died on the cross. It was God's plan for him to save us from sin, so Jesus obeyed and took up his cross, knowing that it would cost him his life. God has a plan for each of us, and we must follow this plan if we are going to be his true followers."

Zuriel's mind was spinning. She was trying to organize all the information inside her head. A disciple was a follower of God. Jesus was obeying God when he died on the cross. God had something for each of his followers to do. Now that Zuriel was one of his disciples, what did God want her to do? She wished she had brought a piece of paper to write all this down.

"When Jesus says to deny yourself, he is talking about putting God's will above your own. You have things that you want to do, and even things that you think God wants you to do. However, we have to be willing to live without these things if we find out that God wants something else for us."

Now she could understand some of the changes in Suzy. It wasn't that Suzy had stopped wanting sex, parties, or drugs; she had chosen to deny herself the right to indulge in them in order to obey God.

"Let me challenge you in this: if Jesus is the most important part of our lives, shouldn't we be willing to give up everything for him? What would our lives look like if we were truly willing to give everything up for Jesus?"

Zuriel thought about that, but she wasn't sure what the answer was. She guessed that living completely for Jesus would be acting the way Suzy and the Lowells had acted, but she wasn't exactly sure how to put her thoughts into words. Zuriel had a strong feeling in her gut that it was going to be difficult for her to follow Jesus. She felt a little bit nervous too. God had told Jesus to die, so what might he ask her to do?

"I want each of you to think about your own lives right now," the man said. "Do you think God might be asking you to do something difficult? Maybe you need to forgive someone, or maybe God wants you to tell someone else about the good news of Jesus."

Zuriel thought hard, but she had no idea. She had only been a Christian for three days. Was she already supposed to know what God wanted her to do? When she had accepted Christ as the sacrifice for her sins, her mind had been at peace, but she didn't hear any audible instructions from God. She tried to think of someone she could talk to about Jesus.

"Let's all take a few moments to silently pray about what God wants us to do."

Zuriel bowed her head and prayed. *Please help me, God; I don't know what I'm doing. What do you want me to do?* Zuriel waited for some sort of voice or sign, but she couldn't hear anything. She peeked one of her eyes open and saw that everyone else still had theirs closed. She wished she knew how to pray longer. She started to think about Matt and wondered if he had ever prayed. Maybe he had prayed when Lena had the abortion. Zuriel wondered if Matt had ever thought about his past with Lena while they were together. She wondered what had become of the poor girl.

Finally, Zuriel heard everyone start to move and it was safe to stop bowing her head and closing her eyes. Many of the people shared what they were going to do to follow Christ for the next week. Many had specific people they were going to pray for or talk to. Some had goals for themselves, like reading the Bible more or spending more time in prayer. Zuriel, of course, had nothing to say, and that made her sad. She wished she had a purpose like the rest of them.

They finished up with the prayer time and began to talk and slowly depart. Each person in the group made it a point to introduce himself or herself to Zuriel and tell her they would pray for her. Zuriel felt overwhelmed and excited at the same time. She hoped that one day she could have their faith and knowledge of God, but she also felt confused and worried that she wouldn't become the person God wanted her to be. She was relieved when she and Suzy got back on the bus.

"Suzy, when you prayed, did God tell you anything?"

"What do you mean? Did God tell you something?" Suzy asked, looking puzzled.

"No, he didn't tell me a thing. I don't know what's wrong with me."

"Oh, Zuriel," Suzy began, using a slightly more serious tone, "when I'm praying and ask God a question, I don't hear a voice. Usually I feel peaceful because I know God is going to answer my questions in his time. Or sometimes I'll just think of a person or a situation that I might be able to change and I feel like God wants me to do something about it. Don't worry; I'm still learning how to pray too."

Zuriel felt relieved to discover that Suzy was doing just fine being a Christian, even without hearing a voice from heaven.

"Did you ever feel like God was telling you something about me?" she asked.

"Yes! I remember I was praying about being able to share my faith. I kept thinking about you every time I prayed. At first, I felt like my mind was just getting distracted from praying, but after a couple of days I wondered if God wanted me to find you and talk with you about him. It was scary because I felt like I barely knew God myself."

Zuriel smiled and then suddenly thought of Lena. She had thought about her during the prayer time too. Maybe God wanted her to tell Lena about him?

"Really? That's cool! During the prayer time tonight, I kept thinking about Lena, Matt's ex-girlfriend. You know … the one who had the abortion?"

"That's interesting. I wonder if you guys will ever meet."

"But what if I'm wrong, Suzy? What if God wasn't the one telling me that? What if I was just thinking about her because I'm jealous that Matt probably slept with her more than he slept with me?"

Suzy laughed, and Zuriel was confused. What was she missing here? "You're laughing, Suzy, but I'm being serious!"

"Zuriel, God wants everyone to know about Jesus. You can be 100 percent sure that God will always want you to tell others about him. And if you're jealous because of her, then what would be a better cure than praying for her and telling her about Jesus? I think a lot of times we just have to do what the Bible says and know that God will take care of the rest."

"The problem is, though, that I don't really know what the Bible says yet," Zuriel said soulfully.

"That will come with time. That's why I bought you a Bible of your own. And you already know that it's good when we tell others about God, so pray that Lena will become a Christian!"

Zuriel suddenly felt peaceful inside. She would pray for Lena. Not only that, she would find out from Drew where Lena lived. Maybe, just maybe, God had a mission for her. Maybe she could do something right for once, and possibly even learn to let go of Matt in the process. Zuriel smiled. Maybe she would like going to church after all!

 *Chapter 17*

"So you're a Christian now?" Drew asked, glaring at Suzy as he spoke.

"Yes I am, and don't blame Suzy for it. I learned today that the Holy Spirit is the one who draws people to God," Zuriel explained, showing off what little Bible knowledge she had.

"Ha! The Holy Spirit? So Casper the friendly ghost has been visiting you secretly and telling you to believe in God?" Drew mocked her.

"No, it's not really like that."

"Well then, Zuriel, tell me what it's like. It sounds to me like you became a Christian without finding out very much about the religion first."

Drew's challenge made Zuriel feel uncomfortable. She didn't know very much about Christianity, but she did know that her life was much better because of it.

"Oh, you mean the same way we investigated the long-lasting effects of drugs and alcohol before we got involved with those?" Suzy snapped at him.

Zuriel smiled and was surprised by what a good point her friend had made.

"You can't compare joining a cult to having a good time," Drew said, laughing at her.

"So now you're assuming that choosing to follow Jesus is not a good time, like I was forced into this somehow?" Suzy asked.

"I actually just think you're nuts!"

"Nuts for Jesus. Don't forget that part!" Zuriel tried to make peace. "Remember when you told me about Lena?"

"What, did she become a Christian too?" Drew asked, teasing her.

"I don't know. I was just wondering if you knew where she was or what she was up to."

"I have no idea. I'm sorry, but I don't keep tabs on my friends' ex-girlfriends."

"For some reason I kind of doubt that," Suzy declared, rolling her eyes. She was obviously frustrated with him.

"Do you know anybody who knows her, or how I can find out where she lives?" Zuriel asked, trying to keep things focused.

"Why do you want to find her? Is this part of your quest to discover more of Matt's past? I thought you were finally starting to give that up."

"I'm not really sure what it is. You were the one who was so determined that I get to know about her in the first place. I'm just thinking it might actually be a good idea." Zuriel saw that he didn't seem willing to help her. She put her arm on his shoulder in an attempt to make him understand how important this was to her. "Please, Drew. Just let me do this."

"Okay, fine. I still have her old number in my phone, but who knows if she still has the same one."

"Thank you!" Zuriel quickly copied the number into her own phone and thanked God for it in her heart. She really hoped things would work out. She wasn't sure why, but having a mission of her own was making life suddenly much better. She still missed Matt terribly but felt more loved now than she ever had in the past.

Her phone rang with an unknown number. Zuriel almost never answered those kinds of calls, but this time she welcomed the interruption.

"Hello?" She walked to her bedroom for privacy.

"Hi, this is Christina Lowell, is this Zuriel?"

"Yes. How are you?" Zuriel hadn't talked to her since the funeral. She felt the memories of going through Matt's pictures with Christina flood her mind.

"I'm wonderful! How are you?"

"Well, things are getting better. It's hard to believe it's almost been six months already."

"I know. So much has changed for me in that time too."

Changed? Zuriel wondered what she meant. "Oh really, how's your family doing?"

"We're doing all right. We're all just learning to trust God through everything and get back to a normal life. It's hardest for my mom. Samuel has been very helpful with everything, though."

Zuriel was sincerely happy for them. In fact, she was considering telling Christina about her own recent change but decided not to. For some reason, she felt like it would be awkward to explain right now.

"I'm glad to hear it."

"I have some exciting news!" Christina shrieked.

"Tell me!"

"I'm engaged!"

Zuriel smiled and squealed in delight; she was happy for her. Her fiancé, Michael, seemed like a really nice guy and was definitely a Christian. An event like that would bring a lot of much-needed joy into the family's life.

"Congratulations! I'm so happy for you. Michael seems like the best kind of guy."

"Thank you! I have to agree!"

"Well, of course you would!" Zuriel laughed but suddenly grew solemn. She remembered what it felt like to be engaged. It was blissful, horrifying, and exciting all at once. Zuriel thought back to Matt's accident again and wondered how things would have been if they had gotten married. She wondered if she would have found God if Matt hadn't died. The idea was painful, but at least she was happy to have her newfound faith. She just wished she could've had both God and Matt.

Zuriel talked for a little longer and heard how Michael had proposed in the Lowells' backyard. Zuriel was happy but felt her eyes moisten. She wanted to be loved by a human man, not only Jesus. However, she knew she needed time to grow in her faith and learn more about God first. She knew that if she were ever to marry anyone, he would have to be a Christian. She wondered how different her relationship with Matt would have been if they were both seeking God. Zuriel was sure Christina would have a wonderful marriage because she and Michael would always be held together by their common love for God.

Zuriel got off the phone and was happy to see that Drew was leaving. She wasn't sure why she had stayed friends with him. He constantly got into arguments with her, but she had always felt like he held the key to the secrets of Matt's past. She wondered if she had only been using him to keep Matt alive inside her heart.

"Well, Zuriel," Suzy said after their apartment door slammed shut, "I squeezed some more information out of him. I tried to imagine you just calling this chick up, and then I figured he had to know where she lived. I think Drew knew Lena better than he let on." Suzy smiled, clearly proud of her endeavors.

"Well, that was sneaky of you! Is that what you'd call a WWJD moment?" Zuriel asked humorously.

"I think Jesus would appreciate my being smart." Suzy winked at her and grinned. "So how do you plan to meet this girl?"

"I'm not really sure. I guess I should probably call her or text her. I think this is going to be awkward whatever way I do it."

"Yeah, I'm not really sure about it either."

"I kind of just want to show up at her house and say, 'Hey, I'm Zuriel.' Would that be creepy? I mean, what else am I supposed to do?"

"Maybe just a little creepy," Suzy replied.

"Okay, fine. I'll text her a little, call her, and then show up." Zuriel realized how far out of her comfort zone she would have to go in order to meet Matt's ex.

"That sounds better. So who was on the phone?"

"Oh yeah, it was Christina Lowell. She's engaged!"

"Wow, good for her! Did you tell her your news?"

Zuriel felt bad after hearing her question. Suzy's voice seemed to indicate that she was hoping Zuriel had told Christina about her faith. Zuriel wasn't sure why she didn't want to.

"No."

"No?"

"No, I just didn't feel like it. I mean, they all love Jesus, and if I told them, they would want to talk to me even more. Who knows, I might even end up adopted into their family."

"And that would be terrible, because …?"

Zuriel felt self-conscious; she didn't really know why she was so afraid to let them into her life. "It wouldn't be that bad, I guess, it's just that it will be a long story and then they'll have different expectations of me. I guess Sam will probably want to talk to me about it too. I'm just not sure if I'm ready for the world to know I'm a Christian when I'm still so new at it."

"Sam might want to talk to you? And what's this about not being sure if you want people to know? You just told Drew, and you're planning to tell a complete stranger who also happens to be Matt's ex-girlfriend!"

Zuriel knew that her excuses sounded ridiculous. She hadn't realized how afraid she was to see Sam again. Apparently he had become this wonderful youth pastor. Now that she had become a Christian, she felt terrible for the things she had told him out in the woods that June day. She thought of how she had lain in the grass and thought he was Matt. She certainly didn't want to get her feelings for Matt confused with Sam.

"I don't know why I can't. I just feel like I can only take one big change at a time. Besides, right now I need to focus on getting to know God and finding Lena."

"Okay, whatever, but I think that you should pray about it. I'll pray too. They did have a hand in leading you to Christ, and I know they are praying for your salvation still."

Zuriel agreed to pray about it, but she didn't really want to. She knew that underneath it all she was just embarrassed about it.

Zuriel pulled out her phone and decided to be brave and send Lena a text. She typed out the message and prayed that it would go over well.

"Suz, how does this sound? 'Hey, Lena, this is Zuriel, I'm a friend of Drew's. I got this number from him and I was thinking that maybe we could hang out sometime.'"

"Well, I guess that's the best you can do. I suppose you don't really want to tell her, 'Hi, I was your ex's fiancée and, guess what else, he's dead, and I decided I wanted to come find you so we can talk about God.'"

"Yeah, I guess this will have to do." Zuriel pushed send and waited for what seemed like an eternity. Finally, her phone vibrated. She read it and almost threw her phone across the room. The text read, "Sorry I think you have the wrong number."

"Suzy, we're going to have to try the address. She has a different number now."

"Well, then I guess it's a good thing I investigated further."

"Yes it is! How long will it take to get there?" She was determined to find Lena and hoped with all her heart that she could find her today. Zuriel would be working for the next couple of days, and she knew herself. She would have to act now, or she might never go to meet Lena.

"I'm not exactly sure; I think it's a trailer park somewhere. Are you actually thinking of going today?"

"I have to. I don't want to sit around here all day and wonder about her. I just feel like I have to do this now before I chicken out and never do it." Zuriel felt her adrenaline level rising. The truth of the matter was that she was horrified to go, but she knew that God wanted her to. She felt a reckless abandonment of all her misgivings. Zuriel wondered if her desire to go had anything to do with the fact that otherwise she would be stuck sitting around all day thinking. Those kinds of days were always the most difficult. Thankfully, those days were getting better, because now she could think about God instead of just Matt. There was so much to learn about her new faith that she wondered if she would ever graduate from being a baby Christian. Maybe doing something reckless for God would help.

"Maybe you should pray about this before you act rashly." Suzy made her suggestion calmly, but Zuriel felt more intense than ever.

"Okay, but you pray too. I really want to go and see this girl right now."

Suzy nodded and Zuriel went to her room. She plopped onto her bed and began to pray. She wanted to do what God wanted her to do, but she found herself praying that Suzy would agree to come with her. Zuriel tried to focus on praying, but she couldn't. Finally she decided she would just go. There was a good chance Lena had moved somewhere else anyway. It had been more than four years since Matt had dated her, and a lot could change in that kind of time frame.

"Suzy, I'm going. Plus, my dad said I could use his old car if I had to. We just need to ride the bus over to my dad's and then we can drive there." Zuriel was so thankful that she would finally be getting a car. It was an old Buick, but that was better than taking buses everywhere and relying on other people for rides.

Suzy looked amused. Zuriel knew she was being absurd, but what else were they going to do for the rest of the afternoon?

"All right. I still think you're insane, but let's go meet this girl."

Zuriel gathered her things, and they were soon on their way out the door. She grew more nervous as she boarded the bus. She prayed, *Dear God, please let her get saved. She needs you and I need you too. Help me to know how to be a better Christian. Help me to heal from losing Matt. Please let this trip make me feel better. Amen.*

 *Chapter 18*

The yelling was as loud as ever. It was almost impossible to keep things quiet in a small trailer. Lena Rose had heard noises like these while growing up. She had promised herself that she wouldn't move back in, but after Garrett dumped her, she had nowhere else to go. She had hoped things would be different now, especially since her parents had finally gotten divorced. In fact, it almost seemed like things had actually changed when she was alone in the house with her mom. The feeling never lasted for long, though, because the people always came back for their drugs. It was how they survived and the way they coped.

Lena's hand shook. It wasn't the effect of any drugs, though. She had stayed away from them because of what she had seen them do to others. She shook because she was terrified. She had been there when the drug dealers fought. She had heard their threats and seen their violence, but she was used to that. She wasn't afraid of them, or at least she knew how to act like she wasn't. This time things were different. Her father had returned and demanded that her mother give him money. He didn't like being told no, and the war had begun. Lena had wanted to call the police so many times before, but then they would just find the drugs hidden throughout the little trailer. That would be a disaster for everyone! She wished she could escape, but there was nowhere to go.

Lena sat on the bathroom floor, peeking around the door, waiting for an opportunity to go outside. She was sure the screams and slapping coming from the other room could be heard by all the neighbors. If something more serious was going to happen, she didn't want to be here for it because there was nothing she could do to stop it. She whispered the Lord's Prayer as she checked for a clear pathway to the door, waiting for an opportunity. *Our Father, who art in heaven …*

She saw the flamboyant figures move to another room, so she decided to make a run for it. Lena swiftly moved through the door and closed it. She zipped up her jacket as she walked down the steps to meet the brisk October air. She wished she could feel free, but she knew better. The life her mother had chosen for them wasn't an easy one.

Lena's mother had grown up in the ghetto, but no one would guess by looking at her. She was beautiful, with big brown eyes and dark Spanish hair. Her mother had fallen in love with a rich man who came from a somewhat normal life. Although at first he appeared to be the better of the two of them, he turned out to be far worse than any thug on the streets. As it turned out, he was actually the leader of a crime ring and one of the main drug lords on the block. He was controlling and abusive, and now he was back in their lives to prove he still had power over them.

She went to the side of the trailer and sat on the broken bench. She breathed in slowly as she placed her hands over her stomach. Lena was pregnant again, but she wasn't ready to deal with another hard choice. She didn't have a job, a boyfriend, or a true home. She hated the mess her life had become. Lena hadn't gone to Mass in years, but last week she had decided to finally show up again. She didn't understand God, but she knew she had done so many things wrong. Maybe that's why her life was so terrible? She had been afraid to go, afraid God would strike her dead, but now she was starting to get desperate. She wondered if God would help her if she went to Mass and made an effort to live better, but she highly doubted it. Matt's words still echoed in her head like they were the very voice of God: "Abortion is murder, Lena, and you can't ever bring my son back. You killed my son!" She would never forget those words.

She had fallen genuinely in love with Matt and had given herself entirely to him. She thought at the time that she was doing him a favor by having the abortion. He had been so concerned that he wouldn't be able to take care of the baby and was starting to wonder if he should go back to his family. Lena thought she would make his life better by removing the problem, but instead she had made it so much worse. He had not only dumped her, he promised she would regret what she'd done to the baby. She did regret what she'd done, and not just because Matt had left her. Her heart was broken over and over again whenever she thought about the baby she had aborted. Her love for Matt had long-since turned to hatred and disgust, and now she barely missed him. She did, however, continue to miss the baby that would have brought comfort to her during this time of hell on earth. Part of her heart was missing. Part of her soul had died. She felt so worthless.

Lena saw an old Buick slowly coming up the road. It stopped a few times and then continued on. Another drug pick up? This would be the worst possible time.

She headed away from the trailer. She wasn't sure what was going to happen. When those kinds of people didn't get what they asked for, they almost always hurt or killed someone. She hated living in the world as a drug trafficker's daughter. She had been told that if you dreamed big you could get anywhere, but she hadn't dreamt anything since she was eighteen and thought she was in love. Her heart had been smashed into a million pieces and then broken into smaller and smaller segments. Sometimes she wasn't sure if she had any heart left, yet her heart desperately wanted to keep this baby. Her heart wanted to love something again.

She heard a car coming up behind her and turned to see the same Buick. She was surprised it wasn't a drug stop but was more surprised when the car pulled over in front of her and a woman came rushing out. The small blonde almost ran to her, and Lena felt frozen in place, wondering what she could possibly have to say.

"I'm sorry; I just was wondering if you were Lena Rose?"

Lena wasn't sure if she should answer, but the woman looked innocent enough. "Who's asking?"

"My name is Zuriel; I'm a friend of Drew Jacobs's."

Lena shuddered at the name of another ex-boyfriend and wondered if she could ever escape her past.

"Oh. Yeah, I'm Lena. Is there something wrong?"

"No, nothing's wrong. I … um … well, I just wanted to meet you."

The woman stood nervously and Lena felt awkward. What did this Zuriel woman want with her? "Why?"

"My fiancé died recently and I thought my life was over. God found me, and I feel like we need to talk. I don't know why."

Lena could see Zuriel's hands shaking. Her voice was strained like she was holding back tears. "I was coming to your house for a visit. When I saw you walking, I took a wild guess that you were … well you."

"Well, I don't actually live here." Lena had been sleeping here, but she refused to acknowledge that she lived here. She wanted to get away more than anything else.

"Oh, then I can't believe I found you."

"I don't really live anywhere."

"Do you need a place to stay?"

Was this woman really offering her a place to live? Lena glanced back at her house and felt ill. She did need a place to stay. She needed somewhere safe to decide what to do about this baby.

"I'm not staying anywhere else right now."

"You can come live with Suzy and me. We have an apartment downtown, and it's pretty decent."

She felt relieved, but she wondered if she should accept. She didn't know this woman or her friend. Plus she was Drew's friend, and Lena was sure she didn't want to see him again.

"I don't know. Why would you come find me? I still don't understand."

"I'm not really sure how to say this, or how it's going to sound …" Zuriel paused and stuck her hands in her jean pockets. "When my fiancé died, I discovered he was different than I thought he was. I tried to dig into his past, and I realized that, just like me, he wasn't perfect. I can't change the things he did, and I can barely change myself, although I'm trying hard to be a better person … I'm sorry; I should just get to the point."

Zuriel caught her breath before continuing. "Lena, I loved my fiancé, and I believe at one point you loved him too. Do you remember Matt Lowell?"

Lena's heart rate climbed rapidly. Matt was dead and now his fiancée had come looking for her. She didn't know what to say. "I remember him." Lena felt her stomach through her pockets and tried to keep her breathing steady.

"I don't know all that happened between you guys, but when I found out about you, I just really wanted to meet you. I can't explain it, but I think you had a strong impact on his life, which in turn has impacted mine. I know this probably sounds weird, and I'm sorry for how random it seems. If you need a place to stay, though, I'd be happy to let you stay with me."

Lena's head spun. This woman had loved the same man she had once loved more than life. She didn't understand Zuriel's kindness or what could possibly possess a woman to befriend her dead fiancé's ex-girlfriend.

"This is really weird." Lena looked around, wondering what to say. "I'm fine. Thanks for your concern, but I really don't want anything to do with Matt." Lena turned toward the trailer. She felt a secret pleasure knowing Matt was dead, yet she felt a strange sense of sympathy for this woman. Suddenly she heard a loud crash and looked up just in time to see a window shatter. She heard the screams and yelling inside the trailer escalating to a ferocious pitch.

She turned back to Zuriel. "Please take me out of here," she begged. She didn't even care if these women ended up harming her. She just needed to get out of here now. The only thing worse than facing her past would be marching back into that hell hole. She was going home with a complete stranger, but she just didn't care anymore. The only thing she knew was that she couldn't stay in this place for one more second.

∾෨෨

Samuel Lowell dismissed the youth group after the final prayer. It was amazing to see all that God had done in the past months. Samuel was well aware that he was a different man now and that this was a different youth group. Instead of looking at each kid like another Matt or some kind of project, he was able to love them for who they were. He honestly wanted them to find salvation—to do things God's way and not his own. The conversations in the group had deepened and become more real. He had stopped telling them how they should act and had started encouraging them to find out how God wanted them to act. Then, when one told Samuel what he felt God wanted him to do, Samuel held him directly accountable for being obedient to that calling. Youth group was now personal, powerful, and life-changing.

Samuel had seen his brother turn a youth pastor into a substitute for God. It was always, "Pastor said this," or "Pastor said that." When John Carter let Matt down, Matt felt as though everything he had learned at church was a lie. Now Samuel realized the importance of teaching the kids that "*Jesus* said this." It didn't matter if Pastor Sam failed; Jesus would still be perfect.

Samuel had most enjoyed watching his sister's spiritual growth. Elizabeth had completely dedicated her life to Christ. In fact, Samuel often felt convicted just talking with her. She had become a leader in the youth group, so much so that even many of the seniors looked up to her. Samuel was thankful; he had been praying for her daily, ever since the funeral when they had spent all those hours talking. Their discussions had helped Elizabeth to heal, but he wondered if she knew how much her faithfulness to God was helping him continue healing too. He was finally getting to say the things he wanted to say to Matt. He was finally the brother he'd wanted to be for Matt. Samuel loved how God always worked things out for his good.

He often thought back to the days of the funeral preparations and then to the service itself. As much as he tried not to, he often found himself thinking about Zuriel. While he never wanted to relive the early days of grief, he couldn't think about them without thinking about her. He didn't want to like her, and he didn't really want to date her. After all, she had been engaged to his brother and she wasn't a Christian, yet despite those two factors, he still had to constantly pull his mind away from the picture of her lying in the grass in her black dress. He tried to take these moments and simply pray for her healing and salvation. He knew it was good for him to pray, but the prayers also gave him an excuse to think about her.

Samuel played a few games of pool with some of the youth group guys and answered parents' questions as the teens waited to be picked up. He liked his job, and he liked what God was doing, but he was starting to feel lonely. He tried to find his fulfillment in God alone, but it wasn't easy being a twenty-six-year-old single guy. Samuel occasionally wondered if it was God's will for him to be single, but he found himself purposely reading verses about the benefits of marriage. He really wanted to find an attractive, godly woman who would serve God beside him at youth group. Michael had tried to set him up on many dates, but none of these women had been his type. He wondered if he was being too picky—no one was perfect, after all. The problem was that every time he talked to these potential dates, he found himself comparing them to Zuriel. Even though she wasn't knowledgeable in the things of God, she seemed more honest and genuine than any of the other women.

Samuel said good-bye to last teenager and gathered up his things. He was ready to go to bed; the kids had really tuckered him out his time. He headed home, knowing that Michael would probably not be there yet. It felt kind of like training. Michael would be moving out pretty soon to marry Christina, leaving Sam an even lonelier bachelor. He could hardly believe his little sister was going to get married. He was happy for her and happy for his best friend too. They were a couple of his favorite people, and he thanked God when he heard that they had gotten engaged. The next thing he did was pray that God would help him guard his heart against jealousy. He wanted to be in love—not only with God but with the woman he hoped God would choose for him.

Samuel walked through the door of his apartment and was surprised to see Michael hard at work playing the Xbox. "Wow, you're home early tonight," he remarked.

Michael glanced over at him for a split second before returning to his game. "Yeah, Christina went to hang out with some of her friends right after church, so I came straight home to start practicing for that gaming overnighter. Those guys are insanely good at this!"

"I was going to say… it's not usual for you to be away from your woman. Did you try to invite Christina to the guys' overnighter too?" Samuel asked sarcastically.

"I wish I could!" Michael shut off the game and then turned around on the couch to face Samuel. "And what about you? When are you going to get yourself a woman?"

"Who knows if I ever will."

"The only people who say that are desperate singles. Come on! I've tried to set you up on so many dates. When are you going to connect?"

Samuel laughed. Michael had always been more popular with the ladies. "Well, maybe you need to set me up with better dates!"

"Or maybe you need to man up and set up your own. I can't believe all the gorgeous, Jesus-loving ladies you've let pass by."

"Michael, you have my sister. Think of what would have happened if you hadn't let so many other Jesus-loving ladies walk past you. I haven't met the right one yet, and I'm not going to get married just to please you."

"Oh, 'cause that would just make *me* happy and have nothing to do with you at all, huh?" Michael laughed and followed Samuel into the kitchen. "But seriously, man, I have a theory."

"A theory, huh? This could be amusing."

"I think you already have a girl in mind. That's the only way to explain this."

"Oh? And who is this girl, Mr. Theory?" Samuel asked the question confidently but hoped Michael hadn't actually figured him out.

"I think you have a crush on your brother's ex."

"Zuriel?"

"Yes, and don't look so shocked, Romeo."

Samuel wished his friend didn't know him so well. He wished he could hide his feelings better. "She was engaged to my brother and she's not a Christian."

"I know. That's why I'm so concerned about you. I know you still like her. If you were taking her off your list, then you would have moved on by now."

"I'll get over her soon enough." Even as Samuel said it, he hoped it was actually true. He prayed that God would help him not to pine away for someone he couldn't have … and he prayed that the woman he was supposed to marry would show up soon!

 *Chapter 19*

Zuriel sat up in bed and glanced at the clock. It was almost two in the morning. She had tried to sleep but was too restless. Zuriel could hardly believe the events of that day had actually happened. She had just randomly decided to go to this girl's house. She went to her dad's house to pick up the car and ended up driving around a rundown trailer park. When Zuriel saw a beautiful young girl walking by herself, she'd experienced a sudden intuition that this was Lena. Her black hair was blowing in the wind, and her shoulders were slouched as she walked. Zuriel hadn't been sure what to do but felt an urgent need to speak to her. She had lunged out of the car and invited Lena to stay in her apartment, and now there was a strange woman sleeping on her living room couch.

The evening had been spent almost in complete silence. Zuriel could tell Lena had a lot on her mind. When she saw the window break at the trailer park and then observed Lena's reaction to it, she got the feeling this woman was more complicated than she looked. Lena was clearly grateful, but she didn't want to talk. It would have been too painful for both of them. Zuriel wanted to get to know Lena and help her, but she was well aware of her own hurts as well.

Matt had always made it clear that he wanted their relationship to be based on respect, and Zuriel thought he was just being romantic and old-fashioned. When she discovered that his previous girlfriend had aborted his child, it was hard for Zuriel not to at least be frustrated. It was obvious Matt didn't want to put her in the same kind of situation Lena was in, and he probably meant well, but now she was wondering more and more about what made him fall for Lena so intensely when he had mostly been so self-controlled around her. But he was dead, so he would never be able to explain himself.

Zuriel turned her thoughts back to the present. She began to wonder what role God wanted her to play in this new situation.

In previous talks, Suzy had told Zuriel that it was challenging living with her before she became a Christian. She said that knowing an unbeliever was watching made her extra careful to do what was right. Zuriel was so thankful that Suzy had tried so hard. Watching her friend's life was the very thing that had convinced Zuriel that Christianity was not only real, but worth considering for herself. She prayed she could offer Lena as much.

Zuriel decided to get something to drink. She had lost all hope of falling asleep again and knew work was going to be difficult today. She would be exhausted, and distracted thinking about the woman waiting in her apartment.

As she crossed through the living room, she was surprised to find Lena sitting up, staring out the large window. Zuriel was going to turn back to her room, but Lena turned abruptly.

"You can't sleep either?" Zuriel asked, realizing she had been caught.

"No, I haven't been able to sleep well for a long time," Lena said solemnly.

Zuriel felt sorry for her and wondered what kind of life she had been living. Zuriel sat beside her and stared out into the night.

"I've always liked this window. I've spent many nights staring out of it and thinking."

"It's a nice apartment."

"Thank you." There was a long silence and Zuriel used it to pray. She felt awkward, and she wondered if sitting down had been such a good idea.

"So, is Matt really gone?" Lena asked, breaking the silence.

"Yes, but I wish he wasn't. He was in car accident. A semi-truck driver fell asleep at the wheel."

"I hadn't seen him in years. Did he ever go back and reconnect with his family?"

Zuriel was surprised by her question. She felt a little hurt too. Matt had told Lena about his family but he hadn't told her? "No. I didn't even know he had a family until after he died."

"Oh. I wish I could have met them. He thought the world of his brother, Sam, and he always seemed a little sad when he talked about the rest of them. I thought I was going to marry Matt, you know. We talked about marriage, a family, God …"

Zuriel's heart was beating fast. It seemed to her Matt had loved Lena much more than he had loved Zuriel. At least he had told Lena the truth about who he was.

"What kind of man did he become?" Lena continued. "I'm sorry—is it hard for you to talk about him?"

"Sometimes, but it's good for me." Zuriel exhaled slowly, hoping God would give her the strength to talk. "I met him about a year ago. He was so sweet and charming, nothing at all like the other guys I had known. He took me on a date and was the perfect gentleman. He told me he had grown up with a single mom who'd died of cancer a few years ago. He said he wanted our relationship to be 'done right,' so he wouldn't move in with me. I thought he was so romantic and traditional."

"I wonder what made him change," Lena interjected, making Zuriel wonder as well.

She gulped back the emotion that was starting to build up. She wished she could bring Matt from the dead and ask him. She knew it was impossible, so she continued.

"He asked me to marry him in a park one night. It was so romantic. I was almost scared to say yes, just because forever seemed like a long time. I did, though, and I couldn't have been happier. It seemed like we were meant to be together forever. Then, one day we were supposed to go out to lunch, because he said he had something important to talk with me about. I waited for him to come, but he never did. I never got to see him again." Zuriel wiped her eyes. It had been a long time since she'd told someone the story. It was painful to remember.

"I'm sorry, Zuriel. It sounds like you were really happy."

"I was, but I had no idea about his past. After he died, I found out about his family and stayed with them during the funeral. It was difficult. I learned he had run away from home when he was eighteen and had never come back. I learned about you and the pregnancy too." Zuriel saw Lena's face grow hard. Zuriel guessed that it was probably weird to hear a stranger talk about her past choices.

"Who told you?"

"I heard it first from the family and then from Drew."

"Yeah, it wasn't pretty. What all did they tell you?"

"Not much. I just heard he was pretty upset about it," Zuriel said, feeling like maybe bringing all this up was a little premature. She was hoping Lena would tell her the story. She knew it would be painful to hear, but she had desperately been trying to put the pieces together.

Lena readjusted her pillow and then began her story. "I met Matt when he was eighteen and had just run away from home. He lived with three other guys, and Drew was one of them.

They thought they were really cool, with their partying, drugs, and newfound freedom. Matt was pretty charming, as I'm sure you know. We got together almost right away. He told me about his past, and we spend a lot of late nights talking about it. He told me he was giving up on God. I didn't know much about God—I had only been baptized as a baby—and I just told him he shouldn't give up like that. He was thinking about visiting his family and making things right again. He even got off the drugs and promised to get an apartment for us to live in. I was so happy. I never imagined that I would find someone so wonderful. That is, until it happened."

"You got pregnant."

"Yeah. Matt was really scared. He started to get stressed out about the future. He told me that he wanted to be a good father, but he didn't think he was ready for it. He started working more and stopped partying. He became really serious and even went to church for a couple Sundays. I didn't understand it at all because all I saw was his charming nature becoming more and more reserved. I didn't see him as often, and when I did get to be with him he seemed distant. So I thought that if there wasn't a baby, he would go back to being his old self. I thought we could go on like we'd been before and maybe even get that apartment together. When I told him I had aborted the baby, he was furious. He told me I had killed his child. He was so angry that he walked out, and I didn't see him again for a long time."

"I can't believe he would do such a thing. I'm so sorry, Lena." Zuriel was thankful that Matt had changed. Maybe Lena had learned about his past and shared more with him than Zuriel had, but it had cost her so much more too.

"It was really hard, but I had to move on. I found another guy, and it wasn't long before I had to find another one. I've always wondered if God could ever forgive me for what I'd done. As much as I hated Matt, I know he was right. It was wrong for me to kill my baby. It left permanent scarring on my heart."

Zuriel's heart ached for Lena; it was so strange to hear her talk about Matt. He didn't seem like the same person she'd known. She was now exposed to a whole new side of him. "I wonder what happened to him in those years that separated our relationships with him."

"It's a mystery. He was the first of many to break my heart."

"Are you with someone now?"

"No." Lena turned her head away and looked like she was fighting the urge to cry. "The last guy broke up with me for the opposite reason Matt did. I'm pregnant again, but this time I refused to have another abortion."

Zuriel felt concern and relief all at once. At least she was letting the baby live.

"I can't believe I'm telling you all this. I hate what I've become." She paused, continuing to successfully control her emotions. "I'm scared, Zuriel. I don't have a job or anyone to support me. I don't know what I'm doing, and sometimes I wonder if this child would be better off dying than entering this world of suffering."

"Don't worry," Zuriel reassured her, "I'll help you find a job. You can stay here as long as you need to. Your baby deserves to live. Suzy and I will help you in any way we can."

"I don't understand why you are both being so kind to me." Lena smiled. "Trying to get brownie points with God or something?"

"I didn't understand why Matt's family was so kind to me, or why Suzy came back into my life after leaving me for her drugs. I learned they loved me because they had come to love God and they knew he loved me."

"I wish Matt had followed their example. My life would have been a lot different," Lena said.

"Jesus does love you, even if everyone else treats you poorly," Zuriel explained, trying to introduce her own testimony. "I recently asked Jesus to make me his follower. I'm so happy now, Lena, and I really want to share that happiness with others."

"I'm glad things worked out for you. There's nothing I can do to change the wrong I did though. Ever since the abortion …" Lena's voice trailed off. She couldn't hold back her feelings anymore.

"God will forgive you if you ask him to. If you believe in Jesus and choose to follow him, he will forgive you. I thought he hated me for most of my life, but now I know what it's like to feel his love all the time. Jesus loves you too, Lena." Zuriel could tell Lena was listening closely.

"I used to go to church, but God's love never seemed real. I know my love for him wasn't real either, so I guess we were just incompatible."

"I'm still learning about what a love relationship means. It was hard accepting that a loving God didn't stop Matt from dying. But, it was easy to accept that Jesus died for me and wanted to give me peace," Zuriel replied, praying she was saying the right things.

"If that's what he's offering, I guess I'll take it," Lena said softly.

Zuriel could hardly believe her ears. God had been working on Lena, and somehow he had allowed Zuriel to be the one to lead her the rest of the way. She thanked God as she heard Lena pray out loud and ask Jesus to forgive her for having an abortion and for all of her other sins. It was amazing that God was changing another life. Zuriel was barely a Christian herself, and now here she was leading others to the faith. She felt blessed to be part of it and so grateful that God had used her to deliver his message.

⚬☙☙◎

"So this is it?" Lena asked as they stood freezing on the snowy sidewalks.

"Yes, this is the place. They help all sorts of women, and I think they would be able to help you too," Zuriel replied.

They walked through the doorway, happy to get out of the cold. Thanksgiving decorations were still up, even though it was now December. Zuriel saw several coloring pages of turkeys taped to the walls. She was amused by how many of the turkeys were uncommon colors, like purple and pink. She hoped she had brought Lena to the right place.

"Can I help you, ladies?" a white-haired woman with long, dangly earrings asked them.

"I think so," Zuriel said. "My friend is pregnant, and we don't really know where to go for care and checkups. She doesn't have insurance, and she doesn't want to have an abortion, so we thought this might be a good place to come."

"Yes, we can help you. Here is a form that you can fill out while I see if we have any openings today. Dr. Carson is here, so you might be able to talk to her and ask any questions you might have. I'm June, by the way; and you are?"

"Zuriel."

"Lena."

"Wonderful. And do you have a name yet for the little person inside you?" June asked sweetly.

Zuriel found her question amusing. Lena was only two months' pregnant, but June looked like she was ready to shake the baby's hand in introduction.

"No, not yet."

"Well then, nice to meet you, baby!" June exclaimed, speaking in the direction of Lena's belly. She excused herself to go talk to the doctor, and the girls found a seat in the waiting room.

"Well, she seems very friendly. I think this was a good idea," Lena said hopefully as she began to fill out the paperwork.

"Yes, a lady at church told me about this women's center. She said they can help with everything from ultrasounds to buying diapers."

"I hope so."

June came out from the hallway and took a seat beside them. Zuriel and Lena exchanged glances. They felt a little awkward. This woman was possibly too friendly.

"Dr. Carson can fit you in. We don't have another scheduled appointment for a while. So you can go back whenever you finish that paperwork." She delivered the message but didn't make an effort to move or get up. "I just want you to know, Lena that it's so wonderful that you are going to keep the baby. Children are a blessing from God. You see those coloring pages on the wall? Those were colored by children whose mothers came here for help. Many of those mothers were planning on having an abortion."

Zuriel had been praying about today. She knew having a baby would be a difficult process for Lena, especially after her first child had been aborted.

"I'm glad too. I just wish I would have done the same thing for my first baby." Lena reached for a tissue and Zuriel was surprised that she had confessed so much to this woman.

However, despite her over-friendliness, there was something about June that was warm and inviting. "Oh, darling, part of your heart will always be with that baby. You can know, though, that Jesus is taking good care of that little person. I'm so proud of you for doing the right thing now."

"I wouldn't have, if God hadn't changed me," Lena explained. "I wish I could forgive myself."

"I'm so glad you have the Lord to help you. I'll be praying for you, Lena."

Zuriel was flooded with thankfulness. It seemed prayer warriors and counselors were turning up everywhere.

"Is there anything I can specifically pray about?" June asked.

"Well, I really need a job, one where they won't mind when I have to leave for a while."

June smiled at Lena's words and went back to her desk to retrieve something. It appeared to be an application.

"I'm retiring soon, and I'm going to volunteer here as a counselor. I need someone to take my place, and it seems like you are the perfect candidate. You know the horror of abortion, but soon you will also know the joy of having a baby. I think you could really make a difference in the lives of the women who come through these doors. Why don't you fill out the application?" June handed her the application, but not without first giving Lena a hug.

Although they didn't know the woman, it seemed entirely appropriate given the situation. God was clearly watching out for them, and Zuriel could not stop thanking him.

 *Chapter 20*

Zuriel closed her phone and surveyed the apartment. The whole place was beautifully decorated for Christmas. It was amazing how meaningful the season had become now that she knew the real reason for celebrating. In fact, almost everything in her life had more meaning now. She could honestly say she was happy. She had left her old life behind and was enjoying her new one very much. She still missed Matt, but she understood that Matt had made mistakes and her life with him wouldn't have been the fairy tale she had thought it would be. She still loved Matt, but she loved Jesus so much more. Her heart was slowly healing.

It had been wonderful living with Lena and Suzy. They were squeezed into the two-bedroom apartment, but they all felt freer than they had ever been before. They were in love with God and no longer trapped by their need for guys and attention. Life was beautiful and hopeful now. The three women were desperately seeking God, despite their insane pasts. Adding to their happiness was excitement for the new addition to their little family: Lena's baby girl, who would come soon. Everything was so peaceful yet overwhelming, more so than they could ever explain.

Now it was the night before Christmas, and they were bringing a handful of friends to the Christmas Eve service at the local church. After the service, they were hosting a Christmas party back at the apartment. They had been praying and inviting people for several weeks, hoping their friends would be willing to investigate the idea of redemption. Each knew what life was like without Christ, and the memory often moved Zuriel to tears. She was proud of the woman God was turning her into but was growing increasingly more heartbroken for the lost. She was so thankful for the opportunity that lay before her. Hopefully tonight her friends would see a new side of church and a new side of God. What could be better than a candlelight service to help people remember the true meaning of Christmas? It seemed like the perfect time for them to come. The women were nervous but thankful God was using them.

Anne Lowell had called yesterday to invite her over for Christmas. Zuriel explained that she couldn't come because she already had plans to bring some of her friends to Christmas Eve service. It was then that Zuriel finally spilled the beans about her salvation story. She just couldn't keep it inside anymore and felt ashamed for not telling Anne sooner. Anne wept openly over the phone and insisted they should see each other soon. Zuriel was okay with the idea for the first time since leaving their house. She knew the importance of surrounding herself with Christian people and sharing with others what God was doing. She knew it had been wrong to keep her testimony a secret from them, but she felt that she needed space at the time. Now it felt like God had filled her emptiness and allowed her to trust other people again. She had seen such incredible healing in her life. Her relationships with Matt, Suzy, Lena, her dad, her grandparents, and, most importantly, with God were all good now. It was time to share this healing with the Lowells.

Zuriel's conversation with Anne was brief, but by the end of it she was looking forward to talking with all of them some more. Truthfully, though, she was looking forward to talking with Sam the most. Zuriel found that thought to be strange and wondered what it meant. Why did she want to talk to him so badly? She felt guilty because she often found herself day dreaming about him. Was she betraying Matt with her thoughts? Other days she wondered if Sam would be like an older brother to her. She missed the rest of the family too, though. Maybe she should plan to embrace the Lowells as if she had married Matt.

Zuriel heard Lena answering the door and the voices of people entering the apartment. It was Drew and Andy, along with Andy's new girlfriend, Chloe. Zuriel went to meet them, thrilled they had come. It didn't seem possible, but here they were. She prayed as more people came to the door. Diana from work arrived, along with Mara and Cassy, friends of Suzy's. They were coming together to learn about the true meaning of Christmas, the meaning Zuriel wished she had understood years ago. She felt in her heart that this would be the most beautiful Christmas she would ever have. Zuriel gathered everyone together, and Suzy distributed them into the cars to bring them all to the church.

The ceremony began and Zuriel was thrilled. She had only been to a candlelight service once, and it had been a long time ago. She felt like a child again as she tightly held her candle. Carols were sung, and Zuriel had never before realized just how much the classic Christmas songs carried the message of salvation. How could she have been blind to it for so long? She frequently glanced down the aisle, trying to read the expressions of her guests. She desperately wanted them to like the service and to fall in love with God more than anything else. This was a huge step for them, something she never thought would happen.

It was funny how easy it had been to lead Lena to Christ. She had been ready, searching, and asking God for help. These people, however, were far away from God and their hearts were hard as stone, yet even the hardest ones seemed to be softening. It was just as Suzy had said: it was motivating to do the right thing when other people were watching. Not that it was a fake performance for her; it was simply an effort to grow as close to God as possible, so that she could be a better example of Jesus' love. The process had been painful, but it was the most worthwhile and beautiful thing she had ever been a part of. It felt so wonderful to have a purpose and to know that life was more than just dragging through another day. The purpose of her life was to live for Christ, and standing in church with her candle in hand, she had never felt more in love with him. Her eyes watered and she could feel God's arms surrounding her. Jesus had come to earth for her! Zuriel let the notion sink in. Jesus came for her. He came to rescue her and all others who were willing to receive his sacrifice.

When the service ended, they dropped their used candles into a bucket. Many of the church members came and introduced themselves to the visitors. Zuriel felt a little embarrassed for them. She felt like she should have warned the church that these were not the kind of people who loved God and liked having strangers ask them questions. Still, maybe it was a good thing for them to be overwhelmed with concerned people. It was a foreign concept to them that so many people could be concerned about others and willing to love and accept them.

"The ceremony was beautiful," Lena said softly, rubbing her protruding belly.

"It was beautiful. I have never felt so connected to Christmas," Zuriel agreed.

"I just hope the others were affected the same way. It was hard to tell. They seemed dazed and a few of them looked scared. I

178 REBECCA FELLRATH

loved it, though, because it reminded me of the Catholic church I used to go to. There were so many rituals and ceremonies. I know those don't save you, but there is something to be said about having traditions and a structured service."

"Yes, I agree. That's why I like it when we have communion. There is something really cool about doing an activity that's so symbolic." Zuriel enjoyed doing anything that made her feel closer to God. She always imagined Jesus drinking the wine and eating the bread whenever she had communion. By taking communion, she was actually doing something that Jesus had done. The thought of following in his footsteps made her happy.

Zuriel wanted to stay and talk with more people, but she could see that her guests were feeling uncomfortable. They headed out to the parking lot and got into the cars. There would be snacks, cookies, eggnog, coffee, and some random types of candy waiting for them back at the apartment. It sounded good, and she was hoping the party would allow her to spark up some good conversations.

They arrived and began to devour the food. Christmas music was turned on and the Christmas tree lights were blinking. Everything looked perfect and beautiful.

"I love this, Zuriel. Our little apartment is so cute and crowded. This is a great Christmas!" Suzy commented.

"I think so too." Zuriel smiled at her friend and then noticed that Suzy's smile was exceptionally brighter than usual. "What is it?"

Suzy looked around, leaned over, and whispered, "After the service, Fred asked me if I wanted to meet him sometime for coffee."

"Fred? Oh, I'm so excited for you! He seems like such a good guy." Zuriel was happy for her friend. Suzy had found a guy who loved God and wanted to do his will. She imagined what a marriage would look like if both people were serving God. Every marriage and relationship she had ever seen had failed, and at one time she had wondered why. Now she knew that a desire to follow God and put others first was the key to having a long and happy marriage. Zuriel hoped Lena would also meet "the one."

As the evening progressed, Zuriel started to feel a little bit disappointed. She tried to find out what people were thinking about the service, but it didn't seem like anyone else had been overly affected.

Drew took a seat beside her, and she attempted yet again to start a spiritual conversation. "So what did you think?"

"About what?"

"Oh, don't be silly. What did you think about the Christmas Eve service?" Zuriel prayed silently that God would help her say the right words.

"It was okay. It's just a bunch of church people singing and praying. You know I'm not into that stuff."

"Well, for someone who's not into that stuff, I'm still glad you came."

"Yeah, I put up with a lot for you."

"For me?"

"Waiting around for you to heal isn't easy, you know."

Zuriel's face reddened. She suddenly realized why he'd agreed to come, and why he had stayed single for the past several months. Zuriel didn't like it one bit, and she knew that even if she ever healed completely, she would never be interested in a relationship with Drew.

"I'm not sure I understand," Zuriel sheepishly said.

"Zuriel, don't you get it? I like you."

"Well, of course you do. And I like all of you guys too: Andy, Suzy, and everyone. I am so thankful God has blessed me with such good friends."

"I like you much more than that. I like you—not your God, and not your friends—just you. You know I've been here for you through this whole thing. I've been willing to do whatever it takes."

Zuriel thought back over the time that had passed since the accident. He had been there, but he wasn't as selfless as he thought. Zuriel prayed that God would help her know how to handle this situation.

"Drew, I—"

"You at least owe me a date or something! Maybe you're not ready for a long-term relationship at this point, but it's been a long time since the accident. You deserve to do more than sit around in loneliness clinging to those church people."

"Please don't think that following Jesus is some kind of cover up for wanting a relationship. I don't think you realize how important he is to me, and how important is for me be around people who love him like I do."

"So I'm being ruled out because of some religious preferences? Did they tell you not to date outsiders?" His sarcasm was brash.

She hoped no one else was listening. This wasn't the conversation she was hoping to have with him about God. "I'm willing to put my relationship with Jesus above a relationship with any man."

"That sounds sick, like you're dating Jesus or something. I don't get you at all. I couldn't understand Matt either, so why should I try to understand you!"

Zuriel was shocked by what he had just said. Drew was putting her in the same category as Matt? But Matt wasn't a Christian …

"What do you mean, you couldn't understand Matt? You guys had the same religious beliefs."

"Yeah, well, we did until a few weeks before he died. I wasn't going to tell you this because I was afraid you would try to connect with him by becoming a Christian. But of course you had to go and turn into one anyway. I think it's high time you knew what happens to people who trust in God!"

Zuriel's head was spinning. What was Drew saying? "Matt became a Christian a few weeks before he died?" Zuriel asked, not realizing how loudly she had said it. The attention of everyone else in the room was now on her. Zuriel felt her hands trembling.

"Did you just say that Matt came back to God before he died?" Lena asked, as the whole room seemed to lean in.

"Let me tell you a little story then, shall I?"

Suzy came and sat beside Zuriel, gripping her hand tightly as Drew began.

"Throughout the time that I knew Matt, he would get into random philosophical moods. For about a week he would be researching evidence for God's existence and arguing with anyone who disagreed. It wasn't long, though, before he would conclude again that God did not exist and forget about it for several months. Two weeks before he died, he got into another one of those moods. He wanted to talk about God, but I was sick of hearing it."

Zuriel felt her heart swelling. Could it be that her beloved had actually come to know Jesus? She was hoping so desperately that Drew would tell them that he had.

"We were walking home after hanging out with some friends from work. We were both pretty drunk, but there was this guy on the street talking to a group of homeless kids about God. Matt recognized him and started screaming and cussing at him. I held Matt back and was trying to figure out what was going on. Matt kept calling him a traitor and told him the guy had ruined his faith. It was really weird, because the guy dropped to his knees and started to ask for forgiveness. I wondered what in the world he had done. Matt wasn't usually violent like that. What really creeped me out was when Matt started to sob. I let go of him and he slumped down on the sidewalk. The man came up and hugged him. He was praying out loud and things got really uncomfortable. They exchanged phone numbers and then we went home."

"It was John Carter, wasn't it? He ran into his old youth pastor? I can't believe it!" Zuriel's eyes watered, as she realized what Drew was saying. There was hope. She might actually get to see Matt again!

"Yeah, it was his old youth pastor. They went out for breakfast the day after you guys got engaged. When Matt came back he told me he was a new man and that he had some things in his life to change. He started reading his Bible and went to church that Sunday. It was weird and I hated every second of it. Matt told me he was going to take you out to lunch and finally tell you the truth about his past. He told me he was going to tell you about his faith, and that he was praying you would become a Christian too. Well, the rest is history, because he died on the way to pick you up for lunch. If God is so good, why didn't he stop Matt from dying?"

An icy silence hung over the room. Zuriel saw that Suzy and Lena were in shock too. Their guests looked dazed and confused. Zuriel felt peace wash over her, along with a real sense of relief that could never be explained. Matt had turned back to God. He wasn't burning in hell, even after all he had done and all the pain he had caused. Zuriel was so thankful. Now she knew this would definitely be the best Christmas of her life. There was no greater gift than salvation, but knowing Matt was saved too was a very close second. She was happy and thankful yet still haunted by Drew's last question.

Zuriel had come to believe that, because of Matt's death, she had been able to find God. It was the pain, her stay with the Lowells, and finally Suzy's new lifestyle that had led her to salvation. Now she wondered what the real purpose of the accident was. Zuriel realized she could have become a Christian without Matt's death. If Matt hadn't died, he would have met her for lunch and explained salvation to her. She would have met his family, come to the truth, and lived the rest of her life with the godly man she loved. Zuriel didn't understand, but she knew she needed to find John Carter. She had to know more.

"Where is John Carter now?" Zuriel asked Drew. "I want to talk to him."

"I don't know. I don't keep track of those kinds of people."

"I know where he is," Suzy replied, to everyone's surprise. "Remember how I told you I was offered a free meal? I think he was the same guy. The name sounds familiar. I didn't think of it before, because I assumed that since John had stolen money, he probably wasn't doing God stuff anymore."

Oh, Suz, please take me to him." Suzy and Zuriel hugged tightly.

Zuriel couldn't wait to find him and talk. She had spent so much time trying to let go of Matt and excepting that he was lost forever. She had even been able to thank God for the trials she had gone through, because they led her to him. Now, however, she wondered how to process this new information. She wasn't sure. In fact, she was scared. What did this mean for her faith? At least she could ask Matt about all this when she saw him in heaven.

"I don't think you heard me right," Drew exclaimed, clearly annoyed by the way the news was taken. "Matt became a Christian and he died!"

"I don't think *you* are hearing right," Lena responded boldly. "Before Matt became a Christian, he was already dead!"

 *Chapter 21*

Samuel heard his phone vibrating on the night stand beside his bed. He stretched and yawned before leaning over to see who was calling at this absurd hour. It was five in the morning on Christmas day. If it was one of the youth group kids pulling a prank, there would certainly be payback.

He glanced at his phone and was startled to see that Zuriel Rawson had just called. He stared at the screen, trying to figure out what to do. He had been trying to move on and forget his childish crush until his mother told him that Zuriel had become a Christian. Not only that, she had been one for a couple months now and was bringing a group of friends to church. Samuel was excited, confused, and surprised by how much he had started thinking about her again. And now she had just called him. Should he call her back?

His phone vibrated. She was calling again, which quickly answered Samuel's question. "Hello."

"Hey, Sam. I … um … I'm sorry for calling so early. Did I wake you?" Her voice sounded shaky. He remembered that voice from their walk through the woods.

"Yeah, actually, you did. It's okay though. Is something wrong?" Samuel sat up in bed and located his shoes. He would be ready to go if she needed him.

"No, it's not really an emergency or anything like that. I just need to tell you something."

"Oh, my mom told me you're a Christian now. I'm so happy for you!" He tried to figure out why she would suddenly feel a need to call him at five a.m. He didn't mind; it just meant she had been thinking about him.

"Thank you. I'm really happy too. I want to thank you for everything. I thought a lot about the things you said after I left. It really meant a lot to me. God used you quite a bit in my life—and Matt's too."

Samuel was happy to hear her words but saddened by the mention of his brother. He wondered if he would ever have a chance with Zuriel because of her relationship with Matt. He prayed silently, surrendering his will to God's plan. He needed to focus on what God wanted him to say and on finding out why she had called so early. The romance needed to be forgotten.

"I've been praying for you," he said, "and I know my family has too. We're all really proud of you. It sounds like you've come a long way in a very short time."

"I feel like I have too; it's just that recently things have gotten complicated, but in a good way, I think. I found out more about Matt and I don't think I can sleep until I tell you."

Samuel braced himself.

"Drew was one of the people I brought to church with me, and he wasn't happy that I had become a Christian. In his anger, he told me more about Matt. He told me about John Carter too."

Samuel's ears perked up. John Carter? What did Drew know about Carter? What did it have to do with Matt, and why was it keeping Zuriel awake? "Interesting … what did he have to say?"

"He told me that a few weeks before Matt died, he turned his life back over to Christ."

Samuel's mouth went dry. He couldn't believe what he was hearing, but he hoped with all his heart it was true. Was his brother the ultimate Prodigal Son? He waited in silence, stunned and in shock as she continued.

"He apparently was a bit of a philosopher and would periodically wrestle with the idea of God's existence. Drew said that one night they saw John Carter telling some homeless kids about Jesus. Matt recognized him and started yelling and cussing. John dropped to his knees and asked for forgiveness. Matt cried in his arms while John prayed for him. Drew said the two later met for breakfast and Matt came back proclaiming to have changed."

Samuel's heart swelled. All his bitterness, all his anger, and all his strife had been for nothing in the end. God had saved his brother and his long-lost friend despite his own failed attempts. How could this be? It seemed far too good to be true. "I don't know what to say."

"I know what you mean. Drew told me Matt planned to tell me everything about his past and his newfound faith at lunch that day. He died on his way to my apartment to tell me."

Samuel was amazed. He was so happy that his brother had been saved and so overwhelmed with thankfulness. He would get to see his brother again someday in heaven. Yet even in this, he wondered what God's will was. Samuel had gotten through the pain of the situation and had tried to figure out God's reasons. Now he had to cope with it all over again—but he liked this way better. He couldn't wait to tell his parents!

"Zuriel, I can't tell you how glad I am you told me this. I am so thankful!" Samuel felt his emotions slipping into his voice. He was in awe. He thanked God for Zuriel over and over in his heart, but most of all, he thanked God that his brother was alive in heaven.

"Oh, you're welcome. I just had to tell you. I stayed up all night trying to understand what it meant. You needed to know and it was eating away at me. I'm sorry I didn't stay in touch with your family. I felt like I just couldn't do it. It was too painful for me back then."

Samuel could understand and felt immense respect for her. She had changed and become a different woman. Now she wasn't so scared and insecure anymore. She was sensitive and strong instead.

"It's okay; I understand. I'm just glad you found God. So how did it happen?"

She explained her transformation after meeting up with Suzy again, and he could hear in her voice that she was sincere. It was strange to be awakened in the middle of the night to find out that, although he felt like he had failed Matt and Zuriel, they had both found themselves at the foot of the cross anyway.

"That's amazing! I'm so glad Suzy was there for you. And it sounds like you've been trying to duplicate what Suzy did for you. I heard about the Christmas Eve service."

"Yeah, God keeps bringing us new people to talk to. Right after I got saved, I felt like I needed to find Lena, Matt's ex-girlfriend."

Samuel remembered her. Although he had never met her, he would never forget the conversation he had with Matt. Matt had left her because she had an abortion. The memory was painful, and Samuel was glad that God had not failed to bring Matt back that day despite his own failure.

Zuriel told Samuel how she found Lena and invited her to move in with them. She told him about the new baby as well.

As Samuel listened to Zuriel excitedly talk, he couldn't help but marvel at his God. Even Lena had been protected and drawn by the Holy Spirit. It was amazing! How could he have doubted God's faithfulness? He wished he had trusted God to take care of things and not made so many assumptions. He imagined how different his grieving process would have been if he had focused on trusting God and resting in his faith instead of on thoughts of Matt going to hell. Samuel thought of his sisters, mother, and father. What a joy it would be for them to know that God had answered every single one of their prayers. He wondered how many times he had prayed and assumed that God was going to say no. Who was he to make a judgment about what God was or wasn't going to do? This was the infinite, almighty God he was talking about—the one who was responsible for saving his whole family's souls.

"Sam, I really want to meet John."

"That would be cool. You'll have to let me know what you find out." Samuel was certainly curious to learn the whole story.

"Well, don't you want to meet him too? I was kind of thinking that maybe you could come with me."

Samuel was caught off guard by the request. He wanted to be there for Zuriel but was surprised by his own resistance. He had been hurt by the former youth pastor and had never even thought about reconnecting with the guy. Yet, deep inside, Samuel knew he needed to go. He needed to tell John he was forgiven.

"Yeah, I guess that would probably be a good idea," Sam replied hesitantly.

"Probably?"

"It will just be hard after all he put me through. He really made it difficult on a lot of people when he got caught. We all had such faith in him. I probably need to tell him I forgive him."

"Well, I want to thank him. He's my hero!" Zuriel exclaimed.

Her hero …? Samuel had never thought that a man who caused such havoc in the church could be a hero. "I don't know about that, Zuriel."

"Sam, he led Suzy to Christ, which also led me to Christ. Pastor Carter was reconciled with Matt, and as a result, now I know he's in heaven. He led the people I love the most to salvation. For that I will always be thankful."

Samuel was dumbfounded once again. This was not the same woman he had known before. Her perspective was unearthly. Although she was a new Christian, God had given her great wisdom. John Carter had once been his hero as well, but when he was caught taking money, he quickly became a villain. Now John seemed to be a changed man. Or was he? Samuel remembered him teaching with conviction when the youth group was alive and on fire for Christ. Perhaps John was merely a sinner saved by grace—a man of God who had fallen but was redeemed by the one who created him.

"You're right, Zuriel, I should go with you. Do you know where he is?"

"Suzy does, so I can get directions from her. What time frame were you thinking? Because I want to do this soon."

"Soon would be good. We'd better do this before I chicken out." He chuckled.

"Okay, that sounds good. Thanks, Sam."

"Thank you! I'm so glad you called."

"I couldn't help it. I'm sorry for calling so early, though. I should let you get some sleep."

"All right. Thanks again, Zuriel. Merry Christmas!"

"Merry Christmas!" She said it so sweetly.

Samuel put his phone back and stretched out on the bed, feeling happier than he had in a long time. His brother had trusted in Jesus Christ and was not lost forever. John Carter had ruined the church but turned his life around and was now building it back up. And now Zuriel was coming back into his life. He wondered if that was good or bad. He knew he liked her wholeheartedly and that those feelings were steadily increasing. He had used the principle that she was not a Christian to keep himself from "officially" being interested in a relationship with her for so long. Now that she was a sister in Christ, Samuel began to wonder if she might someday become even more.

 *Chapter 22*

Zuriel waited on the couch in her apartment and looked out the window. She felt strange to be waiting on Sam. She remembered waiting for Matt and the torment she had been forced to endure, and now she was waiting for his older brother to come pick her up. They would be going to see John Carter so she could finally fit the last missing piece into the puzzle of Matt's life.

Zuriel felt that after seven months she was moving forward pretty well, but there was still part of her that wanted to know the whole story. She felt she would be able to move on completely once the last few mysteries were put to rest. Zuriel was glad she called Sam and told him about John. He texted her later saying how happy his family was, and how they would all remember this Christmas forever. She was happy for them but still felt bad for calling so early.

Zuriel saw Sam's car pull into the parking lot. She felt herself getting nervous and her cheeks getting rosy. She was glad Sam was coming; she really wanted him to ask the right questions and mend his relationship with John. Now, as she watched his blurry figure walking toward the building, she felt uneasy. Why? She wasn't sure of herself and ran to the mirror to make sure that she looked okay. As she heard a knock on her door, she wished she had worn something else. Her jeans and black long-sleeved shirt seemed too plain. She saw a red scarf lying on the kitchen table and quickly added it to her outfit. Pinching her cheeks, she went to open the door.

"Hello," Zuriel said as she surveyed the man in front of her. He looked a lot like Matt, but taller and older. His face was clean shaven and his hair was cut short around his ears. She was surprised by her attraction. She was afraid she would feel like she was around Matt and do or say something stupid. However, she was keenly aware that this was not Matt. This was Sam. Handsome Sam …

"Hey." He smiled and walked into the apartment. He looked her straight in the eyes, and she wasn't used to that. She wondered why she had been so concerned about the red scarf if he wasn't going to check her out.

"I'm glad you found the place okay. I have directions to John's building. Suzy and I stopped by earlier and read the poster on the door. I think he should be there this afternoon." Zuriel spoke quickly while she gathered her stuff. She had forgotten how attractive Sam was. Thankfully his good looks were serving as a distraction from her fears of meeting with John.

"Your apartment wasn't too hard to find. You have a nice place here."

"Thanks."

"Well, are you ready to go?"

"Yeah." Zuriel followed him out to his car and they made their way through the city. She wished Suzy and Lena could have come, but they both had to work. She felt silly for inviting him and wondered if he had agreed to come because he felt sorry for her. Zuriel prayed Sam would do most of the talking. She just planned to listen and get to the bottom of the whole story. She also wondered if she would find out anything new about Sam. She glanced over at him while he drove, horrified that he would catch her looking. She looked again, and he caught her eye. Zuriel quickly looked out her window and blushed.

"Do I remind you of my brother?" he asked.

"Yes ... and no." Zuriel was surprised by his fearless question. He was up front and perceptive.

"I'm sorry."

"Don't be. You're his brother, so you can't help reminding me of him. That's not a bad thing, though. The purpose of our trip *is* to think about Matt, after all."

"True." He gave her a half-smile.

They arrived at a stop light and he turned, looking into her eyes again. "You mentioned both yes and no. What did you mean by that?"

"You remind me of him, but not so much that I would confuse you with him." Zuriel looked away from his gaze. She was surprised by her own honesty. It was awkward to touch on the subject of attraction. It was obvious that he looked like Matt, and obvious that Zuriel had been attracted to Matt. She felt like she had just told Sam that she thought he was hot, in a creepy, implied way. Or maybe he thought she was trying to tell him that she would never be interested in him the way she was in his brother. He probably didn't care, but she didn't want him to think that either. Zuriel felt funny, why did she care? Did she like him as more than a friend and brother?

"I'm glad you see it that way. Matt and I are different, as you know."

"Yes you are. I suppose we'll find out just how different."

"Indeed!" Sam smiled.

They parked along the street and got out of the car, trying to avoid the piles of snow. They paused for a moment in front of the old building. The windows downstairs were boarded up, but there were crosses spray painted on them. It seemed strange and out of place that a rundown, inner-city building would be a meeting place for Christians.

She led the way to the door and noticed the "open" sign. It made her laugh, wondering what of kind of person would put an "open" sign in front of a church.

Sam stepped ahead of her and opened the door. Zuriel beamed; it had been a while since she had been in the presence of a gentlemen.

They walked into the corridor and saw a thin, elderly woman sitting at a desk surrounded by greeting cards in large stacks. She was hard at work writing messages in them.

"Excuse me, ma'am," Sam said.

The woman was startled and looked up quickly. "Oh, hello! I'm sorry I didn't see you there. What can I help you with?"

"We'd like to see John Carter," Samuel said. "We heard he would be here."

The woman smiled and nodded. "Yes, he's here. Does he know you are coming?"

"No."

"I'll let him know you're here …"

"Samuel Lowell."

"Okay, I'll tell him." The woman headed down a hallway, leaving them alone in the front room.

Zuriel wanted to say something, but she couldn't form any words. She was getting more and more nervous to talk with John and hear the rest of Matt's story. She wondered why Sam hadn't said much, but when she saw his face, she could tell he wasn't feeling overly sure of himself either. They were about to meet the man who could be blamed for most of the bad things that had happened in his life—as well as most of the good.

Zuriel prayed that everything would be all right. She hoped Sam would still feel forgiving when he came face to face with Pastor Carter. Her hands shook.

The sound of footsteps echoed in the narrow hallway, and a man quickly approached, followed by the receptionist. He stopped, not saying a word.

Sam turned to face him and the two stared each other down for a few awkward seconds.

Zuriel didn't know what to do. She wondered if the two men were going to fight.

"Hi, you must be John Carter," Zuriel heard herself say, breaking the silence.

"Yes, I am."

"I'm Zuriel. I was engaged to Matt Lowell. I understand he came to visit you shortly before he died."

John looked at her in surprise as he shook her hand. "He passed away? I hadn't heard that. I was wondering why he never came back to visit. I'm …" John rubbed the back of his bald head, and his eyes moistened. "I'm so sorry."

"I'm sure you remember Sam, Matt's brother." Zuriel felt even more awkward now. She didn't understand why Sam remained so silent.

"Look at you, Sam. Matt told me you were becoming a youth pastor. It's amazing how much can happen in the course of a few years. It's good to see you. I'm so sorry to hear about your brother. I had no idea." John extended his hand and Sam shook it, but still didn't say anything.

Zuriel started to sincerely regret bringing him along. She hadn't planned on things being so uncomfortable. She prayed and waited, and John spoke again.

"Of everybody else at the church, I know I hurt you the most. After everyone found out, I couldn't speak to you because

I was so ashamed. I knew how much you looked up to me at the time. I'm sorry I never faced up to you the way I should have. I'm so sorry for everything, Samuel. I'll regret those decisions until the day I die. If you never forgive me, I can understand why, but I'm so happy you came. I've wanted to tell you that for a long time."

Sam looked at the ceiling and seemed to be avoiding John's direct eye contact. The struggle inside him was all over his face. Zuriel wanted to help him, and she wanted these men to be friends again, but she knew she had no power in this situation. They had gone through experiences that were quite different from her own. It was one thing to be hurt by people whose intentions were evil, but she couldn't imagine being hurt so much by someone who claimed to love God.

"I forgive you," Sam finally said softly.

John put his hand on Sam's shoulder and smiled through his glossy eyes. The two embraced, and Zuriel once again felt out of place. She made eye contact with the receptionist, who returned a sympathetic smile. Zuriel was thankful for her understanding.

"Come back to my office. Let's talk about why you're here," John said, wiping his eyes.

Zuriel followed, praying they would be able to get all of the information she longed for.

They walked down the hall and stopped at a room with no door. The office was small and not very well decorated. There was an old couch, a fold-out table with a chair behind it and a laptop on top of it, and a few random books and papers stacked up on a couple of small bookshelves. They sat on the couch across from the table, and Zuriel felt like she was in a principal's office.

"So, my friends, tell me what happened to Matt. We met several times, and then I couldn't get hold of him again. I haven't heard anything about him yet. I'm really sorry to hear about his death. What happened?" John opened the conversation to what Zuriel was most interested in.

Zuriel explained what happened on that fateful day Matt had never shown up and then added, "He told me he had grown up with his single mom in Detroit, so I was pretty surprised to find out that he had a large Christian family in Toledo that he ran away from at age eighteen."

"I can't imagine getting so much news at once," John exclaimed sympathetically.

"It was certainly a shock. I stayed with the Lowells for the funeral and learned more about who he was as a teen. By the time I left them, my friend Suzy had reappeared in my life. She was my best friend for a long time, but had developed a drug addiction and moved out. She gave her addictions up, though—actually it was largely because of you. She rode a bus over here for free food and heard the gospel. So when she moved back in with me, she spent most of her time praying and talking with me about Jesus. I became a Christian through her example and then we ended up taking in Matt's ex-girlfriend, who is actually about to have a baby."

"Wow, that's a lot to take in such a short amount of time!"

"Yes, but there's even more that came up recently," Sam interjected.

"What do you mean by more?"

"We all knew Matt as an atheist. We thought he had completely turned away from his upbringing. It was hard for everybody because we weren't just losing Matt's body, we felt like his soul was lost to us forever too."

Zuriel cut in. "We all thought he was lost to us. In fact, I was only able to justify his death in my mind by thinking about all the other people, including myself, who turned to God during the mourning period and afterwards too. Then I heard from Matt's friend that he actually gave his life over to God before he died. He was apparently on his way to tell me about his faith when he got into the accident. Now I'm so happy that I get to see him again someday, but I can't help but be angry with God all over again. If he was going to tell me about Jesus, then he didn't need to die in order for me to find salvation." Zuriel finished and realized how much of her soul she had just exposed. She looked at Sam and saw a look in his eyes that she had never seen before. She wondered if he had struggled with those same thoughts.

"When Matt came and talked to me, we talked about you and his family. He was very concerned about how to break the news to you. He wasn't sure how you would respond, so he prayed fervently that you would become a Christian when he shared his faith with you. You could look at the situation as if God killed him without a purpose, but then you would miss out on the miracle that is there. Satan, our enemy, is real. He knew what Matt was up to, and he knew that amazing things would happen if you became a Christian. Satan did his best to stop God's will from happening. Yes, it is very sad that things ended up happening this way, but God wasn't surprised by the accident. God still accomplished his will. God doesn't need bad things or tragedy to occur in order to bring about good things in people's lives. However, bad things happen, because of sin. God used the tragedy for good, anyway."

He paused, and Zuriel listened closely trying to make sense of what he was saying. She felt ashamed for being angry with God, but still confused and wishing that she knew the whole story. She guessed that she wouldn't find out the rest until she got to heaven, though.

Sam nodded in agreement as John continued. "Satan meant to ruin your life and ensure that you would not come to Christ, but God used that very situation as a way to help you find him. I do not pretend to understand why God allows certain things to happen but stops others; I just know God is unstoppable. Satan tried to foil his plans, but God still rescued you."

"Yes, he did rescue me," Zuriel responded.

John continued on in an even more solemn tone. "I wondered why God didn't stop me from acting on my greedy impulse. If I hadn't taken that money, things would have been so much better for everyone. Yet even through that horrible experience, here I am with the opportunity of leading many people to Christ on a regular basis. I would never in my life say that stealing money was a good thing. It is sin. Period. However, God still used it for good. The fact that God used my sin for good doesn't take away the wrongness of the action itself; it just means God is merciful. Not even I could stop God's will by my sinfulness."

"God is so merciful," Zuriel heard Sam say. He had remained silent during so much of the conversation, but apparently his mind had been hard at work. God's will could certainly seem complicated to the human mind, but it was so much clearer when she paused to recognize just how powerful he truly was. She felt overwhelmed.

"Samuel, I'm so glad you're teaching those kids. I was relieved to hear that someone strong in faith had taken over the youth group. I haven't stopped praying for you and those kids ever since."

"Thanks, John."

"So what was Matt like when you knew him? What did he want to say to me before he died?" Zuriel asked, wondering what the rest of the details were. She wanted to know so badly.

"He told me he was going to tell you about his family and about why he ran away from home. He was basically going to tell you his real life story. He wanted you to visit his family and go to church. He was scared you wouldn't like his newfound faith. Mostly, though, he was afraid that you might break off the engagement if you heard about the huge change in his life. I think that's why he waited so long to tell you."

"I don't understand why everything had to happen the way it did, but I guess I'll just have to trust God on this one." Zuriel was desperately trying to make sense of it all. She didn't know the reasons God had put her on the path she was on, but she did know he had been faithful to her throughout the whole torturous journey.

Sam spoke up. "John, you've got to talk to my father. He needs to hear about Matt from you. He really needs to hear the whole story, and I think a lot of people would be encouraged to know what you've been up to. Have you talked with the pastor recently?" Sam rubbed his chin thoughtfully. His problem-solving mind was at work.

"I want to, but I don't think they would listen or want me back."

"I'm here with you now, and my brother is alive in heaven because of your work. I think knowing you're doing well will be important to many people. We've all been praying for you and Matt for the last five years!" Sam leaned over the fold-out table. He looked John directly in the eyes. "Please talk to my dad. Come over for dinner sometime."

"All right." John nodded.

Zuriel thought back to a few days ago when she challenged Sam to meet up with John. She could tell the same struggle was going on inside both men.

"So what happened, anyway? You took money to pay off your debts, right?" Sam boldly asked.

"It's more complicated than that. I'm sure the rumors must have gotten pretty big and pretty ugly."

"I've heard a few, but my brother was drowning in pain after you left, and I was living in denial. Pastor Ben never went into all the details; I just had to go through a very intense interview process when I took over as youth pastor because of whatever happened. I could never understand what would make you walk down that kind of road." Sam spoke sternly and slowly. He was clearly having trouble dealing with this particular part of his past.

"My wife, Shirley, dreamed of redecorating the house and home-schooling our kids. I still had loans from school and some credit card debt from my life before Christ. I wanted so badly to give her what she wanted and get out of debt at the same time."

"Why didn't you talk to the church about your debt?"

"I didn't want to borrow anymore money or take charity"— he sighed heavily before continuing—"so I stole the money and was caught red-handed. My wife didn't know what I was doing, so when she found out, she was very surprised and upset. Unfortunately, I was stupid enough to blame her for what I did. I knew in my heart that she had nothing to do with my sin, but I tried to justify it because of her demands. The first year after we left the church was extremely painful. Thankfully, Pastor refused to press charges as long as I repaid the money, but I didn't have a job anymore and I sat around wallowing in bitterness and self-pity. My wife and I were separated for a few weeks before I finally came crawling back to her, begging for forgiveness.

"During that time, I worked several odd jobs, and we barely made ends meet. I knew God had still called me to ministry, so I started telling street kids about Jesus and am now partnered with a bigger church uptown for this mission work."

Zuriel was amazed by this story. She wondered how many of the corrupt pastors she had heard about had stories like this: good intentions without wisdom to back them up.

"Wow … John, I didn't know it was like that. I'm glad the two of you stuck together," Sam said thoughtfully.

"I'm glad too. I don't think I would have made it without her help."

"That's incredible." Zuriel agreed, imagining what kind of woman Shirley must be. She knew this woman had to be a strong woman of God in order to go through all that and still be faithful to her husband.

"And for some reason, God continues to bless us, even though I don't deserve it at all. A few months after beginning our ministry here, one of the church members volunteered to pay off my debt in full. There aren't any words that can describe the depth of my thankfulness. It amazes me so …" John stopped and took a few deep breaths. He was getting choked up.

Zuriel thought it was so encouraging to hear that God was doing amazing things everywhere. He was the same God in every location and person.

"John, I'm so glad I came to see you. Your story has humbled me, and I want you to know that I truly do forgive you." Sam and John stood and embraced again.

Zuriel sensed that it would be time to leave soon. The visit had been very educational, but most of all, it had taught her about the power of God's grace. She was surer than ever before that Christ was the answer to everything.

They walked out to the car in silent reflection until Sam opened the door for her and Zuriel softly said thank you. They were both still thoughtful, revaluating what they knew about God. It was amazing how many prayers had been answered and how many hearts had been healed and changed.

Zuriel wasn't sure what the road ahead would have in store for her, but she knew God was going to make it good. She could finally be at peace with Matt's death and realize that God's will was not something anyone could fully understand. All she knew to do was pray and trust that God was always working out his plan for her life, despite the nasty mess the rest of the world was in.

Chapter 23

Samuel paced in his office waiting for Zuriel to arrive. It was five forty-five on New Year's Eve. His mind was swirling in hundreds of directions. He was thankful he wasn't the main speaker tonight. He hadn't been able to concentrate on much of anything for the last few days, so he was extremely thankful Zuriel had agreed to come and share her testimony with his youth group. He wondered if she was the reason for his fogged mind. He wished so badly that he could just make sense of his emotions and then shut them out. The clock was ticking and he needed to get moving.

The party would start at seven, and there would be games, pizza, and lots of snacks. At nine thirty they would have a worship service, and then Zuriel would give her testimony. After that, he would give the kids a challenge for the New Year in the hopes that they would make resolutions to grow closer to God. Of course after midnight the craziness would begin. Televisions and gaming systems would be pulled out, and the boys would be at it until morning. The board games, art supplies, pillows, and coffee would be thrown into a different room, and the girls would stay up all night telling each other their deepest secrets. It would be a pretty typical New Year's party for the teens; however, it was certain to be anything but typical for Samuel.

Only a few days ago he had driven to see Zuriel and then brought her to visit John. His mind still pondered the absurdity of the event. He never could have imagined that he would have a friendship with either of them. While at the meeting, his mind had been focused for the most part on John and Matt. His thoughts had been concentrated on God's will, as well as on the futility of good intentions, and his own need to offer forgiveness. Every time he thought back to the funeral seven months ago, he was humbled. God had revealed so much to him in that time and had truly changed his perspective and his heart. It was obvious now that God always had a plan and would always accomplish his will regardless of the circumstances.

After Samuel had mulled through his emotions, he thought about Zuriel. He couldn't help remembering her sensitive nature and marked questions. He wondered why God kept using her over and over again to heal him and bring him to a better understanding of his purpose in life. He liked being around her, and he liked that she always challenged him to do what was right and made him desire God more. She had done that even before she was a Christian too. Samuel wondered what it all meant. He tried to remind himself that she had been Matt's fiancée. Even if something were to happen between them, it would probably be awkward and emotionally loaded. He tried to block her from his mind, but there wasn't any point. Zuriel would be arriving at the church soon to prepare for the night ahead. He wondered if maybe he shouldn't have asked her to speak.

Samuel recalled her face when he dropped her off after meeting with John. She looked so nervous and shy. Her blonde hair was pulled back into a ponytail, revealing her pearl earrings. Her green eyes seemed to flash with fire and a strong desire for life, and he felt himself fall in love. Instead of realizing what was happening to him, he had translated the emotion of the moment into spiritual admiration. It was then that Samuel had told her about the party and persuaded her to come and speak. He helped her out of the car and waved good-bye, feeling good about himself and his ministry. But it wasn't until he got home that he realized his true excitement for her to share her story was because it meant he got to see her again sooner.

He walked out of his office to the lobby. It was finally six o'clock. Zuriel would be there any minute, and Samuel couldn't wait. He thought of how amazing it was that the last time she had entered this building she didn't believe in God and was only coming because of death. Now she was returning as a Christian who loved the Lord, and she was here to share her story about the new life she had been given. He marveled and felt his heart quicken as he saw the petite and curvaceous woman walk toward the glass doors at the entrance to the church. He caught his breath, surprised by how much he was affected by her presence. He moved quickly and beat her to the doors to open them.

"Hello. I finally made it!" she said sweetly. Her smile was intoxicating.

"I hope it wasn't too hard to find."

"Oh, no, I remembered most of it from the last time I was here." Zuriel took off her black coat and the familiar red scarf. He shook her hand awkwardly, once again surprised by how small and delicate she seemed. "It's hard to believe that last time I was here, I hated the very thought of church. I never could have guessed that I would be speaking here."

"I was just thinking about that too."

"Oh, I'm so nervous though!"

"I'm sure you'll do fine. I think it will be a really great story for the kids to hear, and very meaningful too. You are an amazing woman and God just keeps using you for his glory."

He led her to the sanctuary and showed her where she would stand while giving her testimony. He gave her a brief outline of the program and then began a tour of the church. Zuriel would not only be speaking tonight, she would also be a chaperon. The classrooms for the girls to stay in were toured, as well as the kitchen and the gaming room.

Samuel loved showing Zuriel around the church. He knew she had been there before, but it felt different this time. Now he was sharing his ministry and work with her. He knew that if he were to get married, the woman would have to be willing to work alongside him. Zuriel's willingness to speak and help out at the church was very attractive. He prayed that God would help him concentrate on the task at hand.

After a while the kids started to arrive, and immediately the smack talk over the video games began.

Michael arrived, hauling several gaming systems with him. Samuel was glad his friend would be there to hear Zuriel's testimony. He needed an outside voice of reason. Was he crazy for daring to hope that something might happen between them?

He shifted his thoughts back to the party. It was youth group time, and the kids deserved his full attention.

He motioned for everyone to come into the kitchen. The pizza had been delivered, so it was time for them all to pray and chow down. Elizabeth and Zuriel had found each other and were talking happily. This was going to be a great evening.

Samuel ate his pizza with some of the visitors and was floored by the amount of kids that showed up. He prayed for God to use this event to grow the youth group and lead more teens to Christ. He also wanted more than anything for these kids to be grounded in their faith. Samuel would never stop encouraging them to know God more. He didn't want anyone in the group to slip through the cracks while still being labeled a church kid, the way Matt had. His goal was to disciple the youth and teach them how to reach out to others as well. While playing a game of ping pong with some of the guys, he prayed for opportunities to really have an impact on these kids.

Eventually, it was time for the main service to begin, and they all started to gather in the sanctuary. Samuel saw Zuriel walking in with Shannon and Jamie. They were the "drama queens" of the youth group, and he was excited to see them talking to Zuriel. Maybe tonight they would finally put their trust in Jesus. He prayed they would and that God would bless Zuriel's testimony with strength and power.

The music began and Samuel quieted his heart. He had so much to be thankful for. Worshiping God meant so much more to him now than it ever had before, because his heart was fully involved. Samuel stood at the back of the room and could see all the kids singing. He wanted so badly for them to know who God was. He wanted them to find the same joy and peace that he had found. The burden God had laid on his heart hurt him as he surveyed the worshipers in front of him. He prayed for the Holy Spirit to move in their lives as well as his own.

From the corner of his eye he saw Zuriel hugging herself tightly as she sang. It was the most beautiful picture he had ever seen. Samuel turned away and tried to regain his focus on the words of the song he was singing. He would not allow himself to get distracted! The last song was almost over and again he glanced in Zuriel's direction. He saw her drop to her knees. For a moment, he wondered if she was trying to show off or seem spiritual, but when he saw her shoulders shaking, he knew she was sincere. God was going to use her in a huge way tonight; Samuel was sure of that.

Once Shane, the worship leader, had led them in a closing prayer, Samuel took the stage to announce the main speaker. "Welcome, everyone, to the best New Year's Eve party ever! I hope you're all having a good time. Isn't it such a wonderful thing to get together and worship God?"

Samuel paused to make sure Zuriel was ready. She smiled at him and nodded.

"Tonight we have a guest speaker for you. Let me start by asking this: How many of you have had a rough life?" Samuel saw many hands go up. Many of the kids really had gone through a lot, and most of the rest at least felt like they had. "How many of you have lost someone you were very close to?" Hands went up, and he made eye contact with Elizabeth.

"Many of you know that about seven months ago, my younger brother died in a car accident. I hadn't seen him in about five years, so the news was very hard to deal with. It's true that life can be extremely difficult, but we always have an opportunity to turn to God. There is a woman here today who has also been through a lot of hardships in her life but has come out stronger and full of faith as a result. You see, when my brother died, he was engaged to Zuriel Rawson. She is here tonight to tell you her story. Ladies and gentlemen: here's Zuriel!"

Zuriel shyly made her way to the platform as the kids clapped. She looked nervous, but she was smiling brightly. Samuel hadn't seen her smile like that very often. He had mainly seen her during her times of grief and loneliness.

He breathed deeply and began to pray. He had to concentrate on the purpose of this evening. These kids were hungry for fulfillment and in desperate need of truth. He prayed that God would make their hearts receptive to Zuriel's message.

"Hello, everyone, I'm Zuriel, as you just heard. Tonight I want to tell you my story." She began simply and smoothly by explaining her own beginning. Samuel found himself in awe. He hadn't heard the full details of her story yet, and hearing them made him love her all the more. She described her childhood, her family life, her time in high school, and her best friend's drug addiction. It was a story of incredible turmoil. Then Zuriel shared how she fell in love with Matt. The story was beautiful, even though it was tough to hear and painful to remember. Zuriel talked about the grief, the surprise, and the anger she dealt with. When she got to the part about her salvation, the room was silent.

Samuel looked around and saw the whole room leaning in. They were listening closer than he had ever seen them listen before. Zuriel explained salvation in simple terms and encouraged them to talk to God and ask him to come into their lives. She didn't lead a prayer, or even tell them how to pray, she just let a silence hang over them for a few moments. It wasn't a natural silence, though; it was pensive. The way she had spoken had made it impossible to write the message off as a typical invitation.

Samuel found himself reexamining his own heart. It had cost Zuriel a lot to change, because the "right thing to do" hadn't been drilled into her head from childhood. What was God calling him to do? What kind of faith did the next step require?

Zuriel prayed for the group, announcing that if anyone had received Christ, he or she should come to the front of the stage to get some booklets about the meaning of salvation. Samuel watched, almost frightened that no one would respond. Several seconds passed and no one moved. Then he saw Shannon and Jamie stand up and walk hand in hand to the front. On the other side of the sanctuary a few new kids walked up too. Then, from the back row, he saw Harrison and Mitch move to the front. Samuel was overwhelmed with thankfulness. God was saving more souls.

❧

Samuel and Michael unplugged the video-game systems and started stacking up the games, separating which ones were whose.

Samuel felt rushed; he wanted to finish as soon as he could. He hadn't seen Zuriel since she gave her testimony the night before. Right away students had swarmed her, asking her questions and telling their own stories. He was busy handing out bibles and information to those who had been saved. It didn't take long for him to be challenged to a game of Madden Football. One game always led to another, and Samuel had not gotten one second of sleep. He wondered how the girls had fared, but based on the laughing and high-pitched squeals he had heard throughout the night, he guessed Zuriel would be just as tired as he was.

His parents were going to have a New Year's lunch, and he couldn't wait to find Zuriel and ask her if she wanted to come. He didn't want to say good-bye, but he could understand if she was too tired. Still, Samuel prayed she would want to come.

"All right, so now I know why you weren't interested in all the women I recommended!" Michael said playfully.

"Well, she *is* a Christian now, but I just don't know if it's a good idea for us to get together. She hasn't been a Christian for very long yet, and she was going to marry my brother," Samuel explained, confessing his own personal war.

"Man, it's obvious you're in love. You both love God, you both have a knack for youth ministry, and you both suffered because of Matt. I think it's more a question of God's timing and her feelings."

"Yeah, I guess I am in love with her." Samuel liked hearing Michael lay it out with logic for him.

"Well, just keep praying and find out if she returns the same feelings."

"Sounds simple enough." Samuel hoped it really would be that simple.

He brought the last few games out of the room and shut off the light. Many of the kids had already left, but a few were waiting for their parents in the lobby.

Zuriel was sitting in the corner with Jamie. They seemed to be deep in conversation. Samuel decided he should wait to invite her over, but he was so anxious, hoping with all his heart that she would say yes. Shane challenged him to one last game of ping pong before he left, so Samuel took him up on it. Maybe he could work off some of his nervous energy. The game was close, but Samuel managed to win right at the end. He said good-bye to Shane and went back to the lobby. The last kid was leaving, and Samuel waved to him before getting his stuff to bring out to the car.

Suddenly he felt panicked. Where was Zuriel? He rushed outside just in time to see Zuriel putting her things in her car. He walked swiftly over to her. "Hey, were you going to leave without saying good-bye?"

"No," she said playfully, turning around. "I just thought I would put my stuff in the car first." Her blonde hair was down around her shoulders now and blowing gently in the icy breeze. He tried to focus on what he had actually come over to say.

"So, my family is having a New Year's lunch at their house. You want to come?"

"That sounds wonderful, but I really have to get back home so I can take Suzy to visit her family."

Samuel felt immediate disappointment. He really wanted to see her longer. "Aw, well it's nice of you do that for her. My family will miss you, though, and I will too."

Zuriel looked thoughtful and stared at the ground. "Well, maybe I can stop by for an hour or so. I *would* like to see everyone again, but I can't stay for long."

Samuel smiled, thanking God in his heart. Was she coming just because he said he would miss her? He wondered and secretly hoped it was true. "I'm glad to hear it. Do you want to follow me over there?"

"Actually, I want to stop at Matt's gravesite first, if you don't mind."

Samuel reviewed her request in his mind, remembering the reality of the situation. "Of course we can stop there! I'll drive separately and meet you there so you can have some time alone."

"Thank you," Zuriel said solemnly. "I guess I'll see you there." This time she smiled at him as she spoke.

Samuel nodded and headed to his car. He put his stuff in the backseat and drove away. He had been to Matt's grave many times since the funeral. He wasn't in the mood for going to the gravesite again or for grieving, but he knew this was where Zuriel needed to be right now. She needed closure.

Samuel parked close to Matt's grave and got out of the car. He wasn't sure how this was going to go. Zuriel opened her door and got out. Samuel waited, unsure of what to do.

"Do you want to go alone?" he asked, wondering if he should have stayed in the car. She nodded and walked slowly toward the grave. He went back to his car and watched, remembering the day he came back here and found her lying in the grass. He prayed for her and her healing as he waited.

Fifteen minutes passed before Samuel saw her coming back. It was so strange loving someone who had been in love with his dead brother … or might possibly still be in love with said brother.

He got out and met her by her car. "Are you all right?"

"Yeah, I'm okay. It's just weird coming back to this place and remembering everything. I'm definitely healing, but it's still painful. I wish he could have seen me last night, sharing my testimony with all those kids."

Samuel's heart ached. He wanted to be with her so badly, but he knew it wasn't time yet. She was healing more and more each day, but she wasn't quite ready for another relationship. If he really loved her, he would have to comfort her and let her heal on her own time. He tried to prepare himself for the journey ahead. He would have to wait longer for her, but even after all that waiting, she still might not want to be with him. He was Matt's brother, after all.

 *Chapter 24*

Zuriel opened the door for Lena as they entered the apartment. Zuriel watched Lena waddle past her, as she was already six months pregnant. It seemed like the last several months had flown by, but Lena kept complaining that time was going incredibly slow. It was March and spring was finally approaching; however, the Michigan weather was never very consistent with the calendar. There was almost as much snow outside as there had been on New Years' day, when she had finally been able to visit Matt's grave. Zuriel had expected the visit to be very painful and wasn't sure about having Sam there. She feared she would have some sort of breakdown. However, she had surprised herself. It didn't invoke the same pain as it had before. She felt the ache and absence of his companionship, but wasn't without hope. Now that she knew he was with the Lord, his death wasn't nearly as sorrowful. In fact, as strange as it might seem, she was happy for him.

Zuriel wished Matt could have heard her speak at the youth group. He would have been proud of her journey, and relieved that she came to Christ. Zuriel prayed silently that somehow God would let him know. She no longer thought of him as a lover lost. No, she looked on him with a sisterly affection, and a fondness more connected to Christ than to him. He was her friend, a friend that understood redemption. She wanted to talk to him about his conversion and beliefs more than she longed for his kiss. She knew that if she were to fall in love again, things would have to be different. She had become a new person after his death; completely new. Her old self had been in love, but this new person had a different notion of what love was. She wasn't in love with Matt anymore, and it was a great relief to her when she made that realization. Zuriel had been falling in love with someone much more important: Jesus Christ. She was amazed that the more she learned about his love, the more she wanted to know. She was studying the Bible like she never had before and was becoming more confident as a result.

Her phone vibrated in her pocket and she smiled, hoping it was Sam. Sam didn't text her often, but would occasionally send updates on the youth group and ask her how she was doing. She really appreciated everything he had done for her. Zuriel opened her phone hoping to find out what was new with him. When she saw that the text message was actually from Drew, she rolled her eyes as she read it.

Hey. When are we going to hang out? Let's see a movie.

Zuriel wanted to believe he was finally over her, but now here he was, back at it again. He was furious when he found out she actually met with Matt's old youth pastor, John Carter. He was intimidated by anything relating to her ex-fiancé. Thankfully Drew had given up on converting her back to atheism. His weary ranting and teasing was not missed. She just wished he would give up trying to convince her to be his date.

Zuriel tried to figure out how to get out of this movie night. She replied: *Okay. I think Lena, Suzy, and I are free next week.* She hoped this would be a kind way of letting him know that a date was not something she was interested in. She hoped …

Her phone vibrated again, almost as soon as she had sent the message. *I don't want them to come. Darn you, girl, when will you get it?*

Zuriel got it all too well and knew his pursuit was strictly romantic. She had tried to explain her disinterest many times.

Lena laughed from across the room, causing her swollen stomach to shake. Lena had all sorts of ideas how to get rid of Drew, but Zuriel thought they were too extreme. Eventually Drew would just have to give up. Zuriel squeezed her phone against her chest, wishing Sam had been the one to text her. He never said anything out of line and always kept their conversations focused on day-to-day life or on what God was doing for them. It was refreshing, non-threatening, and comfortable. Drew didn't have the ability to listen or even just to talk without trying to get more out of her than what she was willing to give. She begrudgingly replied to his message.

I do get it, Drew. We've already talked about this. We're friends. Nothing else!

Zuriel pressed send and felt a pang of guilt. Her text felt harsh, but enough was enough. She had tried to convince herself that being nice about it might bring an opportunity to lead him to Christ. She had almost decided to go on a date with him for the chance to win him over to God. Suzy's boyfriend, Fred, heard about her plans and quickly advised her against it. His older brother like advice was often forceful, but he did have her best interest in mind. When several minutes went by without a reply from Drew, a smile crept on her face. Zuriel wondered if she might finally be free of Drew's pursuits.

"Ha! Victory!" she said in a mocking way.

"What did the old thorn want this time?" Lena asked, fluffing pillows around the lump on her stomach.

"A date. Real shocker, I know!"

"He's still trying to make a move?" Suzy exclaimed, laughing as she came out of the bathroom sporting pajama pants, a tank top, and wet hair.

"Sadly, yes, but I don't think he will in the future. I reminded him again that we're just friends." Zuriel took a seat on the living room couch.

Suzy followed, and all three of them were squeezed together.

"Good for you! So Fred's advice is finally sticking," Lena teased.

"Maybe it's starting to. I don't know. I feel a little guilty for hurting Drew's feelings," Zuriel sheepishly admitted.

"Oh, that's ridiculous. If he had feelings he would have cared about yours a long time ago!" Suzy interjected.

"True, but all guys aren't like Fred. Some of us might have to settle for a lack of feeling." Zuriel chuckled, raising her eyebrows at Suzy.

"Thank you, Suzy, for knowing one of the only decent bachelors around!" Lena added, pulling Suzy's hand over her belly to feel the baby kick.

"There is a lack of decent men in the world. I am lucky!" Suzy agreed.

"What about Sam? He's a good guy, isn't he?" Zuriel remarked before she was aware of what she was saying.

"Oh, that's right." Suzy jeered. "So now you're planning on being in a relationship too, are you?"

Zuriel was stunned by Suzy's question. A relationship? With Sam? She didn't think that her feelings for him were like that. She liked him and thought he was attractive, but he was Matt's brother, for pity's sake! How would that ever work out?

"No way! I only brought him up because he's a good guy."

"A good guy who would be perfect for you," Lena clarified, winking at her.

"I think that would be totally weird!" Zuriel said overconfidently. She didn't like where this conversation was going.

"Well, I guess it might be a little weird since he is Matt's brother. Actually, it would probably be even weirder for him than for you," Lena conceded, finally introducing some sense into the discussion.

"Yeah, I can't imagine him being okay with dating his brother's ex. He's a good, Christian guy too, whereas I've done drugs and partied like nobody's business. He needs a pure, churchy girl who has a past that would be better suited to the things he's trying to do for God," Zuriel rationalized. Hearing herself say it was sad. She wasn't sure if it was because she wished she hadn't done those things or because those things were preventing Sam from being a prospective date. Either way, she felt a growing sense of insecurity.

"But, Zuriel, if he wasn't Matt's brother, and you had grown up in church, would you be considering him?" Suzy put her hand on Zuriel's shoulder and tilted her head in a reprimanding glare.

Zuriel tried to think things through. It all seemed so silly. She knew the most important part of a relationship was putting God first, and she knew Sam would do that.

"I guess that since he's one of the few decent guys, he would be a possibility, but only a possibility! It would never happen," she confessed, feeling uncomfortable.

"Aha! So there is a glimmer of something!" Suzy exclaimed with a laugh.

"Well, only time will tell," Lena chimed in. "I wonder what he thinks about you. I mean, he does text you, doesn't he?"

"Yes, but not very often. He's a pastor, so of course he checks up on people," Zuriel said.

"But he's also a man, so of course he checks up on *attractive* people like you!" Suzy exclaimed, surprising them all.

"Suzan!"

"Oh, please, Zuriel! You have to consider that no matter how good a guy is, he is still a guy. There is a strong chance that he likes you if he's taking time out of his busy schedule to text you," Lena logically explained. "So if you aren't interested, you might want to be careful what you say or how far you let this thing go. He might have a crush on you."

Zuriel thought about Lena's words and was mortified. She didn't want to lead anyone on, and Fred had explained to her just how easy that was to do. She had already failed in that area with Drew. Zuriel wondered if texting Sam was such a good idea after all. She felt her phone vibrate in her pocket and had a gut feeling Sam had just texted her. She decided not to check it. She didn't want her friends to know, and she wondered if she should be short with him anyway. Maybe she needed to be more careful. She wasn't ready for a relationship right now.

"I guess I should be careful. I just won't talk to him as much," Zuriel said.

"We'll see how that goes," Suzy teased, playfully elbowing her.

The conversation moved on to other things, but Zuriel felt like her phone was burning in her pocket. What did Sam really think of her? Why did he text her once a week anyway? Was it really because he was her friend, or was he interested in becoming something more? It didn't seem possible because he hadn't made a move. He wasn't hinting around for more either—he was just there, always available to offer his concern and prayers. She could hardly consider that a pursuit, but at the same time it was the most genuine love she had ever received from a guy. He seemed to be only saying and doing things for her benefit, nothing more. Zuriel wasn't sure what it all meant. She decided to pray about the subject and text him less in the meantime. She had never considered the situation from her friends' perspective before. What if he really did like her? Zuriel was going to visit her dad next week. Maybe she should talk to him about it. She had never shared anything like this with him before, and she wondered if he could help.

Peter Rawson sat next to Zuriel on the front porch of his folks' old house. He was happier than he had been in a long time. His daughter had long been a stranger to him and a reminder of the woman who had broken his heart. Now, however, they had some sort of connection. They both knew what it was like to fall in love, only to lose the object of their affections. He couldn't deny there was something else going on too, though. It wasn't just their common bond of love once lost; no, Zuriel had drastically changed in the last several months. No longer was she the selfish, fearful brat he had once thought her to be. She had become a genuinely loving and good person, so much so that he often felt guilty when he was around her. He was thankful she had somehow turned out to be a good person despite everything she had gone through. She wasn't going to live a waste of a life like he had. There was something about her that he greatly coveted: she had hope for the future.

Peter knew he was rough around the edges, and he had become very bitter. He was angry with God, Amour, his parents, and even Zuriel. Now it felt as if his heart was softening a little, but he wasn't sure if he liked it or not. All he knew is that he felt so relieved that his daughter hadn't disowned him forever. When he thought about how many times he had treated his own parents badly, he felt a twinge of guilt. He was glad that he hadn't left them alone, despite the many times he had wanted to. People always said that what goes around comes around, so maybe he was being rewarded for sticking with them? He wasn't sure, but it didn't matter. He would enjoy seeing his daughter whenever she wanted to come over.

"Hey, Dad. Did you ever think about getting into a new relationship after Mom left?" Zuriel asked him.

He didn't feel like talking about this, but he also knew she wouldn't have brought it up without a reason. She used to bring things like that up to cause him pain, but not since her fiancé's accident.

"Yeah, I did think about it, but I was too angry and didn't want to get hurt again."

"Oh."

Her short response implied that she was disappointed. "Why do you ask? Are you gonna try to get with another guy?"

"No!" she abruptly exclaimed, but then began again with a completely different tone of voice. "Well, I don't know. I was just trying to figure it out. I'm not in love or anything; I'm just wondering when it will be a healthy time for me to get back into life."

"You're healing pretty fast. It sounds like you're already back to life."

"I guess I mean I'm wondering if finding a husband is okay. I don't want to betray Matt, but I really am over him. I love him, but not in the way that I plan on loving my future husband, if I do ever get married."

Her words startled him. He didn't understand why she wanted a husband. Wasn't losing a fiancé hard enough? She seemed almost happier after Matt died, which didn't make any sense whatsoever. He wondered what was wrong with her. "It does seem like you got over Matt pretty quick."

"He died when I was a different person, Dad. When I dated him and got engaged, I wasn't right inside. This new person doesn't want to go back. I don't know who I would have become if the accident hadn't happened, but that doesn't matter. I am who I am, and my life's goals are different now. I miss Matt, but I know God has bigger plans for me than mourning his loss for my whole life."

Peter was amazed by her wisdom. He wished he were as smart as she and could offer some good advice. She knew herself—who she had been and who she was becoming. He wished he knew that much about himself.

"I envy the fact that you know who you are. I don't think you'll have a problem living a good life."

"I don't want to just live a good life, though. I really want to do what God wants me to do. I just wonder if getting in a relationship, even if it's with a Christian guy, would be a part of that plan."

"You're always so concerned about what God wants now. I don't get it." He scoffed. He marveled why "God's will" was suddenly so important to her. Religion had changed her for the better, but he had seen so many before her change for the worse.

"Aren't you concerned about what's going to happen to you when you die, Dad? You've seen what God has done in my life. You've seen how much happier he's made me. Don't you want him to make you feel better too?" Zuriel's eyebrows narrowed as she spoke.

Peter felt pangs of sorrow rush through his chest. He respected the person she had become very much, but he seriously doubted there was any hope for him. "Zuriel, you know I could never have your faith."

"I don't want you to have mine. You would be so much happier if you had your own!"

Peter rolled his eyes and muttered a few curses under his breath. He felt uncomfortable. "Happiness for me is that you're okay. I don't care about God; I care about you. I was hurt by so many people and God did nothing to stop it."

"I know I hurt you a lot, Dad, but God stopped me from continuing to hurt you even more, didn't he?"

Her point made sense, and he hadn't thought of it that way before. God had given him a new daughter. Was God capable of giving her a new father? She deserved as much. "I don't know about this God stuff, Zuriel, but you've definitely changed for the better, I'll give you that much. I've just refused to heal for so long that I don't think it'll happen overnight."

Zuriel smiled, and he felt glad that she liked what he said. As much as he hated the idea of going to church, he agreed he would tag along once or twice for her sake.

"Thanks, Dad. That means a lot to me."

"I know. I'll come with you to church, I guess, just as long as you don't tell your grandparents. I don't want them to start giving me religious crap too." He smiled playfully and Zuriel laughed.

"Dad, I just don't know what to do. Do you think I should open myself up to a relationship?"

"Zuriel, that's up to you. Only you can know when you're ready."

"I don't think I do." She was staring at her feet, and he realized how much this question had been eating at her. He had never been good at these types of conversations, and he hated being reminded of his past love life. His head began to ache as she continued.

"Before all this, I only liked a guy if he was fun and attractive. Now, though, I realize those things don't last and I should choose a guy because of his soul rather than his appearance. I just don't know how to go about all this. I wonder if it's happening too soon."

"Zuriel I won't pretend to understand this new person you've turned into or whatever psychology you're using for picking a lover. I just know that you shouldn't do what I did. Don't lock the rest of the world out. Just make sure you find what you want and don't compromise." Peter's heart was pounding. He felt that for once he was being a good father. He had finally given advice that was worth something. When he saw his daughter in thoughtful contemplation of what he had just said, he was proud of himself.

"Well, there is a guy who might be attracted to me, but I don't know what to think about him," she said shyly.

"Is he a good guy?"

"Yeah, he's incredible! He loves God, he's a gentleman, and he loves his family. I mean, he's a youth pastor, for goodness' sake!"

"Then what's holding you back? You seem like you really like him a lot."

"Dad, its Matt's brother, Sam! I can't fall for him!" Zuriel's expression had become agitated, and he again felt inadequate to handle this.

He was bad with emotions. It did seem like it would be a strange situation, if this worked out, but Peter liked Sam. He was a good guy, and he was concerned about Zuriel being taken care of. He knew that Sam would rise to the challenge if given the opportunity. "Sam is definitely a good guy. That's for sure."

"Yeah, I wish you knew him more. Then you could tell me what to do."

"He does call from time to time, and our conversations have been good ones."

Zuriel was dumbfounded. She stared at him blankly for several seconds. "He calls you?"

"Yeah. Well, he called me twice. He was just checking in on us all."

"I can't believe this." She fidgeted with her hair and paced back and forth on the porch.

"It's true. He called. I like him." He chuckled, fascinated by her response.

Zuriel plopped back down on the plastic lawn chair. She shook her head in wonder.

Peter wondered why it was such a big deal. He would never understand women!

 *Chapter 25*

Zuriel watched the kids running through the church yard looking for eggs. They were so adorable. On Easter Sunday, one of the little girls had prayed that Easter would come again very soon because she loved candy so much. It gave Zuriel an idea. Since all the Easter candy was on sale, she bought a bunch of it and gave them all Easter for the second week in a row. It was so fun to watch their excitement.

"This was a good idea, Zuriel. They love it," Lena said, leaning against the brick church.

"Yeah, it sure looks that way," Zuriel replied with a smile.

"Oh, I think your phone was going off earlier. I forgot to tell you."

"I'll check it when we get back inside."

"I brought it with me." Lena giggled, handing the phone over.

Zuriel saw an unopened message from Sam. Zuriel looked at Lena and attempted to send her a reprimanding glare.

"So you checked to see who the text was from and thought that this was going to be important?"

"Well, I just thought you would want to know," Lena clarified.

"I'm not leading him on, remember? I've been texting him less and creating more space," Zuriel explained, annoyed that her friend was making it more difficult.

"I know. But you still get excited when he does send you a message, whether or not you reply."

Zuriel rolled her eyes, pretending it wasn't true, but she knew she liked getting his texts. She had to stay focused, though; she didn't want to create a relationship that would lead to nowhere. Her heart could only take so much heartbreak. Letting herself get attached to someone else right now was a recipe for disaster. She opened the text. *Hey, Zuriel, are you doing okay? Can I call you after church?*

Zuriel read the message again and was surprised. Of course she was doing okay; why was he so concerned? And to top that off, he wanted to talk after church. She felt nervous. What was going on? She hoped everything was okay and that nothing had gone wrong. She had texted Jamie from youth group that morning, so at least she knew the kids were fine. Was it his family? What was going on?

She quickly texted a reply and shoved her phone into her pocket. She would hear the whole story after church. She dreaded hearing what he might have to say, but at the same time she couldn't wait to talk with him again. Zuriel gathered the kids together to head back inside; their parents would be picking them up soon.

"So are you going to tell me what the text said?" Lena asked, after the last kid was picked up.

"He asked if I was all right and if he could call me."

"Seriously?"

"Yeah, so he is going to call me after he gets home from church." Zuriel felt weird saying it out loud. She wasn't sure why. She didn't have a problem talking on the phone; it's just that she would be talking to Sam.

"So, does that mean you aren't coming to lunch with us?" Lena asked, and then winked dramatically.

"I guess not," Zuriel replied, trying not to smile.

They gathered up their things and Zuriel left alone. She had been looking forward to having lunch with the Bible study group, but this felt more important. She was excited to talk with Sam again. Because Zuriel wasn't texting Sam as much, she hadn't heard about what was going on in his life recently. She didn't initiate conversations anymore, and her replies were always kept short.

As she entered her apartment, she realized how much she missed hearing his voice. It had been about a month of this limited contact, but it felt like much longer. Zuriel felt silly. Why did she care so much? Why was she so excited to talk with this guy?

Zuriel pulled out a can of Campbell's soup and poured it into a bowl before throwing it in the microwave. Usually she heated it on the stove, but today she was in a hurry. Sam might call her at any moment. She grabbed a spoon and snuggled up on the couch, pushing Lena's pillow and blankets to the side. She tried to eat slowly and normally but found herself eating quickly and glancing at her phone every few seconds. Before she knew it, she was finished eating and had been staring out the window for almost thirty minutes. She hated waiting.

Her phone rang. Her heart rate quickened and she answered uneasily.

"Zuriel, it's so good to hear your voice."

"It's good to hear yours too. Is everything okay? Your text made me kinda nervous." She felt awkward. She hadn't planned on voicing her concerns so quickly.

"Oh yeah, things are fine. I was mostly calling to see if everything is okay with you. I haven't really heard from you lately, and I just wanted to make sure you were doing all right."

"Yes, I'm doing fine." Zuriel laughed a little, finding it ironic that she had been so afraid. Everything was fine, thank God. "Things have been going really well. Today I had my Sunday school kids do another Easter egg hunt. One of the little girls prayed that Easter would come again soon, which gave me the idea to have it again."

She heard his laughter over the phone. Was her heart swelling? She had forgotten how much she liked the sound of his voice and his laughter. "That's a great idea. I'm sure they loved that."

"I think the candy they found is what made it a good time."

"Candy is always a good time for me." Sam chuckled, but this time, Zuriel sensed his laugh was forced. It seemed like he had something else to say. What had he really called about?

Suddenly she felt anxious all over again. She couldn't wait for the conversation to end. "Yeah, I kept some candy for myself too," she awkwardly replied.

"Very nice." There was silence.

Zuriel breathed deeply and waited.

"Zuriel, you know I care about you. I need to know if I did something to offend you."

What was he saying?

"I'm not sure how you feel about me ... I guess that's not really the issue. I just want to know if I did something wrong."

"What do you mean? I don't understand," Zuriel said, knowing she probably sounded stupid, but she had no idea what was going on. Why would he think he had offended her? Did he think he had done something wrong? She thought about how she hadn't been texting him as much. Had he really been paying such close attention to her texts that he actually missed them?

"Well, it just seemed like you were possibly avoiding my messages," he began, soulfully. "I just wanted to make sure everything was okay. If you don't want me to text you, I understand. I just wanted to ask and make sure things were cool."

Zuriel's face felt like it was on fire. She didn't want him to think she was avoiding him on purpose. She was, but not for the reason he thought. Did she even want to tell him the reason?

"You've done nothing to offend me, Sam. I'm doing fine. I appreciate your texts, and always have." She wondered if she was being too vague, but what else was she supposed to say? She couldn't just explain to him that she didn't want to lead him on, could she?

"Are you sure everything's okay?"

"Yes, I'm definitely sure. I've been pretty busy these last few weeks trying to work out my priorities." Zuriel regretted her words as soon as she said them. She had made it sound like Sam was a low priority, which wasn't completely false. She just hated the way he would take it. He probably thought she didn't care about him anymore. This was nothing at all against him, though; it was entirely about her feelings.

"I see. I guess I understand." He spoke solemnly, and Zuriel couldn't stand it. She didn't know what to do or how to explain things better to make the situation right. She wanted to say something but was too afraid to talk; she didn't know her feelings well enough yet. Zuriel didn't want this misunderstanding to lead to another one. She would rather have him think she was uninterested than to assume that she was. However, Zuriel was horrified of losing Sam's friendship to either her feelings or to her lack of communication. He was just a very good friend—right?

"I'm trying so hard to figure out what the right thing to do is in every situation. I don't know the answer to that yet, so for now I've been spending most of my time trying to learn what God wants for me. I don't mean to isolate myself from you, though, or from anyone else either." Zuriel paused, unsure of what she was trying to say. She prayed that he would understand. "There are questions that I need to find the answer to. I didn't mean to make you worry about me, and I don't want you to feel like I don't appreciate you. You've been an amazing encouragement and one of the truest friends I've ever had." Zuriel bit her lip, waiting for his response. What must he be thinking about her now?

"Zuriel, just do what you need to do. I'll be praying for you as always."

"Thank you, Sam. You have no idea what that means to me." Zuriel realized her eyes were watering. She didn't know exactly why she was crying, but she felt like a horrible person. He had appeared to understand what she was trying to say, but she was terrified that he didn't really. Sam was Matt's brother, so in a sense, he was her brother too wasn't he? She didn't think she liked it that way. Zuriel knew in her heart that she had contemplated the idea of him being more than a friend or brother to her. She felt like it was impossible for them to ever have a relationship, though, so instead of just being his friend, she had put more distance between them.

"If you ever need anything, or if you just need to talk, let me know. I'm always here for you," he offered somberly.

"Thanks. You're an amazing guy, Sam. I hope you know that." Zuriel said the words, believing them to be true with all her heart. She wished the absolute best for him.

"Thanks, Zuriel. You're pretty amazing yourself."

Zuriel felt shy now. He was complimenting her, and that meant a lot. She was thankful for a friend like him, but his kindness made her feel even worse for the space she had put between them. She tried to focus on the purpose for the distance she had created. It was important for her to make sure that she wasn't leading anyone on, and that she was focusing only on what God wanted her to do.

"You're sweet," Zuriel said, wondering what to say next. "How is the youth group doing?"

"Oh, good! Everyone is growing in their faith, and we've had some new kids start coming too. We've got youth group tonight, so that will be pretty exciting."

"I'm glad to hear it. You have a great group there."

"I'm blessed, that's for sure." He spoke without emotion.

Zuriel wondered if he was okay. He seemed tired, and not at all like his usual self. She hoped it wasn't because of her. "I'm planning on coming to your sister's wedding next month. I'm excited for her. She is an awesome girl!" Zuriel exclaimed, trying to brighten the mood.

"Yeah, it's coming up pretty fast. Everyone is rushing around making last-minute plans. I think Michael is the only calm one."

"I'll bet; that'll be great to see." Zuriel felt that her words were hollow. The silence between them lingered, and she felt her chest tighten up. Why did she feel this way?

"Well, I'm glad you're doing okay, Zuriel. I should probably let you go. I have to prepare for tonight." He seemed desperate to get off the phone.

"Okay, well, it was good talking. I guess I'll talk to you later then."

"Sounds good to me. Bye."

"Bye," Zuriel whispered as she hung up and slid her phone into her pocket. She felt an overwhelming desire to cry. She didn't like how the conversation had gone. She didn't understand her own feelings, and she felt that she had just ruined any chances of having a relationship with him. What had she been thinking? She wasn't sure of her goals or of what she was even trying to figure out.

Suddenly, a new emotion presented itself. Zuriel was afraid. She was afraid of losing her friendship with Sam. She wished he could know how much his texts meant to her. She wished he knew how much she thought about him and the things he said. She wanted him to know, but she didn't know how much would be too much to say. The fact that he was Matt's brother still made things complicated, and she couldn't afford to be attracted to anyone right now, especially Sam. Still, she was alarmed by how much the conversation had shaken her up. Zuriel was concerned that he might not text her anymore. She had certainly given him the impression that she didn't want to text or talk. Her goal had been accomplished, but she had broken her own heart in the process.

Zuriel tried to pray, but all she could think about was Sam. She hated how things had turned out, and she felt like she had just been dumped—but why? Sam was just a friend. He was just a brother, or so she had convinced herself, but Zuriel knew he had become something much more. He was the godliest man she knew, and the kindest and gentlest. If she ignored the fact that he was Matt's brother, he would be the most logical person for her to fall in love with. Yet this single fact was making her question what she should do. No matter how hard she tried, she couldn't stand the idea of only talking with him every once in a while. Just thinking about it made her miss him.

A warm tear slid down her face. The reality of how much she cared about him dawned on her like never before. Was she in love? This wasn't the feeling she had when she fell in love with Matt. No, this was different—it was deeper. This had nothing to do with Sam's appearance, although he was very handsome. This had everything to do with his heart for God and his love for people. She wanted to marry someone just like him. She had been in love with the idea of Sam for so long that she began to wonder if she had really been in love with Sam himself. Suddenly the fact that he was Matt's brother didn't matter at all. She knew she loved Sam.

Zuriel started to laugh, and a few more tears glided down her face. She was in love! The realization was overwhelming and wonderful. She was in love with Samuel Lowell! Not the shaking, insecure love she had felt for Matt, but the kind that ran deep into her soul. She wanted to talk to him, to lead the youth with him, to know him better, and to love him more. Zuriel wondered what she should do. She thought about their phone conversation and knew immediate action was necessary. Maybe she didn't need to vocally declare her love for him, but she had to at least let him see that she cared.

She decided she would go to youth group that very evening to surprise him. She could walk in a little bit late to make sure he'd notice her. Then she would wait patiently until it was over so they could talk. She had no idea what she would say, but she knew she had to be there. Zuriel had to make sure Sam knew she wasn't ever going to avoid him again. She loved him very much—so much more than she had ever thought possible.

Chapter 26

Samuel sat in his office and tried to talk himself into getting up. He was disappointed. He had been trying to wait patiently for Zuriel to be ready to start a new relationship, but was beginning to feel discouraged. For the last three months they had texted each other roughly once a week for no more than an hour each time. It wasn't anything special, though; just a basic conversation to keep their friendship alive. He was thankful for their discussions, despite the fact that they were so infrequent. Samuel determined to do what was best for her, no matter the cost.

Recently, however, Zuriel had stopped replying to most of his messages. Even when she did reply, her responses were always short and to the point. At first he thought that she was just busy, but when three weeks went by without hearing anything from her, he started to get concerned. Samuel felt that he was losing ground. He knew it would probably be best to just let some time go by and maybe talk to her at his sister's wedding, but that seemed so far away. He imagined her showing up with another guy hanging onto her arm and started to panic. His situation was like that of a high school guy hoping to get a date for prom.

Zuriel didn't have to be romantically interested in him, but he begged God that she would be. The fact of the matter was this: Zuriel was a beautiful woman who genuinely loved God. These two attributes alone would make her highly attractive to any churchgoing bachelor. Samuel guessed she probably thought of him as baggage associated with her old life and possibly didn't want to commute from Detroit. He knew he would probably never have a chance with her, but he was still very hurt when she stopped texting him. Didn't their friendship mean more to her than this? He had planned on just waiting it out, but he couldn't stand it. He needed to know what was going on.

So Samuel had called her and investigated further. She hadn't revealed much to him, other than the fact that her feelings of friendship toward him hadn't changed. She didn't seem like she was ready for any relationships yet, but he wondered if it was wise for him to assume that. Waiting around for a few more months might profit him something, but he wondered what the point would be. Was she getting closer to another guy? Is that why she was backing away from him? He just didn't understand.

Samuel felt like a fool for coddling his feelings for Zuriel. He should of have let them die instead of holding on to a vain hope for something more. He prayed that God would give him the strength to teach youth group tonight, because he definitely wasn't in the mood. His lesson was about how Christ submitted to God in everything. Given his current circumstances, he knew it would be a convicting sermon to preach. Was he himself willing to submit to God and let Zuriel go?

As he left his office and walked into the sanctuary, Samuel offered up a silent prayer. The worship band was practicing, and a few of the guys from youth group were playing hacky sack in the corner. He gathered his notes and took a few breaths. Christ's strength would be made perfect in his weakness tonight. Samuel held on to that promise as the kids began to arrive. He had a feeling he would never again think of the teens' relationship drama as petty. How could his heart be breaking like this when he wasn't even in a relationship?

The worship service began. Samuel stood in the front row and tried to concentrate on the words he was singing. He felt so broken inside, and it made him feel guilty. His life was going really well, and God was doing amazing things, so he shouldn't be hurting like this. The pain of missing Zuriel wasn't anything like the pain of dealing with Matt's death, but it still hurt much more than he could have expected. He would continue to be patient, though. He needed to believe God had someone else for him and that everything was going to be okay. The group sang "I surrender all," and Samuel felt his burden slowly lifting. God knew what he wanted, but more importantly, God knew what he needed. If that meant that Samuel would be single for the rest of his life in order to do God's will, he would accept it.

Samuel stood on the platform and welcomed everyone. He asked everyone to bow their heads and pray with him. "Dear God, thank you for this day. Thank you so much for bringing us together to worship you. We are so grateful that we can bring our burdens to you, no matter what they are. We surrender everything to you. Help us obey you in all that we do. We love you so much, Father. Amen."

Samuel closed his prayer and opened his Bible to find the Scripture for the evening. He heard the door close a little too loudly and looked up, wondering which one of his hooligans was disrupting the service. To his surprise, he saw a young woman walking to the back of the room and taking a seat.

Samuel's heart stopped and he could hardly believe what he was seeing. Was that Zuriel? It was! His breath caught in his throat and he exhaled slowly, trying to focus on flipping through his Bible. What was Zuriel doing here? What had made her drive all this way, and that without telling him or warning him? His adrenaline was racing full throttle and he prayed for strength. How was he going to teach now?

Finally the words came, and he began to talk about submitting to God no matter what. Jesus obeyed to the point of death and Samuel prayed that, as followers of Jesus, the youth would be willing to do the same. Living life without Zuriel was hardly as bad as dying on a cross, but a small part of him wondered which form of torment he would prefer. Her hair was draped gracefully around her shoulders, and her perfect face looked lost in thought. Her Bible was sitting on her lap, and he used it as a reminder to concentrate on the lesson he was teaching. Seeing her was almost too good to be true, but he was afraid of what the reason might be. He could at least find out additional details about their talk this morning. Maybe there was more to the story than what she had told him.

Samuel finally finished his message and closed with prayer. He felt guilty for being happy that his own lesson had ended. He was just dying to talk with Zuriel. As he gathered his things, many of the teens swarmed her. He would have to wait even longer now. He quickly tried to think of ways to make more time to talk with her, so that they wouldn't be interrupted by anyone else. He wondered if getting coffee would be too much like a date. Once again Samuel felt like a lost child. He needed to be patient, but he was certainly ready to act when the time came.

Samuel talked with some of the guys while he waited. He looked over at Zuriel, and their eyes met. They both smiled, and he saw her blush. She was blushing? It was torture to even consider that she might like him after all.

She turned away shyly, and he was even more excited to talk to her. The kids finally cleared away, and he quickly walked over to her.

"Well, this is certainly a pleasant surprise!"

"It is for me too," she replied, still blushing.

"What made you decide to come?" he asked, wondering if he was being too direct.

"I just thought I would come and visit, I guess. It's been a while since I've been here."

"It's great that you came. I think everyone has missed you."

"Well, I've missed you too." She stopped suddenly and looked embarrassed. "I've missed everyone."

Samuel smiled. She seemed different. Was she possibly flirting with him a little?

"Well, do you want to grab some coffee? Maybe we could catch up? I know we talked earlier, but, you know ..." Samuel felt silly. He hadn't actually planned on asking her out, but here he was. He tried to justify it in his mind. They were just good friends catching up, right? However, he couldn't ignore his burning desire to have more than just a friendship with her. She looked amazing. Oh, how he prayed she would say yes.

"That sounds great!" Her words were surprising and beautiful to hear. Something must have happened that afternoon. He wasn't sure what it could possibly be, but he knew that God answered prayers. Hope was not lost after all!

"Let's meet at Starbucks then. We can probably go in about twenty minutes."

"Okay." Zuriel smiled and would've said more, but she was abruptly attacked with hugs as some of the other girls discovered her presence.

Samuel turned to find Shane standing there smiling at him. "What?" he asked, afraid Shane had been standing there the whole time.

"You're going on a date tonight, aren't you?" Shane asked, grinning and raising his eyebrows.

"We're just going to catch up and hang out."

"Okay, but drive separately, don't stay out too late, and keep your hands to yourself, son!" Shane lectured playfully.

Samuel laughed and nudged Shane's shoulder with his fist. "Yes, sir!"

Time seemed to crawl as Samuel gathered his things and headed to the lobby. Zuriel was waiting, examining the artwork on the walls. He smiled as he approached.

Zuriel returned his smile and said, "These are really neat."

"Yeah, there are a few artists here in the church. They donated these paintings."

"I love them all!"

Samuel watched her admire the art and knew his heart was melting. He had only seen glimpses of her peppy, happy side up to this point. It was tremendously attractive.

"Well, shall we go? You can follow me there?"

"Okay. Sounds good." She nodded.

They got into their separate cars and Samuel pulled out. He thanked God out loud and tried to calm his nerves. Only a few hours ago, he had lost any chance of ever being with Zuriel, and now they were going to get coffee. It was almost too good to be true! He tried to be sober-minded about it, but he could barely contain his excitement. They pulled in and he jumped out of the car as quickly as he could. She must have been pretty excited too, because she beat him to the door. Samuel hurried ahead to get the door for her. He was determined to win her heart.

They went to the front counter and Zuriel ordered her drink. He interrupted the cashier to let her know that he was paying for them both. Zuriel quietly said thank you, and he saw her cheeks get rosy again. Tonight was the big chance that Samuel had been waiting and praying for. He picked up his mocha and they found a table close to a window.

"Thanks for the coffee. It was really sweet of you," she said.

"No problem. It was really sweet of you to come tonight! I think the whole youth group was really glad to see you again."

"I'm glad I came. I really like talking to all of them. They're all so much better off than I was at that age. I guess it just makes me want to help them even more."

"Well, you're the perfect gal to do it." He caught a half-smile and felt even more relaxed. It was okay for him to just enjoy spending time with her and trust God for the rest. God had already blessed him beyond his wildest dreams.

"It's really cool that you're working with the kids like this. I think John Carter would be proud."

"I hope so. Thank you so much, by the way, for convincing me to go see him. He took my dad out for breakfast recently. It's just amazing to see how God continues to heal people."

"I'm glad." Zuriel took a sip of her coffee and then stared down at her cup.

"The whole thing has caused me become a much better youth pastor," Samuel continued. "My dream is for the kids to really take ownership of their faith. I can only pray God will keep using me to help them."

"I think he will. That's a very good dream to have." She took another sip and looked out the window. She seemed thoughtful, like there was something else on her mind.

"What about you? What's your dream?" He wanted to get inside her head and find out what she was thinking.

"I would love to help other girls and young women. I wish so much that I had followed God sooner! I just want people to know more about the true meaning of love. The story of what happened with Matt and me is such a powerful one that I feel like I should be sharing it more often."

"It's true. You did a really good job sharing with the youth group on New Year's Eve. I think God has just begun to use you." Samuel spoke while praying in his heart that he would be able to see God use her with his own eyes.

"Thanks. I'm glad you asked me to do it. It got me out of my comfort zone, but it was definitely good for me."

"You have a way of getting me out my comfort zone too. I will never forget that day we met in the woods." Samuel remembered when he first saw her there and how much he had wanted to run away. However, through that simple conversation, he had been convicted and started a healing process that changed him forever.

"I remember that too. I'm sure I must have said some things that hurt you very much that day."

"Oh no, it was all deserved. God used you even before you knew Christ." He looked at her, wondering what to do. He was talking fast, and probably sounded nervous. He was throwing out "youth pastor" compliments and realized how out of touch he was with women his own age.

He wanted to bring up their earlier phone conversation, but he wasn't sure how. "I'm sorry for calling you so suddenly the way I did. I didn't mean to assume that something was wrong. You don't have to keep me updated on everything that goes on in your life if you don't want to. You are obviously doing really well."

She avoided eye contact and held her coffee tightly. "No, I'm sorry." Zuriel confessed. "I've been really scared of getting to know new people, mainly guys, because I didn't want to betray Matt or lose his memory. I've healed so much recently, though, and I know the person I fell in love with isn't the same person I want to love now. It's been a confusing journey for me. I'm sorry I made you worry about me."

Samuel felt honored that she had shared that part of her heart with him. What did she mean by "Matt isn't the same person I want to love now"? Could she be referring to him?

"I understand. If you would rather I didn't text you, I really won't be offended. I know I acted immaturely about it this afternoon. You just do what you need to do," Sam said, trying to sound sincere.

"Oh no, please don't take anything I said this afternoon seriously!" Zuriel said quickly. She paused and took a breath, proceeding more slowly. "Your texts mean a lot to me. I really don't want to lose you just because I'm scared of getting close to someone."

Samuel couldn't believe his ears. She wanted him to text her? She had stopped texting him because she was afraid of getting close? Was she afraid that he would die just like his brother had? Had she only been keeping her distance because she didn't want to betray Matt? Her side of the story was starting to make sense, and Samuel was overwhelmed with excitement. She was more interested in him than he had ever dreamed could be true.

"Zuriel, I'm not going anywhere. God will protect us both, and he has the ability to lead us where he wants us to go. I know this probably feels weird to you right now, especially because of our relationships with Matt. We can get to know each other as slowly as you want to." Samuel hoped he hadn't spoken out of turn. He was in love, and his willingness to wait even longer for her if he had to was full proof of that fact.

"I think getting to know each other better would be a good idea." Zuriel almost whispered the words. She was staring at her coffee again, clearly trying to disguise the intensity of her resolve, as well as trying to hide her blush from Samuel's gaze.

He thanked God over and over again for giving him this day. In one day his dreams had been dashed to pieces and then rebuilt to twice the size they had been before.

"Well, how about if I give you a call this week then?"

"I would like that a lot," Zuriel replied, making Sam's heart pound even faster than it already was. She finally looked up and they met eye contact for a few seconds. The look in her eye might as well have been a kiss. He knew in that moment that his heart was gone forever.

Samuel looked at his watch and saw that it was getting late. They needed to wrap things up, although he could have talked all night. He threw away their plastic coffee containers and walked out to the cars. She had at least an hour drive back home.

"Thank you so much for coming, Zuriel. I can't express to you how much it meant to me," Samuel said, helping her into her car.

"I'm glad I came too. Thanks again for everything," she replied.

Samuel nodded and whispered a good-bye. It took all the strength he could muster to shut the door and walk back to his own car. He waited inside while he watched her drive away. Samuel smiled widely; this had been the best day of his entire life!

 *Chapter 27*

Sam's car pulled into the parking lot. Zuriel quickly gathered her purse, the gift, and the dress she planned to wear later. She slipped her shoes on her feet as Lena and Suzy sat on the couch laughing.

"I knew this would happen! You guys are totally going to get married!" Suzy exclaimed.

"Oh please, we're just friends," Zuriel replied defensively.

"You've been talking to him a regular basis, and you go out for coffee after youth group every week. Girl, you are totally *not* just friends," Lena pointed out, to Zuriel's amusement.

She and Sam hadn't really talked about what they "were" yet. They were really good friends, after all, and Zuriel was sure he was the kind of man she wanted to marry. She just really hoped he felt the same way about her. Maybe they would get married someday. Zuriel had been praying nonstop that God would tell them what to do.

"Okay, whatever, but we aren't even dating yet," Zuriel explained.

"Then why is he picking you up early for breakfast right ⁐ his sister's wedding?" Suzy asked, raising her eyebrows and

Zuriel decided to ignore her comment. "I'll see you ladies at the wedding!" she stated.

She shut the door as she left. She knew going on dates meant you were dating, but she was afraid to refer to him as a boyfriend. He was a pastor—did they have special rules about dating? She didn't know how the Christian dating was supposed to go.

When she got to the lobby, she saw Sam coming through the double doors. She felt her temperature rise, just like every other time she had ever seen him.

"Well, you look like you're all ready to go!" Sam smiled brightly.

"Yes, I figured we'd be in a hurry. There are only a few hours left before you have to be there."

"Right you are." He held the door open and they made their way to the car. He helped her in and they were off. As they drove, Zuriel seized the opportunity to take a good, long look at him. Sam's side profile was attractive and strong. His dark hair was freshly cut and spiked slightly in the front. His face was clean-shaven, but she could see that he had missed a spot. It was so adorable! She knew she was in love.

They pulled into IHOP and Zuriel was excited. She loved breakfast food, but more than that, it felt like they were on a real date. She wondered if they would officially be girlfriend and boyfriend soon. The longing for Sam had recently grown into a burning desire for much more than just friendship. In her heart, she knew he was the one for her, but she also knew the waiting period would require a lot of patience on her part.

They were seated immediately, and Zuriel looked through the menu, but somehow she just couldn't concentrate. She was happier than she had ever been before and was so thankful God had led them to each other. Who knew what the future might hold?

They ordered their food and talked briefly about pancakes and the many other breakfast foods of the world. She was amazed at how enjoyable such a basic conversation with Sam could be. Zuriel was thankful there wasn't anything special required in order for her to be in his presence. She could just enjoy being with him.

The food came and they ate, continuing their small talk. Zuriel loved to hear him laugh, especially when it was because of something she said. It felt so good to have the full attention of a handsome guy again. Zuriel slowly ate, trying not to watch his mouth while he chewed. If they were going to be more than friends, Zuriel knew she was going to do things God's way and wait on his timing, but she missed physical affection. She imagined what it would be like to kiss Sam, and her face warmed. She wondered if he noticed and knew she would be embarrassed if he knew the focus of her contemplation.

"So how does the older brother feel on his sister's wedding day?" she asked, trying to get her mind back to reality.

"Well, he feels … old!" They laughed together before he continued. "I'm really happy for her and for Michael. It's just weird that Christiana is the first one to get married. I guess I always expected Matt and I would be married long before this. It's strange how things work out sometimes."

"I can imagine! I'm an only child, so I have no idea about that aspect of family life."

"Yeah, it's okay though. I don't think I would've been ready any sooner than now anyway. I've been through a lot this year. It's almost embarrassing to think about how immature I was before."

He smiled, and she loved seeing him so happy.

"You weren't immature before. You really helped me out a lot, even before all those changes," Zuriel explained.

"If I remember correctly, you're the one who helped me the most," Sam corrected her.

"That wasn't my intention back then, I'm afraid. I'm so thankful, though, that God took my selfishness and somehow used it for good."

"Intentions are interesting things," Sam said, suppressing a smile. He glanced down at his coffee and then slowly lifted his eyes to meet hers. He smiled, and Zuriel felt her face growing pink. Intentions? What did he mean?

"How are intentions interesting?" Zuriel asked before she could stop herself. She wanted him to clarify and guessed her intentions were now pretty obvious.

"Well, they are a very important part of relationships." He surveyed the room and paused. Zuriel was starting to feel excited. She hoped she could guess where this was going. She tried to keep her breathing natural as he continued. "Some of the youth group guys have been noticing your regular attendance. They keep asking me what my intentions are toward you."

Zuriel's heart almost pounded out of her chest. "Oh, that's funny," she said nonchalantly, looking at the table and hoping he wouldn't see her crimson face.

"I didn't really give them an answer because I didn't want them to say something to you before I got the chance to bring it up." There was a silence, and Zuriel lifted her head to see him staring at her. His face was serious, but his eyes were inviting. She couldn't look away. "I'm sure you have wondered, Zuriel, what my intentions are. At first I didn't think there would be a chance of anything happening between us because of our relationships with Matt. I had almost lost all hope of there ever being anything more than just friendship, but then you showed up to youth group, and I couldn't help wondering if I might actually get that chance."

"I still feel horrible about that phone conversation," Zuriel sorrowfully mentioned, feeling excited and scared about what Sam was probably about to say.

"Well, you more than made up for it, Zuriel. I have really enjoyed seeing you and chatting over coffee. I tried to tell myself that we were just friends catching up. However, if you go out for coffee every week with a very attractive member of the opposite sex, it can hardly be justified as anything else but dating," he stated.

Zuriel's breath caught in her throat. Had Sam just called her attractive—very attractive, in fact?

Sam continued. "As far as intentions are concerned, I've been intending and hoping that we could get to know each other better. I'll admit I have thought as far ahead as marriage, but I really don't want to make you feel rushed. So if you need more time before we take the next steps toward a more serious relationship, I think we should rethink these coffee dates. I just need to know what you're thinking."

Zuriel looked at Sam again and was met with the same intense stare as before. He was asking her to be his girl! She tried to stay composed and think before she spoke. She so wanted God to be involved in every part of this. Surprise lingered in her mind that he had thought as far ahead as marriage, but then again, hadn't she? He was by far the best man she knew, and definitely the most handsome. She knew her love for him had nothing to do with rebounding from Matt. Her emotions were quite clear: this man in front of her was Samuel Lowell, the man of her dreams. She wanted nothing less than to be in a relationship with him. Zuriel couldn't imagine missing out on these coffee dates or texting those sweet messages back and forth. She had been praying about this for a long time, and her opportunity was finally here.

"Sam, I would love to get to know you more. My intentions are the same as yours." She laughed when Sam's stare turned into a wide smile. He laughed too, out of what appeared to be relief.

"I'm so glad," he said, reaching his hand across the table to find hers. Zuriel was slightly surprised by it and hesitated before weaving her fingers through his. She blushed again and was startled. Things like this never used to make her blush, but now she felt so innocent and nervous.

"Me too," was all she could say in response. They both giggled and continued to just stare. Sam traced her fingers and kissed her hand. She loved the feeling of his warm mouth against her skin. She felt tingly all down her spine. Time seemed to stand completely still, and staring was all she wanted to do.

The sound of Sam's phone vibrating against the table broke their trance. He checked his phone and looked startled. "We're going to be late! I was so busy staring at you that I almost forgot about my sister!"

Zuriel laughed as they got up to leave. Sam helped her into the car, gently kissing her hand again before letting go. He climbed in on his side and drove to the Lowells' house.

She couldn't stop smiling, and she also couldn't wait to tell Lena and Suzy.

"Oh, and just to make sure we are on the same page," Sam began while they were stopped at a red light, "our relationship will be about getting to know each other and discovering more about those intentions we talked about earlier. We will keep our relationship pure." His voice was serious, but Zuriel felt comforted by what he said. She knew that if God was going to bless their relationship, they needed to do things his way.

"Yes, that's important to me too." Zuriel winked and clasped his hand once again.

Sam nodded and kissed her hand again.

He pulled into his parents' driveway and quickly walked around to help her out of the car. She was so thankful that he was such a gentleman. He made her feel like a little schoolgirl who had just received her first love note. The feeling amused her as she realized how far from her old life she had come.

Sam went ahead quickly to get ready so they would hopefully not be too late. While he was gone, Zuriel changed into her dress in the bathroom. She looked in the mirror and examined herself in her new white dress with pale pink flowers. She felt pretty. Her green eyes seemed more vibrant than usual, and her hair wasn't frizzing all over the place for once. Zuriel was so thankful that God had given her this day. It was more wonderful than any other day she had known. How could she ever have doubted that God loved her? How could she not be passionately in love with her Creator on a day like this?

After stealing a quick glimpse of the bride to be, Zuriel met Sam in the living room. When she saw him in his tux, she couldn't help but notice how striking he was. He studied her for a moment and she could see the joy in his eyes. He thought she was beautiful. She could tell just by the way he looked at her. She gracefully took his arm and they went back to the car.

"You look gorgeous, by the way," he told her, turning the key in the ignition. She laughed, unfamiliar with compliments like these.

"You're looking pretty good yourself!" Zuriel said with a smile. He winked at her.

They drove to the church, laughing more than they actually talked. Both were so giddy and relieved that their questions regarding mutual affection were finally gone. When they arrived at the church, Zuriel waited in the sanctuary as guests started to arrive and the last-minute wedding preparations were made.

Lena and Suzy finally arrived and sat next to her.

"What is with you? Are you blushing?" Suzy enquired as she took a seat.

"I don't know; I might be. Guess what!"

"What?" the girls asked at the same time.

"We're officially together now!" Zuriel squealed, probably louder than necessary. There were many shrieks of laughter as the full story was told.

"You were together long before today, you silly goose!" Lena teased.

"But it wasn't official. Now I can call him by boyfriend!" Zuriel responded defensively.

"A rose by any other name would smell as sweet!" Suzy snapped.

Zuriel rolled her eyes, accepting the teasing as a rite of passage.

The music began, and the girls quieted down, to survey the procession. The church had been decorated brilliantly with red and white crinoline and candles. The flowers were classic red roses, surrounded by baby's breath. Everything was beautiful. Michael stood beside the pastor, looking taller than she had ever seen him before. His red tie complemented the surroundings and seemed to be an arrow pointing to his nervous grin.

Zuriel, of course, very much noticed the best man. Sam smiled at Michael to reassure him, and Zuriel dreamed of the day Michael would be reassuring Sam in a similar way. It was too easy to imagine her own wedding.

The wedding guests stood, as the pianist began to play the Wedding March. Christina looked breathtaking. Her dark hair was curled carefully around her face, with a beautiful rose holding back a lock of hair. The simple white dress looked classic and seductive, especially as she walked, never breaking eye contact with her future husband. Will seemed to be holding on to her very tightly, almost holding her back. He surveyed the guests as he walked with watery eyes.

Zuriel had once hated the thought of her own father walking her down the aisle, but now that they were getting close, she imagined it being emotional for her father as well. Good thing he liked Sam so much!

Samuel finished his food and immediately began tapping the side of his glass with a butter knife. Michael nudged him and smiled as other guests joined in. The groom turned to his new bride and he gave her a kiss, sending applause through the whole reception hall.

"Thanks, man," Michael said, winking at Samuel. "I promise to return the favor!"

"You bet!" he affirmed enthusiastically.

The thought of Michael someday returning the favor was a notion Samuel enjoyed entertaining. He pictured Zuriel's perfect mouth across from him at breakfast, and he couldn't stop smiling. She really did like him, and she had thought about marriage too. It was amazing. If it was God's will, he would be having a wedding soon too. He hoped as much. He looked for her amongst her friends. They were sitting at a round table several feet away. He was rendered nearly breathless at the sight of her in her stunning white dress. Zuriel was laughing, which caused her head to lean back, as though she was receiving a kiss. Samuel was hit by an overwhelming sense of longing. He was the luckiest man in the world. It would be heaven to have her at his side, but he was a groomsman, the best man, in fact. He wished he could go sit beside her and see what was so amusing to her.

Michael and Christina rose from their seats to go cut the cake. Samuel moved as well, hoping to quickly find Zuriel. He had been missing her. The guests noticed what was going on and a crowd formed around the cake.

Samuel walked through the cluster of people until he found her. She stood next to her friends, giggling and whispering about something. His chest swelled as he took a long breath and tapped her on the shoulder opposite him. She turned and looked the wrong way, falling for the classic trick.

Laughing, she shifted her body back around to face him. "Why, hello there!"

"Hello," he responded. "What are you ladies giggling about?"

"Oh, just girly stuff," Zuriel replied shyly. Was she blushing again? It was hard to tell in the dimly lit room.

"We're imagining our own weddings," Suzy interjected while giving Zuriel a playful look.

Samuel wondered if they were talking about the possibility of Zuriel marrying him. He hoped so! "I see. Well, it looks like the cake will be cut soon. Let's move to the front so you little ladies can actually see."

They liked his charming statement and followed him to a better viewing spot. Samuel tried to concentrate on actually watching the cake cutting, but he was far more interested in watching the woman next to him. He wrapped his arm around her waist, feeling how small and soft she was. She looked up at him, looking vulnerable and sweet. He hardly noticed the crowd disappearing to the dance floor. Zuriel broke the trance and led him by the hand to the edge of the dance floor.

Samuel watched his best friend hold his little sister as they slow danced. He felt so happy for them and so astounded that his kid sister was now a grown woman. She looked gorgeous tonight, and it was obvious that Michael was well aware of that fact. There was a time that Samuel questioned whether marriage was something worth pursing, but with Zuriel's captivating form standing beside him, there was no question marriage had to follow soon. Maybe next summer he would watch her come down the aisle to meet him.

The dances continued, and watching his father dance with Christina was the best part. He could see his father's eyes full of love as he struggled to come up with dance moves. His dad wasn't the emotional type, but Christina could make anyone emotional.

She was his first daughter, and the first of his children to marry. Samuel could only guess his conflicting joy and pain.

At last, the rest of the guests were invited to come to the dance floor. Samuel turned to Zuriel, pulling her in a one-handed sideways hug.

"Would you care to dance?" He held out his free hand, surprised when she didn't take it immediately.

"Well, I don't know …" She looked at the ground to avoid his gaze. "I'm not really that good of a dancer."

"Oh, I'm sure you'll be a wonderful dancer." He gently took her hand and tugged her over to the dance floor. He was aware of her insecurity, but he was sure she would thank him for it later. After all, it was just a dance.

The music started and he put his hands on her waist, feeling her hourglass shape. She put her hands on his shoulders but kept a safe distance between them. Samuel smiled, remembering how she had responded to his touch at breakfast. He looked into her eyes and she looked back, not shying away this time. He loved the rich color of her green eyes and was overwhelmed by the way she looked at him. Her gaze spoke much more than what she was willing to express with words. He knew she was admiring him and she loved him.

Just as Sam had predicted, Zuriel was a good dancer. She was just a little stiff, clearly requiring her space. So he honored her unspoken request as they danced together. He was just thankful she was finally going to be his girl. Suddenly her hands moved to his neck. Samuel smiled, noticing that Zuriel had pulled herself closer in order to better reach his neck. They danced that way for several seconds before he felt her body relax in his arms. Finally he knew she felt safe and comfortable. Samuel loved her surrender.

"You're a wonderful dancer," he whispered in her ear, "and a very beautiful one, I might add."

Zuriel giggled, whispering, "Thank you."

Samuel closed his eyes and thanked God with all his heart for this dance, for this evening, and for this adorable woman he held in his arms. Surely there could be nothing on earth better than this.

Chapter 28

Zuriel woke to the sound of Suzy's voice and wondered what on earth was going on. She looked at the clock and saw that it was four a.m. Jumping out of bed, she rushed to the living room, where a very pregnant Lena was breathing heavily.

"Oh my goodness! Is it time?" Zuriel asked. She was suddenly wide awake.

"I think so," Suzy answered. "She woke me a few minutes ago. Her contractions are only a few minutes apart, but she hasn't lost her water yet." She helped Lena put on her shoes and looked up. "Get dressed, girl, and start the car."

Zuriel didn't need to be told twice. She quickly threw on an outfit and slipped into her flip flops. She pulled out her phone to post the big news on Facebook and send out a few texts. She grabbed her keys and went out to the car. As she started it and waited, she prayed that God would strengthen them all this morning, especially Lena. This would be a big day!

The others came out, still dressed in their pajamas. Lena was holding on to her belly as if the baby would come out any moment. Suzy and Lena looked somewhat comical, hobbling together like two old ladies. Zuriel got out and opened the back door, and they slid inside the car. It was only a matter of seconds before they were off.

"Why did you wait so long to wake us up? You'd better not have this baby in the car. You know I ain't delivering a baby!" Suzy barked.

Lena just rolled her eyes before bracing herself for another contraction. "Zuriel, these bumps are killing me!" Lena moaned.

Zuriel felt sorry for her friend, but there were no smooth roads in Detroit. The best she could do was slow down, but based on the sounds coming from the backseat, Zuriel wasn't sure slowing down was an option.

Zuriel prayed out loud for the birth as they pulled into the hospital entrance. She dropped Suzy and Lena off outside while she went to find a parking spot. It seemed an eternity of searching before she finally found one. Locking the car, she ran inside and caught up with the others. Two nurses were pushing Lena to her room in a wheelchair.

"That was fast," Lena said, breathing more and more heavily as she was pushed along.

"I ran," Zuriel said, breathing almost as loudly as Lena.

They pushed Lena into a room and helped her into a hospital gown. It looked funny stretched over her swollen belly. It took both of them to help her get on the hospital bed so the nurse could connect her to the monitor. The three of them smiled and breathed easier when they heard the steady heartbeat of the baby girl.

"That beat is beautiful," the nurse reassured them. Lena smiled in return but could only do so for a few seconds before another contraction began. Lena clasped the hands of the friends on either side as she panted loudly.

"I'm so proud of you for doing this. You're giving your baby life!" Zuriel said soothingly, rubbing Lena's palm.

Zuriel suddenly felt her phone vibrating in her pocket and saw that it was Sam calling her back. She kissed Lena on the cheek before excusing herself from the room. She didn't want to disturb the birthing mother. Zuriel wanted children someday, but she could only pray to God that she would be brave enough to give birth. Zuriel stepped into the waiting room, and walked to the end of the hallway, away from the noise.

"Sam?" she answered.

"Zuriel. So Lena's in labor, huh?"

"Yes, we're at the hospital right now."

"Okay, I can get ready and head over there."

"Thanks! I would love to have you here, of course, but I don't know how long it's going to be. You might be waiting here for a while." She volunteered the information but hoped desperately that he would still come. She loved his company and support; it made everything better.

"I'll be there. Are you doing okay?"

She was relieved but noticed that his voice sounded solemn and concerned.

"Yes, of course. Why wouldn't I be?" she responded happily.

"I just wanted to make sure, because of what day it is today. I promise I'll still take you to see his grave sometime this week. If it's really important for you to go today, we can do our best to still get you there."

Zuriel's pulse quickened. Of course! She had forgotten that today was June first. Exactly one year ago, Matt was killed by the semi. Sam had planned to come pick her up and take her to the cemetery.

"Oh, I had completely forgotten about that with all the activity this morning. I guess it is June first, isn't it?" she said, expressing her shock.

"Yes … I'm sorry I reminded you." He paused. "This might be a good distraction for you. We can go another day." He paused again, and Zuriel didn't say anything. She was trying to process the reality of the situation. "Are you okay?" he asked, genuine concern resonating in his voice.

She thought about it and found herself feeling surprisingly indifferent. "Well, I think I'll be fine." As Zuriel spoke, she realized how confusing her emotions actually were.

Maybe she wasn't fine, because now the significance of the date was sinking in and she suddenly wanted to cry, but she wasn't sure exactly why. Zuriel had moved on from the pain of Matt's death but still she felt like weeping merely for the sake of weeping. Remembering the pain of last June was an intense recollection. She grieved the loss of her good friend and the knowledge of how lost her soul had been. Her tears might be also mingled with tears of joy. Was it the joy of knowing Matt was in heaven, that her soul was saved, and of being in this new relationship with Sam? Or was it guilt for moving on and finding something in death to celebrate?

Zuriel didn't know how to grieve but didn't really want to. She felt stuck, wondering if Sam would feel like she wanted Matt more than him, if she showed her sorrow. This was a confusing mess of emotions for her. If Matt had lived, she would not have fallen in love with Sam. However, if Matt had lived and continued to love her, would she have cared? Would she ever have realized what she was missing? Zuriel thanked God that he was in control of the universe instead of her. She already struggled enough just trying to make sense of her own thoughts.

"It's okay, Zuriel. I'm glad you're doing all right. I'll be there as soon as I can," Sam said, breaking her train of thought, or emotion, or whatever it was flooding through her head.

"Okay, thanks, Sam," she muttered, concealing her turmoil.

"See ya soon! Bye."

"Bye," Zuriel said before hanging up. She felt shaken and wondered how she was going to get through the rest of this day. She had acted like everything was okay when talking to Sam, and it had been.

She began to pray and asked God for clarity. What was she feeling? Who or what was she grieving for? Was grieving Matt a betrayal to Sam? Was not grieving a betrayal to Matt? She wasn't sure exactly what to do, but it didn't matter. She couldn't control her trail of feelings, no matter who they appeared to be betraying. She had to deal with the pain. She knew she would eventually have to talk with Sam about it, but she would worry about that latter.

She reluctantly allowed herself to daydream and remember all the good times she'd had with Matt. They were somewhat blurry memories, but they represented a very intriguing time in her life. She was thankful for Matt, because without him she might have done some very terrible things in order to drown out the pain of her life. Matt had brought her joy, but it now seemed minuscule compared to the abundance of joy she had in Christ. Zuriel nodded, acknowledging that loving Sam and Matt both could not be a sin. She loved Sam more, but that was because she had more to give. She was empty of God's love when she'd been with Matt.

Hot tears fell faster. She could not deny the fact that she missed Matt. He had been the best friend that she had known up to that point. She couldn't pretend that it wasn't painful and couldn't convince herself not to care. It wasn't that she would trade Sam to get Matt back; they were valuable to her as individuals. God had blessed her with them both. She had to thank him for both.

Zuriel started walking back to Lena's hospital room, deciding to embrace this day for the good in it and not the bad. Lena was done being monitored for now, and moved into a kneeling position. She looked tired, but there were also signs of determination.

"How are you doing?" she asked, feeling like it was a silly question.

"It hurts, but I'm okay," Lena whispered as she grimaced. Another contraction was beginning.

"She's been doing great!" Suzy enthusiastically chimed.

Zuriel took a seat next the bed and looked around, trying to think about the blessings this day would bring. She tried to escape thoughts of Matt, but how could she? Being in a hospital made her envision him mangled and broken, when he was brought here after the accident. Zuriel put her hand over her mouth, wondering if she was going to be sick.

Suzy glanced up from leaning over the birthing mother and rushed to her side. Zuriel felt awful taking the attention off Lena, but she could hold nothing back from her dear friend. She reminded her that today was the anniversary of the accident.

"I'm so sorry, I completely forgot in all the excitement," she replied.

"I did too, Suzy. Don't feel bad. I feel so confused and lost. I really don't know why I'm sad. I really am over it; it's just that this was the day my life began to change. It marks the beginning of finding God and finding Sam. I feel like such an idiot!" Zuriel exclaimed, sniffling to keep from crying.

"You don't have to understand it. You've been through a lot this year. Today probably feels like a day of reflection and memory."

"Yeah, but I don't know if I'm sad or happy," Zuriel explained, and then realized how hilarious her statement was. She began to laugh as tears were still falling down her cheeks. She was so thankful that the year was over, and so thankful God had pulled her through. Zuriel could easily remember the pain she had been through, and her emotions could take her back to those dark moments in a second; however, they were not the same emotions tied to the reality of how she felt now. She was thankful, happy, and content, yet her body, mind, and soul still remembered the past.

Lena moaned. "Umm, I'm glad you're having a come-to-Jesus moment, but I need you to rub my back again."

Zuriel jumped up and began rubbing. The contraction ended, and the lines on Lena's face softened.

"Lena, you look beautiful," Zuriel said, continuing to massage her back.

"Thanks," Lena replied weakly.

"I am so happy for you," Zuriel whispered, taking her hand.

"I am happy for me too. I can't believe I'm going to have a baby." Lena smiled.

"I can't wait to meet your child, Lena. Today represents victory."

"It's true. I know this birth doesn't erase the abortion I had—Jesus alone has that power—however, I have felt a deep sense of healing by carrying this child full-term." Lena's eyes sparkled. Zuriel's own emotional turmoil seemed silly now. Their conversation was ended, with the continuation of the labor process. It was hard to watch her suffer, but each pain brought them closer to seeing the baby.

One of the nurses came in several minutes later.

"There is a Sam Lowell in the waiting room. He said to tell you ladies that he's here."

Zuriel was relieved but wasn't sure if she should leave the room. Suzy and Lena seemed to read her mind and encouraged her to go see him. Zuriel felt slightly bad about leaving them, but she was desperate to see her man.

Zuriel walked to the waiting room and saw Sam sitting there. He looked exhausted but still just as handsome as ever. She rushed over to him and soon found herself safe in his arms. She was so glad to see him and feel his body close to her own. His presence was always comforting.

"Are you okay, sweetie?" Sam asked again, still holding her tightly.

"I am now."

"I had a feeling things were more difficult than you made them sound over the phone." He caressed her cheek.

"Well, I had forgotten what day it was. At first I thought I was fine, but then all of my past emotions hit me at once. I felt like if I grieved for Matt I would be betraying you, and if I didn't, I was betraying Matt." Zuriel felt her eyes getting glossy again. It wasn't because she was sad but because she was embarrassed to admit these feelings to Sam. She groaned, annoyed that she couldn't keep her composure in front of him.

"Oh, Zuriel, you're not betraying me. It's okay for you to miss Matt. I miss him too."

"You're so sweet to say that." She rested her head against his chest and tried to explain the terrible, wonderful hour she'd had with God that morning. She had finally processed her feelings, but communicating them was just as challenging. Emotions were never meant to be explained with logical thoughts, yet Zuriel continued to explain, hoping her words made sense. It all sounded like rambling to her, so she tried to summarize her thoughts with one final statement: "I think it's possible to love you more than Matt, but still miss him. It's strange to grieve and still be so thankful at the same time."

"I understand. I'm so thankful for you, but somehow it feels like I am saying I'm thankful my brother died so I could have you. At the same time, though, I'm very sad that he died. Death in and of itself is not good; however, I can't use that as an excuse to not be thankful for the things God has given me."

"Yes, that's the same conclusion I came to," Zuriel said, feeling relief that he understood.

They sat together in the waiting room, and Sam put his arm around her. It was refreshing to sit in silence, just knowing he was there. She felt a strong surge of love for him in a way she couldn't describe. She laid her head on his shoulder and was relaxed by his steady breathing. She drifted off to sleep.

Samuel stood outside the hospital room and could hear the sounds of a baby crying and several women squealing with delight. It was almost three in the afternoon, and the baby was finally here. She was a girl, and that was, of course, a cause for extra celebration. He picked Zuriel's voice out from the others and chuckled. Samuel had sat with her for hours earlier, holding her and talking with her about life, Matt, God, and all sorts of things. He loved her very much and was almost certain he would marry her someday. She looked tired today, but she was still as gorgeous as ever. She was so concerned about the baby and about the "correct" way to grieve. He loved how she had listened to his advice and responded to the comfort he offered. The feeling of her melting against him and then letting her guard down was precious. He loved her far more than words could express.

Samuel walked into the waiting room and saw that several people had come to show their love and support. June, the elderly woman from women's center, was among them. When she saw Sam, she hugged him. Her wrinkly old arms barely squeezed around him.

"I'm so happy for her, Samuel. Those girls are just great!"

"Yes they are. You should hear them in there. They sound like they just won a million dollars." He saw Drew walking toward him and extended a hand.

"What are you doing here?" Drew asked abruptly while shaking his hand. His eyes were wandering, as if searching for someone.

"I had to come! Zuriel told me Lena was in labor, so I left right away," Samuel replied, trying to be friendly. He wondered what was up with Drew. He seemed a little defensive about something, but Samuel couldn't quite put his finger on it.

"Huh," was all Drew said. He rudely walked past Samuel and saw that Zuriel was coming down the hall. Drew seemed like he was anxious to see her. Samuel realized what the purpose of his rudeness was. He felt sorry for the guy.

"She's beautiful! She's seven pounds and two ounces!" Zuriel announced, practically floating down the hallway.

Drew greeted her coolly. "Why didn't you call me earlier? I would have been here to wait with you."

"Oh, I didn't want to wake you that early. You came at just the right time. I can't wait for you all to meet her. Lena was wonderful too," Zuriel answered sweetly. Her eyes were brighter than they had been all morning.

Samuel couldn't help but notice the joy radiating from her. She was so amazing! Her eyes met his and she brushed past Drew so she could give him a hug.

"I'm so excited, Sam! She's gorgeous!"

"What did Lena name her?" Samuel asked. Zuriel's eyes widened and she let out a cute little giggle before answering.

"June Bethany Rose! I can't believe I never told you what her name was. She actually picked the name out weeks ago. But isn't it just a wonderful name?"

"Yes it is." He smiled and hugged her again. He loved it when she was happy.

"Zuriel, can I talk to you for a minute?" Drew asked, standing a few feet away looking frustrated.

Samuel's guard went up, feeling greatly annoyed that he was calling Zuriel out like that. What was his problem?

"Sure." Zuriel pulled away from his grasp and walked to Drew.

Samuel wanted to follow her, but he knew she could take care of herself. He heard loud whispering and saw Drew was angry. Zuriel answered, talking with her hands.

"Have you forgotten about Matt already?" he heard Drew exclaim, speaking loudly. "You said you needed more time and that you were busy falling in love with your Jesus. What changed, and why I am the last to know?"

Samuel started walking toward them, ready to make Drew understand that this girl was taken!

"I already told you you're just a friend. You were never going to be more than that. I'm with Sam now ... so that subject can be put to rest. As a friend, I am glad you came. The baby is absolutely beautiful!" Zuriel sounded self-confident.

Samuel was so proud of her. She was handling things very well, but he doubted Drew would be able to.

"What do you mean you're with ...?" Drew's voice trailed off as Samuel joined the group and put his arm around Zuriel. Samuel looked Drew in the eye and the tension between them was thick and obvious. He felt Zuriel stiffen. Drew was red in the face now.

"He's not Matt, Zuriel! Matt's dead, and dating his brother won't bring him back."

"I know that," Zuriel said sternly.

Samuel felt her growing even more rigid, and she seemed to be scooting away from him. The space between them was now more than an inch, and it was clear that Zuriel was uncomfortable with the situation. Samuel stepped forward, purposely imposing on Drew's space and forcing him to take a step back.

Drew turned abruptly and stormed down the hallway toward the exit. Samuel was glad he was going. What a jerk! He wondered if the guy actually thought saying things like that would work. He obviously wasn't very good with the ladies!

"Well, it's a good thing he doesn't like you anymore, because lucky for him, you're taken." Samuel put his arm back around Zuriel and pulled her close.

She finally relaxed against him and looked him in the eye. "That was crazy." She sounded exhausted.

He couldn't be irritated with Drew for liking her—that was a difficult thing to avoid—but Samuel was ticked off that he had tried to ruin her good mood.

Samuel brushed Zuriel's hair behind her ear. "Don't worry about Drew. He'll get over it," he explained. "Now what's this you were saying about a new baby? When do I get to take a peek?"

She smiled and took his hand, leading him down the hallway. Samuel was relieved. Zuriel's day wasn't ruined after all, so neither was his.

 *Chapter 29*

Zuriel put on her cream-colored sundress and smoothed her hair behind her ears. Her skin looked tan next to the light fabric. She had been feeling more and more beautiful recently. It seemed as if Sam's constant praise was starting to go to her head. She was no longer the fearful mouse she had once been, and she wasn't sure exactly how she felt about that. How much could a person change in one year and still be healthy? Zuriel could only conclude that all things really were possible with God.

She applied her makeup, carefully choosing which colors would be best to bring out the green in her eyes. She wanted to look stunning for her beloved today. Michael and Christina's wedding had been the last time she had dressed up and really done something fun. Recently she had been busy receiving guests and helping Lena with baby June. Their apartment was small, so none of the girls were getting much sleep. Zuriel was exhausted from continuing to work every day while only getting as much sleep as the new mother. After a few weeks of this madness, she couldn't refuse Sam when he asked her to spend the day with him. They still hadn't been able to visit Matt's grave, and they were long overdue for a date. Zuriel was determined to look her best.

Preparing to go to the gravesite again felt strange. The emotions she felt when she thought about going were neither dread nor sorrow. She was actually looking forward to going and spending time with Sam there. It was as though her past was buried there with Matt—her past with all of its fears, heartache, and mistakes. Now that her future looked so glorious, how could she mourn for her former life?

Zuriel was ready to revisit the gravesite, mostly because she'd have Sam at her side. She was more in love than ever, despite the fears that grew. Just like Matt had been gone in a second, Sam could be taken home at any time. Zuriel didn't want to be afraid of this, but she thought about it more often than she would like to admit. The closer she got to Sam, the less control she had over her heart and her emotions. Everyday felt dangerous, but at the same time everyday she felt alive. She was loved.

Zuriel heard a soft knocking and moved to the door, tip-toeing past the mother and daughter napping on the couch. She answered the door, delighted to see Sam standing in the hallway. His black hair was getting longer and the waves were resting on his forehead, indicating a windy day. His brown V-neck T-shirt was snug around his muscles. Zuriel smiled, looking into his eyes.

Throughout her whole life she had struggled with the meaning of love. She had wondered if anyone could truly love her for who she was, and rarely believed people when they told her they did. However, when she was with Sam she never questioned if he loved her. It wasn't because of what he said to her; it was the look in his eyes, the tone of his voice, and the way he was always there for her to demonstrate his love. She could see that he loved her by the look on his face. It was a priceless picture that she would always treasure. Who could ever unlock the mystery of the unspoken love language between two people? It was a strange language that only God could interpret and reveal to those who noticed it.

She stepped out into the hallway and wrapped her arms around his waist. He hugged her tightly in response, running his fingers through her hair. She didn't understand why God was giving her this chance to be in love. Not only was it a chance to be loved, but one more beautiful than what she could have imagined before.

"You look beautiful, my sweet one," Sam said, kissing the top of her forehead. She smelled his strong cologne as her nose was pressed against his chest. Its aroma was comforting and reminded her that she was safe in his arms. She pulled away from his embrace so she could look into his eyes.

"Thank you." She smiled and tilted her head to admire him. "You are looking mighty fine yourself!"

Sam winked and hugged her again. "Are you ready to go?"

"Yes, I just need to get my purse." Zuriel quickly snuck back into the apartment and grabbed her purse before slipping on her ballet flats. She couldn't wait to spend the rest of the day with the man she loved. Life was so good.

They made their way to the parking lot and Sam helped her into his car. Zuriel loved his special treatment of her. There were times in her life where she thought that this sort of man didn't exist save for movies and fairytales. She wished that she hadn't settled for less in her youth. If only she had known what an amazing man was waiting for her, she would have tossed every other guy to the side, regardless of how good-looking they were. Although she regretted those days, she couldn't think about them without thanking God for his goodness to her. Every event made her the person she was ... the person Sam loved.

"How are you feeling about today?" he asked, reaching for her hand as he drove.

"I feel good. What about you?"

"I feel the same. I think it's a good idea that we're doing this. It will be nice to relax and reflect. Having a romantic dinner afterward doesn't sound too bad either!" Zuriel giggled at his words. She loved how charming he was when he talked. She remembered how he acted the first time she ever saw him, so stoic and high minded. He had the charm of a mother bear. It was funny to think about how much things had changed—how God had caused things to change.

"I don't think a romantic dinner ever sounds anything but good!" Zuriel exclaimed.

"Especially if it's a romantic dinner with you!" Sam added, continuing to flirt.

"Yes, well it wouldn't be much fun without you either," Zuriel played along.

Sam squeezed her hand, and they looked at each other in mutual admiration, feeling childlike and in love. Zuriel relaxed into her seat, enjoying the peace that came from being in Sam's company. She wished she could spend every day exactly like this.

They made comfortable small talk as they drove to the burial grounds. The sun was shining brightly and the grass was glistening as they navigated the cemetery's winding, narrow roads. Sam parked and helped Zuriel out of the car. He offered her his hand, and Zuriel gladly took it. She wanted to feel him close to her; especially right now as they neared Matt's grave.

"It's always fascinated me, how cemeteries tend to be some of the most beautiful places. The grass, flowers, and statues are lovely," Zuriel noticed as she looked around.

"I guess I never really thought of them as lovely, but they aren't exactly haunted like the movies make them seem," Sam replied. They finally arrived at their destination. Zuriel surveyed the tranquil scene and remembered the fateful day when Matt was brought here. It had been a bright, sunny day just like this one. By now, though, the burial plot was completely covered with grass and the stone was slightly weathered and blending in a little better with the rest of its surroundings.

"This spot is beautiful," Zuriel noted. "He was beautiful."

"It's been so many years since I last saw him that I don't know exactly what he looked like before he died. I'm sure he is quite the man up there in heaven, though."

"I guess we'll find out one day." Zuriel stared at his tombstone. It was curiosity that stirred her heart with the desire to meet him. It was almost funny to her to think that she had once loved Matt so much. Her definition of true love had changed so dramatically that she hardly knew what to call the emotion she had felt back then. Zuriel enjoyed this time of reminiscing; it made the present seem so much more real.

"So much has happened to us because of Matt," Sam began. "I don't even know what to say."

Zuriel understood how he felt. Her grieving was over now and her heart was light. She was so thankful for everything that God had done for her, and so in love with the man beside her. How did she put those thoughts into perspective when Matt was buried beneath her?

Zuriel stared at the ground and felt the grass inviting her. As she sat, she felt the warm sun caress her back. She slowly stretched out onto the cool patch of green in front of Matt's grave, letting the sun shine on her face as it had done a year ago. So much had changed for her in that last year. Zuriel now had hope.

Samuel watched Zuriel as she rested. He remembered the time he came to get her and found her lying on the ground in her black funeral dress, so small and afraid. He had been attracted to her back then, but now she looked even more beautiful as she lay here in her sun dress. She looked so peaceful and so content that

angelic was the only way to describe what he saw. He thought
to himself that if the Holy Spirit were to take on human form,
then that form would be no less beautiful than the one that he
was now admiring. Zuriel was so lovely and so feminine. Samuel
didn't think it was possible to love her more, but the sudden surge
of attraction he felt for her in that moment proved him wrong. It
was clearly evident to him that no other woman would ever come
close her. He absolutely had to marry her someday.

Samuel sat on the ground next to her, thinking and enjoying
the beauty that surrounded him. He thought about his brother
and wondered why things happened the way they did. So much
pain and heartache could have been avoided if Matt had stayed at
home. So much sorrow would have been avoided if Matt had not
gotten into his terrible accident. However, so much joy would have
been avoided as well. Samuel realized he would never be able to
fully understand God's will. Why did God allow some bad things
to happen while stopping countless others? Satan must have tried
terribly hard to ruin all of their lives. Samuel was thankful that
the enemy had not prevailed. He knew the ultimate purpose of
his life was to bring glory to God and lead others to salvation.
That purpose had been accomplished, no matter how much the
evil one had tried to destroy.

Zuriel spoke. "I remember lying here the day of the funeral."
Her words brought Samuel out of his reverie. "I remember
thinking about how I was supposed to be married, but instead I
was left all alone. Little did I know how close God was to me. I
thought God hated me, but now I finally realize how much he
used Matt's death to show me his love."

"I remember finding you here and being amazed by how
beautiful you looked. I stood over you, but when you opened your
eyes you looked so disappointed. I could tell you were wishing I
was Matt."

"Yes," Zuriel replied, "I almost thought you were him for a split second. It was painful. I'm glad you came for me, though. I probably would have stayed there for a very long time."

"I had a feeling something was wrong, and I felt compelled to come." Samuel remembered driving back for her. "That's when I was first attracted to you. I felt terrible about it, though, because you were supposed to marry my brother. I wasn't sure how you would feel about my attraction, and I wasn't sure how I felt about it either, especially since you didn't know Christ at the time."

"Our story isn't really an ideal way to fall in love." Zuriel's statement surprised Samuel. They hadn't ever said "I love you" to each other before, though Samuel had known for many months now that he was in love with her.

He turned to face her. Samuel stroked her cheek with the back of his hand. Zuriel opened her eyes and sat up. She was smiling and looked thoughtful.

"It's true, out story isn't ideal, but we fell in love nonetheless." Samuel paused, mesmerized by her eyes. He caught his breath and just had to speak his mind. "I love you, Zuriel … and I know I always will." Samuel saw the joy radiating from her face. It was so amazing to watch Zuriel's heart melting before him. She smiled at his words and looked away shyly before meeting his gaze again.

"I love you," she echoed.

Samuel kissed her on the cheek and shifted so he could put his arm around her as they sat side by side. He was so thankful that she loved him. It blew him away that, despite their unlikely circumstances, they had fallen more deeply in love than most people he had ever known. It was such a relief to know he had found the one person he wanted to be with for the rest of his life. His mind stopped, suddenly aware of what he was thinking. Was he sure he would marry her? Samuel didn't want anything else. He wanted to make this woman his wife.

They sat in silence, enjoying the June weather and each other's company. Samuel wondered when they would get married. He supposed that after a few more months of dating he would pop the question, and a year or so later they could finally be married. At least that was the typical procedure for modern Christian couples. He didn't like it, though, because he knew he was ready now. He was twenty-six years old, for crying out loud! Samuel sighed, preparing himself to be patient and keep on waiting.

"It is wonderful, knowing for sure that someone loves you," Zuriel began, breaking the silence. "I have spent most of my life wondering if people loved me, and doubting whether they really did. I ran from love and never believed anyone else when they told me they were in love. The love of God really changes things. I could probably count on both hands and toes the people who really love me."

Samuel couldn't imagine anyone not loving the beautiful woman beside him. He gently pulled her head to face him and was once again caught off guard by her beauty. He had a sudden, desire to make her realize how lovable she really was. He couldn't stand the thought that she still doubted her own worth. Samuel loved her completely and wanted her to understand that he would never stop loving her. He wanted to reeducate her. He wanted her to see he wasn't like everyone else. Samuel was not only in love, he loved her for who she was, all romance aside.

"I wish you knew just how lovable you really are," Samuel whispered.

Zuriel was quiet and just stared back at him with her piercing green eyes. Her blonde hair was blowing gently about her face, and the strength of his love for her only increased.

He wanted to marry this woman as soon as possible! His heart, mind, and body longed so much for her to be his, but he knew he had to wait. Or did he? Why not just get engaged? Why not marry her soon?

They both loved God and desired to serve him, and they both loved each other. Those were the two most important factors in the lives of a married couple. Those were the things that made marriages successful. So what was he waiting for?

Samuel examined the situation and remembered that they were sitting next to Matt's grave. Maybe he should wait until they were somewhere more romantic—but then again, maybe he couldn't stand to wait another moment!

"Zuriel," Samuel whispered in her ear, pulling her closer and caressing the side of her face and neck. His heart started to pound heavily, and his adrenaline was flowing full force. He couldn't believe he was actually doing this! "Will you marry me?"

Zuriel stared at Sam, barely able to believe what was happening. First he told her he loved her. That by itself was amazing, and Zuriel's head was still swimming with thoughts and emotions. She was so in love with him and knew that he sincerely loved her back. She felt like she had been elevated to heaven right when her life was already so much better than she could have ever imagined it. It felt so good to have her lover hold her in his arms and caress her. Still, nothing could have prepared her for the next four words out of his mouth: "Will you marry me?"

Zuriel had heard the question before. It seemed like so long ago. She could remember wrestling with herself, wondering if she should say yes. The evening had been so romantic and well-planned. She could still visualize the park lampposts, the sound of her feet on the sidewalk, and the precious way that Matt had spoken to her.

"Marry me," Matt had whispered, "and make me the happiest man alive."

His words had made her tremble. She felt like she had been standing on the edge of a cliff and Matt was urging her to jump off. But as his lips pressed against hers, she knew there was no going back.

"Yes," Zuriel had managed to say, looking up at him. "I wouldn't have it any other way." In the back of her mind, though, forever had seemed like such a long time, and love seemed like it couldn't be powerful enough to last.

Now she was being asked the same question again. It was different this time. There wasn't nearly as much romance and careful planning involved. With Matt, she had been swept off her feet and given a ring, but Sam was asking empty-handed, driven by the emotion of the moment. Could a split decision be considered true love? He held her, waiting for some sort of response. She tried to say something but felt numb, so surprised by what he was asking. In fact, she could hardly breathe. She loved him so much. She wanted him so badly. How could she doubt his love?

She knew the love of Jesus Christ had unlimited power. She also knew that, through him, all things were possible. Zuriel looked at Sam and didn't just see an attractive guy whom she enjoyed being with. When she looked at him she saw a leader, minister, friend, and lover. Zuriel knew instantly and without a shadow of a doubt that she wanted to spend the rest of her life with him. She knew what her answer would be.

"Yes," Zuriel said at last. She nodded and smiled, while a few tears trickled down her cheeks. She felt so happy that she couldn't decide whether she should laugh or cry.

Sam gasped in relief and pulled her face close to his. He kissed each of her cheeks and then her forehead and chin. His hands slipped behind her head and around the nape of her neck, up under her hair, as he held her head at eye level. "I love you, my darling."

Zuriel stared back into his brown eyes. He coaxed her closer, and their lips touched at last.

Zuriel thought of the engagement scenes in movies she had seen and in books she had read. They always seemed to end with a "happily ever after" message. As Zuriel tasted Sam's lips for the second time, she knew this was much more than just a "happily ever after." She knew this was a step of faith into the unknown and that there was no going back. This was the man she would marry. She would be Mrs. Lowell, even if it cost her every ounce of love she had.

Zuriel became aware of the gravestone beside them and for a moment felt a wave of fear. Would Sam be taken away from her too? She knew she had to accept that this life was temporary. As much as this moment felt like heaven, it was still very far from the joys of paradise. While they did live on earth, there were sure to be many more trials, tragedies, and pain to come. Zuriel thanked God for the joy and blessing of their engagement and decided to trust him that, if it was his will, she and Sam would be married soon. Then they would take it one day at a time, grateful for everything God had given them, while accepting the fact that he might ask them to give it all back. One day their true "happily ever after" would begin, but that wouldn't be until they reached heaven.

Zuriel laughed softly, thinking about the irony of the situation: she had become engaged to marry Sam while sitting next to Matt's grave. How strange life was. Pain and pleasure always seemed to go hand in hand. As she considered the uniqueness of her engagement, salvation, and life story, she was overwhelmed with thankfulness. Love for her Father in heaven and her new husband-to-be filled her heart.

She remembered the famous words of Job from the Bible: "The LORD gave, and the LORD has taken away; blessed be the name of the LORD."

CPSIA information can be obtained at www.ICGtesting.com
Printed in the USA
BVOW04s1613170314

347872BV00002B/4/P